MURDER AT THE DRESSMAKER'S SALON

A CLEOPATRA FOX MYSTERY, BOOK 4

C.J. ARCHER

WWW.CJARCHER.COM

CHAPTER 1

LONDON, MARCH 1900

*F*lossy flitted around Maison de Poitiers like a butterfly in a cottage garden, her attention captured by one delicate fabric or gown after another. The smile hadn't left her face since we entered, and she didn't mind that we had to wait for Madame Poitiers and her assistant to finish serving another customer.

The dressmaker had asked us to take a seat and begged our forgiveness for the delay before turning back to the sour-faced woman who looked displeased that we'd occupied Madame Poitiers' attention for a mere moment. Aunt Lilian and I sat on one of the blush-pink velvet sofas and watched Flossy lovingly stroke a pale blue silk muslin dress with roses painted on the skirt and a cloud of chiffon gathered at the bosom.

"Isn't this one positively beautiful?" Flossy cooed.

The sour-faced woman's lips pursed harder. She needn't be so annoyed. Her daughter had the undivided attention of Madame Poitiers' assistant in the adjoining changing room.

"It is the latest fashion in Paris," Madame Poitiers was telling the woman in a strong French accent. "I return to my home city at every opportunity and meet other designers. We exchange ideas, but of course I keep the best ones to myself." Madame Poitiers smiled as if she'd made a joke, but the woman didn't respond. She appeared not to be listening. That didn't stop Madame Poitiers from prattling on. "I source only

1

the finest fabrics, and employ only the most talented seam-stresses and embroiderers. Ah! She is ready. Oh! What a vision!"

A girl of no more than seventeen or eighteen emerged from the dressing room wearing an ivory chiffon gown over-laid with black lace at the bodice and hem. The assistant darted around her, adjusting the sleeve and flattening a tiny wrinkle on the skirt.

Madame Poitiers lightly clapped her hands. *"C'est magnifique!"*

The girl stood on the raised dais and smiled at her reflec-tion in the mirror before turning to her mother. The smile slipped off. "Mama? What do you think?" She bit her lip as she waited for her mother's verdict.

"Oh, Cleo, that would look lovely on you," Flossy said. "The black lace makes it suitable for half-mourning."

The girl's mother stiffened and she eyed me up and down coolly. "Your gowns are one-offs, are they not, Madame Poitiers?"

The dressmaker placed a hand to her considerable chest. She looked offended. "But of course! I assure you, Lady Davenport, no two are the same. There will be no one at any of the balls you attend in exactly the same Colette Poitiers dress."

Lady Davenport turned her back to us. "I don't think we have to worry about appearing at the same events."

Beside me, Aunt Lilian stiffened.

Flossy didn't seem to notice the slight and continued to make her way around the room. The salon resembled a small but sumptuous drawing room. The pink color scheme of the sofa, armchairs, cushions and drapes was a little too much for my taste, but it suited the feminine space. A life-sized portrait of a younger, slimmer version of Madame Poitiers wearing a gown in the tight-fitting princess line style, fashionable at the time, reigned over her salon, while the remainder of the walls were covered in floor to ceiling mirrors in gilt frames. Wan morning light reflected in the mirrors, brightening the interior but not so much that the customers noticed every blemish when they studied themselves outfitted in one of Madame Poitiers' splendid creations.

Flossy fingered the white fringing at the waistline of a dress on the headless mannequin beside the counter then moved on to a display of silk fans. I stood to admire the combs arranged under glass on the counter, but didn't set my heart on any in particular. I was here because I'd agreed to attend some parties and dinners during the upcoming social season, but I wasn't going to be put on display myself. Flossy was the main feature. This appointment with London's most sought-after dressmaker was for her benefit.

Madame Poitiers continued to talk to Lady Davenport while her assistant pinned the hem to the correct length for the girl. Lady Davenport appeared not to be listening. I could hardly blame her. Madame Poitiers prattled on about a party she'd attended in Paris years ago where she'd sung all night. According to the story, which she wove in a rather erratic pattern, she'd been forced to give up singing opera, her first love, when she caught a disease of the throat. By the time the assistant finished and stepped back to gain perspective, Madame Poitiers had mentioned the name of every important person who'd attended the party, which arias she'd sung, and given an account of every conversation she'd had and with whom. She'd just begun to list the refreshments when Lady Davenport announced she'd wait for her daughter in the carriage.

Undeterred, Madame Poitiers turned to us with a bright smile. "Now, Lady Bainbridge and Mademoiselle Bainbridge." She clasped her hands. "What a delight it is to see you again. And who is this *jolie fille* you bring to me?"

The assistant ushered Lady Davenport's daughter into the change room while Aunt Lilian introduced me to Madame Poitiers. The dressmaker wore a simple gown in burgundy that fit her figure in such a way that at first glance, her waist appeared smaller than it was. A white lace necktie was the only decoration. The outfit was designed to not distract the customer from the beautiful pieces on the mannequins.

She seemed older than Aunt Lilian, with lines around her eyes that appeared only when she smiled, and a sagging jawline. There was no gray in her hair, however, and her movements were elegant if somewhat drawn out, as if she put thought into each one. She glided rather than walked, keeping her chin raised and her nose in the air as Lady Davenport had done as she strode out of the salon. But with Lady Davenport, the haughty pose seemed natural, as if it was one she'd employed every day of her life. With Madame Poitiers, it was practiced.

She stood back and studied me, one finger making a little circle, asking me to twirl. "Mademoiselle has a lovely shape. *Très elegant*. And what a pretty face, the skin so clear, the eyes so green! She is more like you than your own daughter, *non*?"

Aunt Lilian nodded, smiling. "So they say."

Madame Poitiers turned her attention to Flossy. "And Mademoiselle Bainbridge, how you have blossomed since you were last here. Your hair is the color of the Arabian sunset! And your figure..." The dressmaker turned her attention to Flossy's chest with the discerning eye of a woman who knew the size without measuring. "There will be no need for the embellishments the other girls must use." She indicated the blue dress with the gathered chiffon on the bodice, positioned to subtly disguise a flat chest.

Flossy giggled.

"So I am to outfit both girls for the season, *oui*?" Madame Poitiers spoke to my aunt, not Flossy or me. "And you, Lady Bainbridge? Are you to have new clothes too?"

"Just the one," Aunt Lilian said. "Florence requires four new ball gowns, another four evening gowns. Cleo is still wearing half-mourning for her grandmother, but I think just the two evening gowns, one in a very light shade of gray and the other deep purple. She'll also require four new ball gowns and another two evening dresses in the latest colors and styles. She'll be out of mourning altogether soon."

"I don't think I need quite so many," I said. "I won't be attending all the events with Flossy."

"Of course you will," Flossy said with a pout. "Tell her, Mother."

"We agreed," I told Aunt Lilian.

Aunt Lilian gave me a small but triumphant smile. "We agreed you wouldn't be presented at court. That was all."

My aunt and cousin had tried to convince me to do my debut along with other girls coming out this season. I had refused. For one thing, I felt as though I was too old at twenty-three, and for another, I simply didn't want to. The idea of partaking in an outdated tradition that mattered only to snobs like Lady Davenport sounded like the least enjoyable way to spend a day. I'd expected my aunt to dig her heels in and insist, but she'd given up without much of a fight. Flossy was more disappointed than her mother, but I suspected that was because she wanted to host a ball for me at the hotel.

I leaned closer to my aunt and kept my voice low. "I can't afford all these new gowns and it's not fair that Uncle Ronald pays for it."

"Nonsense. He won't mind." She took my hands in both of hers. "He will want his niece to be as elegantly outfitted as his daughter. Trust me, Cleo. I know my husband."

I didn't doubt her on that score. I was an ornament on the family tree, a representative of the Bainbridges at every event, just as much as Flossy and Floyd. If I were to attend balls and parties alongside my cousins, aunt and uncle, then I must look as though I belonged. It was just that I hadn't expected to be attending as many functions as them.

I had no more opportunity to protest as Aunt Lilian and Flossy launched into descriptions of the outfits they wanted. Madame Poitiers wrote nothing down but listened attentively until Lady Davenport's daughter emerged from the dressing room. The assistant carried out the dress behind her.

Madame Poitiers excused herself and opened the door for the girl who hurried out to join her mother in their waiting conveyance. Once the door was closed, she turned back to us.

"If you admired that gown so, would you like something similar?" She snapped her fingers at the assistant, hovering near the door to the change room, the gown with the black lace draped over her arms.

"I thought all your dresses were unique," Flossy said.

Madame Poitiers laughed, the sound throaty. "I say similar, not the same." She plucked at the lace overlay on the bodice. "A different pattern here, a change of base color, a bow at the shoulder, and *voila*! No one will recognize it. Mademoiselle Fox will be one of a kind." She signaled to her assistant with a wave of her hand and the young woman hung up the gown. "First, we measure."

She stood aside while her assistant took our measurements and wrote them in a book. The young woman had not been introduced to us nor had Madame Poitiers addressed her by name. The only words she spoke were directions to lift our arms, or turn, or be still, and she didn't make eye contact. She couldn't have been older than me, but she was the picture of an obedient shop girl. She was efficient, and needed no direction from Madame Poitiers.

Indeed, the dressmaker took no notice of Flossy and me as she told Aunt Lilian all about the time she'd met Russian jeweler Peter Fabergé in Saint Petersburg and how his designs had influenced her more elaborate jeweled gowns.

"It was a wonderful time for artists like us." Her eyes became dreamy, her husky voice softening. "So many ideas! He adored my collection that year. So elegant, he would say, so modern and fresh."

"Which year was that?" Aunt Lilian asked.

Madame Poitiers shrugged in a gesture both graceful and nonchalant. "I do not recall. I was young and life was amusing and exciting." Her eyes shone, and her secretive smile hinted at more stories that were quite possibly scandalous.

The assistant completed our measurements and, after a nod from Madame Poitiers, disappeared through another door into a back room. I caught a fleeting glimpse of several seamstresses, some concentrating at sewing machines, others standing at the cutting table, and another pinning pieces of cloth over the wooden torso of a dress form.

When the assistant re-emerged, and the door closed behind her, the sounds of the whirring sewing machines was blocked out completely from the salon. The assistant walked carefully towards us, her vision obscured by fabric samples stacked in her arms.

Madame Poitiers directed her to place them on the counter beside the large catalog book. She flipped through the thick pages of hand painted designs until she came to the series she wanted.

"*Ici*, these will look *très elegant* for Mademoiselle Bainbridge with her full bosom. This one is for her, I am certain, and in this shade of green." She touched a bolt of delicate

6

chiffon. "Feel it, Mademoiselle. It's so soft, delicate. And the color is not of grass." She pulled a face. "But pretty, soft."

Flossy pointed to one of three designs on the page. "With rosettes down the front like this."

Madame Poitiers squinted at the image then clasped her hands together as if in prayer. "You have such style, Mademoiselle! Are you sure you are not French?" She laughed that throaty, sensual laugh. "I knew a girl just like you in Paris. She was a model for Pierre Benoit, the designer who took me under his wing. Her hair was like spun gold too, and she had an adorable little puppy nose. Oh, the gentlemen did admire her, very much, as they will admire you when you enter the ballroom dressed in a Madame Poitiers gown."

We spent a long time choosing fabrics and designs. By the end, Aunt Lilian had begun to flag. She kept herself upright on the sofa while Flossy and I looked through the design book, but I suspected it took enormous effort. Her eyelids drooped, her shoulders sagged, and she hardly took any notice of the dressmaker and her assistant as they made a great fuss of Flossy and me.

It wasn't until the front door opened and a woman and her young charge entered that Aunt Lilian rallied. She smoothed her hand down her lap and smiled at the newcomers, although not the smile of recognition.

"Ah, Madame and Mademoiselle Enderby, I do apologize but I will not be much longer." Madame Poitiers briefly looked the young girl up and down and praised her on such a fine figure and pretty face before returning to the counter where the assistant was adding up the cost of our order with the same quiet efficiency she'd shown all morning.

"You are wise to come to Maison de Poitiers early," Madame Poitiers said to us as her assistant worked. "Every year I get busier and busier! So many favorite customers return to the humble designs of Madame Poitiers. You saw the old article in *The Queen*?"

She indicated a page neatly cut from a magazine framed and positioned on a stand at the end of the counter. The paper had yellowed but the type was still clear. One of two color illustrations on the page depicted a younger Madame Poitiers smiling enigmatically. The other was of the famous actress,

Myrtle Langford, wearing a pink and white off-the-shoulder gown with pearls and either beads or jewels sewn across the bodice in a diamond pattern, and a hemline in a more flowing fabric. Even illustrated, the elegance of the gown was unmistakable, although the style was out of date.

Madame Poitiers picked up the frame and studied the article. "They called me an 'extraordinary designer.' Isn't that amusing? Such high praise for a humble dressmaker. Of course, my creations have graced beautiful women all over the world, not just Miss Langford. Actresses, singers, dancers, duchesses and even princesses!" She sighed, deeply satisfied. "They wrote about my past as an opera singer, too. They say I could have sung with Dame Nellie Melba herself if the disease in my throat had not cut my career short."

The assistant closed the order book without showing Madame Poitiers or my aunt the final cost. I suspected that was how these sorts of places worked, unlike the larger department stores. The final bill would be sent to my uncle at the hotel and he would pay after our purchases were delivered. It was all very discreet.

"Ah, we are finished. *Bon.*" Madame Poitiers smiled at Aunt Lilian as she rose. "It has been a pleasure, as always, Lady Bainbridge. You grace my little shop with your elegance and style, as do your daughter and niece." She smiled as she opened the door for us and bade us goodbye.

Flossy was the first to comment on our morning as the carriage set off for the Mayfair Hotel. "Good lord, she hasn't changed from last year. If I have to listen to the story about Peter Fabergé one more time, I'll cover my ears and scream."

"Such a trying woman," Aunt Lilian agreed. "How she prattles on and on. I always leave her salon with a headache." Aunt Lilian's headaches had more to do with her medicinal tonic wearing off than Madame Poitiers, but neither Flossy nor I pointed that out.

"She is quite a unique character," I said. "Her designs are truly beautiful, though. She's extremely talented. It's no wonder they're so sought after."

"We were fortunate to get an appointment," Aunt Lilian said. "It was only because of a cancelation that we could. Everyone wants to wear a Poitiers design."

Flossy smirked. "As she so helpfully pointed out."

"She's simply proud of her achievements, as she has a right to be. Although I doubt she's French."

"Do you speak French, Aunt?" I asked.

"A little." She bestowed a wistful, sad smile on me. "Your mother took to her French lessons better than me. I tried to speak to Madame Poitiers in her native tongue once, and she refused to answer me in that same language. She insisted we speak English, claiming it wasn't fair on her assistant. It was the most attention she paid the poor girl during our entire appointment. Mind you, she was a different girl than the one there today."

Flossy clicked her tongue as she stared out of the window at the shops along New Bond Street. "Is anybody who claims to be French actually from that country? Lady's maids, chefs, artists, dressmakers...all say they trained in Paris. I don't believe them, personally."

"I do believe our last chef was a genuine Frenchman," Aunt Lilian said. "And his replacement doesn't claim to be anything other than English born and bred."

"Father knew her when she was younger," Flossy pointed out. "It's too late to pretend a French heritage."

I watched Aunt Lilian carefully for any sign that it bothered her that the hotel's new *chef de cuisine* knew Uncle Ronald many years ago. But she seemed as serenely distant as always as she too turned to peer out of the window at the passing shops and traffic.

The hotel's coachman deposited us at the front door of the Mayfair Hotel where Frank assisted each of us down from the carriage, all smiles and warm greetings. The friendly doorman act didn't fool me, but Flossy and Aunt Lilian were taken in by it. As soon as their backs were turned, however, he scowled at the workman exiting the building next door, pushing a wheelbarrow laden with rubble. He called out to his colleagues standing on the back of a cart, waiting to toss the wheelbarrow's contents onto the growing pile of bricks.

"Is something the matter?" I asked Frank.

"I've asked them time and again to keep their voices down. We've got distinguished guests staying here and they don't want to listen to those idiots all day."

"You can't hear them from inside the hotel."

My reasoning didn't wipe the scowl from Frank's face. Nothing I could say would cheer him, so I left him to join Flossy and Aunt Lilian who hadn't waited for me.

Guests and staff couldn't hear the workmen talking from inside the hotel, but they could hear muffled sounds of sledgehammers knocking down internal walls. The building next door was being converted from three shops into one large restaurant for the hotel. There was bound to be some disruption for the next few months, and I suspected it would get much worse before it got better. Uncle Ronald had hoped to have the restaurant opened by the height of the social season, but I doubted it would be ready in time.

Society was already beginning to trickle back into the city, although many stayed in their own houses where they would remain throughout spring and part of the summer before returning to their country manors. Those who didn't come from quite the same heights, or who'd had to sell off their London houses as the cost of keeping them rose, stayed at hotels like the Mayfair when they visited the city. They didn't stay as long but came and went as required. A lady and her daughters might stay for a few days to shop and have dress fittings, while her husband attended to business matters. They would return for a ball here and there, but wouldn't stay for the duration of the social season.

International visitors were also increasing, eager to rub shoulders with titled noblemen. American heiresses and wealthy widows in particular were checking into the hotel every day. According to my cousin Floyd, some would stay for three or four months before returning home, hopefully just for a fleeting visit to pack up their belongings and return to England to marry the impoverished lord they'd snared. That was how Floyd described it, with a heavy dose of sarcasm in his voice.

One of those Americans was now complaining in a loud voice to Peter. He'd been recently promoted from the front desk to the position of assistant manager and was still learning everything required of him. Peter was usually very good at placating annoyed guests, but from the way the woman's pitch rose with every word, he was having no luck this time.

"I want to speak to the owner!" she snapped. "If not him, then that Hobart fellow, the manager. I assume he still works here?"

"He does, madam," Peter said. "But I'm afraid Mr. Hobart and Sir Ronald are in a meeting."

"Then get them *out* of the meeting."

The young woman next to her said something to the older woman only to receive a scold for her efforts. The young woman shrank away, quite a feat considering she was taller than every woman in the foyer. They were clearly mother and daughter, going by the similarity in their appearances. Both were tall with sunken chins and narrow faces, but they sported quite different styles. The mother wore a bold moss-green gown, a pearl necklace, large emerald ring, and almost an entire spring garden of silk flowers and leaves on her wide-brimmed hat. Her daughter wore no jewels whatsoever and her outfit of off-white lace would have cost a great deal but it was demure with its high collar. She also wore a simpler hat with just a large bow at the front and not a flower in sight.

"Well?" the woman demanded. "Off you go. Fetch your superior. I want to speak to someone with authority."

Peter glanced around the foyer, his gaze desperate. Flossy and Aunt Lilian were nowhere to be seen. The lift must have been waiting on the ground floor and already taken them up to the fourth floor to their rooms. It was up to me to rescue poor Peter.

CHAPTER 2

$\mathcal{W}$ith a look of relief, he introduced me to Mrs. and Miss Hessing from New York. Miss Hessing gave me a shy smile, but Mrs. Hessing looked me up and down, a deep vertical crevice forming between her brows.

"The niece, you say?" She grunted. "You're a little young to have any influence. Where is your uncle? I want to speak to Sir Ronald about our appalling treatment."

"Mrs. Hessing usually has one of the large suites on the fourth floor," Peter said quickly. "But none become available until tomorrow. They will be accommodated in smaller rooms until then, when we'll move their belongings over as soon as possible."

"My secretary made the reservation weeks ago! Why wasn't I told then?"

"Our records show a letter was sent, explaining the situation. Perhaps your secretary failed to pass it on."

Mrs. Hessing pulled herself up to her considerable height. "This is my third year at the Mayfair, and we plan to stay for ten weeks this time. Surely we have a right to expect the best treatment. Or has the Mayfair lost some of its shine?" She settled her stance and regarded Peter critically. "It wouldn't surprise me, since Mr. Armitage no longer works here. *He* was always so accommodating, so welcoming. He was one of our favorites, was he not, Joan?"

Miss Hessing muttered something under her breath and, rather astonishingly, blushed.

"We'll miss seeing his lovely smile as he greeted us of a morning." Mrs. Hessing sighed. "Which hotel does he work for now?"

"He left the hotel business altogether," I said. "I assure you, Mr. Armitage couldn't have accommodated you on the fourth floor tonight, either." Aware of the curtness of my tone, I forced myself to smile and my voice to soften. "I know nothing can make up for the inconvenience of staying in an inferior room tonight, but if you have no other plans, perhaps you would like to join the Bainbridge family at dinner this evening? It will give us an opportunity to tell you all about our new restaurant. We like to inform our favorite guests of exciting developments and even ask the most discerning for their opinion. I can see you are a lady of style. Your advice on décor would be greatly appreciated."

Mrs. Hessing's frostiness melted into a smile that attempted to be self-deprecating but failed when she said, "My friends do say I have a unique sense of style."

Beside her, Miss Hessing drew in a rallying breath.

"I suppose we will make do for one night." Mrs. Hessing turned to Peter. "See that our things are moved while we're out tomorrow morning. We leave at ten-fifteen sharp."

Peter assured her it would be done and even gave a little bow before mother and daughter strode towards the lift.

"Are all the American guests like her?" I asked.

"Most are very nice, generous too. Mrs. Hessing is rather a unique individual."

"As is her style, so her friends—and that hat—say."

Peter chuckled. "They come every year since Miss Hessing came of age. She's searching for a titled English husband. The moment she catches one, they'll no longer need a hotel. They'll stay at his estate, I suspect."

"I wonder if Mrs. Hessing will live with them or return to New York."

"If she plans to live here too, maybe that's why Miss Hessing hasn't secured a husband yet."

I shook my head but couldn't help my smile. "You are wicked sometimes, Peter."

He watched the lift door open and Floyd step out with his friend, Jonathon. "The daughter seems pleasant enough, although it's hard to tell. She fades away beside her mother."

Floyd greeted the Hessings and introduced Jonathon. The lift operator held the door open while they exchanged pleasantries then the men walked off. Mrs. Hessing rapped her knuckles on her daughter's arm and said something to her. They watched the men for a few moments more then stepped into the lift.

I was about to leave too but hesitated. "Did you notice Miss Hessing blush when Mr. Armitage's name was mentioned? Why do you think that is?"

"He probably paid her more attention than she's ever had from a man before. He was good like that, always making sure he spoke to the quiet ones as much as the loud. It made them feel special. I've got to remember to do that."

He spoke in the past tense, as if Harry Armitage no longer charmed women. I knew first-hand that he still did. Not because he employed that charm on me. Quite the opposite; I seemed to bring out the ill-tempered side of him. Rather, I'd seen him gather information from reluctant or shy female suspects. He had a way of making them feel as though they mattered.

I nodded a greeting at my cousin and his friend, expecting them to bypass us and head for the front door. Floyd started in that direction but had to divert his course when Jonathon approached me.

Peter melted away before I could ask him if he knew my uncle's plans for the evening. Now that I'd invited the Hessings to dine with us, I didn't want to be left alone with them with only Flossy to assist me. My aunt wouldn't feel up to joining us and Floyd wouldn't be in if his father was not.

"Good morning, Cleo," Jonathon said, all smiles. He had the careless good looks of an idle youth with too much money and not enough responsibility. He'd gone to Oxford with Floyd, but he seemed to have no occupation and no cares. I suspected he would inherit wealth one day without having to lift a finger.

Floyd, however, had to work for the hotel, although he spent a great deal of his time out with his friends. My uncle grumbled and berated him for being lazy, but he didn't give him more to do.

"It's afternoon, actually," I said. "Have you two just risen?" Sometimes Jonathon stayed overnight, sleeping on the sofa in Floyd's room. Sometimes they didn't come home at all until dawn. The night porter was given strict instructions not to breathe a word to Uncle Ronald on those occasions.

"We've been up for hours," Floyd said with a wink. "Now we're going out for lunch."

"Want to join us?" Jonathon asked.

Floyd gave his friend a curious look, but Jonathon didn't seem to notice. He smiled back at me, his blue eyes twinkling. With his blond hair flopping over his forehead, he would have passed for a sweet youth, but the small scar on his cheek added a measure of ruggedness that enhanced his good looks. I suspected the women loved the effect.

Not me, however. At least, not to the extent that I wanted to accept his lunch invitation. I didn't want to give Jonathon a reason to expect more than conversation and a friendly smile.

"Not today," I said and turned to Floyd. "Is Uncle Ronald dining in the hotel tonight?"

"He is. Why?"

"Mrs. Hessing was upset that her usual room wasn't available until tomorrow. To appease her, I asked her to join us for dinner. Will you be there too?"

Jonathon hooted a laugh. "Of course he will be. But you'd better watch out, my friend. That Hessing woman has her eye on you. If you're not careful, you'll find yourself married by the time she leaves England."

"Me? Ha!" Floyd clapped his friend on the shoulder. "You're the one the mother covets for her daughter."

"The daughter? No, I meant the mother."

Floyd rolled his eyes. "Very amusing. But I wouldn't be so confident of escaping her clutches if I were you." He gave his friend a smug smile. "I'm not in line to inherit a title. *You* are, and that makes you far more attractive."

"True." Jonathon jerked his head, flicking his hair out of his eyes. "Does that make you want to join us for lunch, Cleo?"

A bubble of laughter rose up. "No."

He sighed theatrically. "So you're condemning me to an afternoon of dull conversation with this lout. That's cruel."

Floyd shoved his hand in his jacket pocket. "If you're finished flirting with my cousin, I'd like to join the others before they order without us."

Jonathon grinned at me before slapping his hat on his head and following Floyd out of the hotel.

I smiled all the way up the stairs until I reached Uncle Ronald's office. I could have sent one of the hotel footmen to deliver a message, but it had been some time since I'd been alone with my uncle and it was probably about time that I talked to him. If nothing else, it would break the ice that had formed after he'd warned me to stay away from Harry Armitage. Uncle Ronald had taken a firm dislike to Harry after he'd learned about his criminal record. It didn't matter that Harry had been a child living on the street at the time. In my uncle's book, Harry was not to be trusted as assistant manager or as a friend to his niece. He'd been fired from his position and warned to stay away from both me and the hotel.

Harry obliged. I did not. Since my uncle paid me a generous allowance each month, I agreed to attend family outings and gave my opinion on his plans for the hotel when asked, but I would not allow him to choose my friends for me.

Fortunately, he seemed to want to forget about our argument once he'd calmed down. While I knew the issue simmered below the surface, ready to boil over at the first sign of provocation, it was better for everyone that we moved on as quickly as possible. My uncle was a stubborn, proud man, so it suited his nature to pretend the argument never happened. I also suspected I was the first person in the family to stand up to him and he wasn't quite sure what to do about it.

I sat in his office and waited while he finished what he was doing. Uncle Ronald gave the papers spread out before him his full attention. He may be a descendent of nobility, but perching on a minor branch of the family tree meant he'd not inherited a title. He had inherited a London mansion, however. Armed with a strong work ethic, and his wife's fortune, he'd turned that mansion into a luxury hotel. I couldn't help but admire his business acumen.

When he finally slotted his pen into the stand, he sat back and placed his clasped hands over his stomach. He considered me as if I were as important as his paperwork. That put me quite high up in his estimation.

"Did you enjoy your morning at the dressmaker's?" he asked.

"It was very pleasant, thank you."

"How many new gowns have you ordered?"

Was he asking because he was worried about the cost? It was difficult to tell. "Only the number Aunt Lilian thought best."

He twiddled his thumbs. "A very diplomatic answer. I'm sure Lilian ordered you as many as she did for Florence. We both want our niece to look her best this season, after all."

I thanked him for his generosity and his features softened.

"You and Florence will be very popular at all the parties, I'm sure." He sat forward and stroked his moustache, pinning me to the seat with his steely stare. "You will be attending quite a number of events, so your aunt tells me. And I'm sure you'll be…amenable."

My heart stilled. "Amenable?"

He waved his hand. "You'll dance, of course, and make new friends."

So that was the price of his generosity—my cooperation.

What if I refused the gowns or refused to attend all the parties? Would he get angry and throw me out? The contrarian in me wanted to try it and see. The sensible part of me did not. I liked living at the hotel. I had a comfortable life and friends among the staff. My two cousins treated me like a sister, which was more than I'd ever hoped for. I didn't want to be thrown out. Not for refusing some beautiful gowns that I wasn't even paying for. I wasn't the sort of person who cut off her nose to spite her face.

"I like to dance," I assured him. "And I enjoy intelligent conversation. If I can't find the latter, I'll resort to the former." There. It was acquiescence but not a promise to court young men of his choosing.

"Speaking of friends, I'm glad to see you've cut ties with some old ones," he went on.

He meant Harry. I kept my features schooled and my mouth shut. I simply met his gaze across the desk.

He held it for a moment before looking away. He pushed the ink stand a few inches back and cleared his throat. "If you go shopping with Florence, be sure to have the bills sent here. No doubt she'll take you to the finest shops."

My heart lifted. Not because I wanted to go shopping, but by not mentioning my aunt, it meant he expected Flossy and me to go out alone and unchaperoned. While we'd done it in the past, my frequent mysterious absences from the hotel during investigations had raised his ire. He'd even hinted that he would assign one of the hotel maids as my chaperone. Thankfully he'd never followed through with the threat. It was yet another sign that he believed I'd put my acquaintance with Harry behind me.

Perhaps I had, but not because I wanted to. Harry's response to the letters I'd sent had been short and formal, without a hint of familiarity. Knowing the predicament I would be in if my uncle discovered we were still friends meant he was reluctant to see me. I could have gone to his office to see him, but I stayed away. I simply had no reason to go.

But staying away wasn't easy.

"I wanted to let you know that the Hessings from America have arrived," I said.

"Ah, the indomitable Mrs. Hessing and her unfortunate daughter."

"Unfortunate?"

"To have an overbearing mother dragging her half way across the world to find a husband she has no hope of catching."

"She might have hope," I said, taking offence on Miss Hessing's behalf.

"You haven't been a part of the social scene here for long, so you don't know what it's like. If Florence couldn't find herself a husband after being out for an entire year, what hope does a meek girl like Miss Hessing have when there are a dozen American heiresses also in London? Her lack of character wouldn't matter if she were a beauty, but unfortunately I've heard her compared to a horse by Floyd's friends." He shrugged. "Her mother brings her back again and again, attaching more and more money to the hook in the hope of catching a duke or, at the very least, a baron. She should have settled for the plain Mister who showed some interest last year. Could have saved herself a fortune."

And her poor daughter the humiliation.

"Her usual room wasn't available until tomorrow, so I invited her to dine with us tonight. I hope that's all right. I couldn't think of any other way to placate her."

His smile began slowly then grew wider and warmer. "It was precisely the right thing to do, Cleo. Thank you." He spoke softly. "You have a good head for the hotel business. It's a pity you're not a man. You'd make an excellent assistant manager."

I bit my tongue but it was no use. It wouldn't remain silent. "You hired a female chef." There were no women employed as head cooks in any of the exclusive London restaurants, so it had come as a surprise when my uncle hired her. Even though Mrs. Poole's reputation was exemplary, she'd not been in charge of a kitchen quite as large as the Mayfair's before.

"Elizabeth Poole is an exception. She's the most sought-after private chef in all of England. She has cooked for princes and dukes. Her cuisine is delicious and the presentation artistic. She teaches cookery classes, writes for cooking journals, and has a reputation second only to Escoffier." His eyes brightened when he spoke about her many achievements. "She is also not here on a permanent basis, as she likes to remind me. There's a task for you, Cleo. See if you can convince her to stay on. I don't want to continue the search for another chef when I have an excellent one already working for me."

It seemed to me that Mrs. Poole had quite a lucrative career and didn't need to work at the Mayfair. "It's fortunate you two are old friends."

"And that she took pity on me." He chuckled. "I hadn't seen her in years, so I wasn't sure she'd accept. I thought she might have forgotten me."

19

"You are not easy to forget, Uncle."

He chuckled again, but it quickly faded. "Are you telling me you want to be assistant manager? Is that why you're reminding me that I hired a woman in a position of authority?"

The rapid flip of topic had me in a spin for a moment. "No! I just don't want you to close your mind to the idea of hiring women for positions they wouldn't usually be considered for. Peter is the right choice for assistant manager."

"He's no—" His lips pinched, cutting off the end of his sentence.

"You're right, he's no Harry Armitage," I said quietly.

It was a response that could have failed miserably and stoked my uncle's temper again. But I'd wanted to remind him how good Harry had been as assistant manager. I wanted him to feel regret for dismissing him.

He snatched the pen out of the stand and pulled a stack of papers closer. I was dismissed.

I headed to my suite, where a maid's cart laden with clean towels, sheets and supplies was parked near the door. Harmony dusted the window sill in my sitting room, but she stopped upon seeing me. She tucked the duster under her arm.

"I hoped you'd be back for lunch," she said, taking a seat on the sofa. "I ordered sandwiches." Indeed she had. Enough for two.

Harmony should only be half way through her shift at this time. She rarely joined me for lunch, but we almost always had breakfast together before she styled my hair.

"This is a treat," I said, choosing a sandwich of cucumber and ham. "To what do I owe the pleasure?"

"No reason." She picked up a newspaper and handed one to me then retrieved a second for herself from the small stack. She read as she nibbled a sandwich.

It had become our breakfast ritual to scour the newspapers for potential clients—victims of burglary, kidnappings, that sort of thing. I'd hoped Harry would pass on more clients to me, but so far, he'd sent none my way since the Warrington divorce case that had turned into a murder investigation. The lack of co-operation was further evidence that he wanted as little to do with me as possible.

This morning I'd hurried out after breakfast for the appointment at Maison de Poiters so we hadn't finished reading through the papers. I'd assumed we'd leave it at that, but Harmony clearly wanted to read all the copies front to back.

I flipped the page and scanned the columns. "A shop burned down in Whitechapel." I tapped my finger on the headline. "Arson is suspected after witnesses saw a man run away. I could approach the shopkeeper and offer to find the arsonist."

"No shopkeeper in Whitechapel has enough money to hire a private detective, and there's a good chance the building's owner started the fire himself to claim the insurance."

Harmony's opinion of people was generally harsher than mine, but it wasn't surprising, considering our different upbringings. Mine had been thoroughly upper middle class, raised by an academic father and a mother whose wealthy family had cut her off upon her marriage. Harmony lived in a slum all her life until she moved into the Mayfair's staff accommodation. She'd once told me she'd seen the worst of humanity, as poverty made people desperate and desperate people did terrible things to survive. I used to subscribe to that opinion too until I started investigating murders and saw first-hand how cruel and devious folk in the middle and upper classes could be. There were good and bad in all walks of life.

Harmony folded up the newspaper she was reading and reached for another sandwich. "I should resume my chores." She didn't rise, however, and continued nibbling her sandwich, lost in thought. When she finished, she offered the plate of sandwiches to me. "You should call on him."

"Who?" I asked, oh-so-innocently.

"You know who. Go and visit him and see if he has a case for you. Tell him you'll take anything, even the unhappy spouses."

Harry had vowed he wouldn't investigate the numerous cases that came across his desk where husbands and wives wished to employ his services to catch their spouse with a lover. Proving adultery was the easiest route to divorce, but I'd been surprised at how many couples wanted to formally end their marriage. Harmony wasn't.

"If Harry wishes to pass them on to me, he'll send them my way," I said. "He hasn't. I have no interest in going to his office, cap in hand. I'm above begging."

Harmony gave me an arched look. "For now."

She had a point. I couldn't go on like this much longer. It wasn't so much the money I needed—although the dream of moving out of the hotel got further and further away the longer I was without work—but I had to do *something* with my time. There was only so much shopping and afternoon teas I could take before I went mad. I'd visited all the museums and art galleries several times, and I took walks most days, even in the rain. That was more than my cousin ever did.

Harmony left to resume her duties, and I spent the afternoon reading newspapers and writing letters, pausing to have afternoon tea in the hotel's large sitting room with Flossy. We'd just finished and were about to leave when Aunt Lilian hurried in. She looked as though she'd just woken up after a restless night. Her eyes were hooded, the eyelids dark and ribbed with veins. Her hair was flat on one side and messy on the other, and the top button of her collar was undone at her throat. She searched the room and a look of utter relief washed over her face when she spotted Flossy and me.

She rushed forward, hands outstretched. "Florence, Cleo, there you are."

I took one hand and Flossy took the other. "What is it, Mother?" Flossy asked. "Are you unwell? Shall I send for the doctor?"

"I don't need a doctor, just my tonic." She blinked back tears. "I can't find it. I think it fell out of my purse at Maison de Poitiers."

"You took it with you?"

"I thought I might need it, but I didn't take any, even though I felt a headache coming on. I know you don't want me to, but I carried it with me anyway. Just for an emergency, you understand."

The tonic had been prescribed by her doctor to cure her

melancholy disposition. It achieved that rather well. When-ever she took a dose, she always cheered up. It gave her energy and vitality. She was a different person when she took it, not faded and frayed like a flag left out in the weather too long.

But the tonic also made her condition so much worse when it wore off. Not only did she suffer from crippling headaches, but her moods also became very low. And the more she took of it, the more often she needed the next dose and the next, and the worse she felt in between. Flossy and I had tried to tell her it was making her sicker, so some days she agreed not to take it at all. But on those occasions, she kept to her bed in her darkened room, as even the wan London sunlight hurt her eyes.

"Can you return to the salon to see if it fell behind the sofa cushions?" Aunt Lilian asked.

"It'll be closed by the time we get there," I said. "I'll go tomorrow, first thing."

"But it's all I have left, and I need it for tonight." Her voice thinned to a whine. "I hear we're dining with Mrs. Hessing, and I ought to be there. She's one of our best guests."

Her desperate plea had caught the attention of three women seated nearby. One pursed her lips in disapproval.

I steered my aunt out of earshot. "Flossy and I will be hostesses in your stead. Mrs. Hessing will understand."

Flossy tried to give her mother a reassuring smile. "Do try not to worry."

Aunt Lilian chewed her lower lip, leaving behind teeth marks. "Even so, I need my tonic. What time is it, Cleo? Perhaps you can make it before the shop closes, after all. Our carriages are very swift."

"Not with the end of day traffic." I grasped her hand again, feeling it tremble before she snatched it away.

She rubbed her temple. "I'll send for the doctor. He can bring me another bottle."

"It's not an emergency, Mother." Flossy gripped Aunt Lilian's elbow, only to be shaken off. "You can go without for tonight."

Aunt Lilian bared her teeth in a snarl. "Don't speak to me

like that." She turned and rushed out, brushing past Mr. Chapman the steward without responding to his greeting.

Beside me, Flossy sniffed. "I wish she wouldn't rely on it so much."

"Do you think she'll call the doctor?"

"She doesn't know how to use the telephone, but that might not stop her asking Mr. Hobart to call on her behalf."

Aunt Lilian didn't join us for dinner. It was a long evening with Mrs. Hessing dominating the conversation, criticizing everything from the weather to the prime minister. Her daughter sat mostly silent, despite my efforts to draw her out. Despite her silence, or perhaps because of it, her mother spoke about her as if she weren't there. At one point or other, she managed to mention all of Miss Hessing's good qualities as well as the amount of her inheritance. My uncle looked interested. Floyd did not.

The following morning, after breakfast, I walked to Maison de Poitiers. I planned my journey so I'd be there when Madame Poitiers opened the salon. I wanted to be back at the hotel before my aunt awoke. It wasn't far, but my aunt and cousin had insisted on taking one of the hotel carriages yesterday. As Flossy put it, only those who can't afford private vehicles walk, even short distances.

As I approached the shop on New Bond Street, Madame Poitiers' assistant approached from the opposite direction. She didn't see me as she dug through her bag. She pulled out a key and inserted it into the lock.

"Good morning," I said.

She jumped at the sound of my voice. "Oh! Miss Fox. You surprised me. Did you forget something yesterday?"

"My aunt thinks she dropped her medicine here. Did you happen to find a small bottle of tonic caught in the sofa cushions?"

"No, but come in and we'll look together."

"I'm afraid I don't know your name," I said apologetically.

She smiled as she opened the door. "It's Anna Newland."

She had a warm smile and a pleasant face with almond colored eyes and dark brown hair fixed in a simple bun high on her head. A straw hat sat in front of the bun, the brim decorated with yellow and orange ribbons arranged to look like a sunburst. It was simple yet stylish, much like the woman herself. She couldn't have been more than my age. She wore no jewelry and a plain black dress, but like Madame Poitiers' dress, it was well made and fit her frame perfectly.

Yesterday, I'd thought her shy, but her easy manner this morning made me think she was simply staying quiet to counter-balance her exuberant employer. Inside, she opened the curtains, flooding the salon with light. I crossed the room to the sofa on which my aunt had sat but stopped before I reached it.

The sight of two legs had me clutching my throat as bile rose. The rest of the body was hidden by the sofa.

I rounded it cautiously, reluctantly, and gasped. Madame Poitiers lay on the floor, her blood-red eyes staring sightlessly up at the ceiling, a white strip of lace wrapped around her throat. I didn't need to feel her pulse to know she was dead.

CHAPTER 3

 iss Newland's scream brought the entire sewing team into the salon, as well as the shoemaker from next door. He immediately left again to telephone the police, since the salon didn't have a device, and returned a few minutes later. By then, Miss Newland had calmed down. She sat on the second sofa, as far away from the body as possible. One of the seamstresses brought her a cup of tea from the back room and offered me one.

I politely declined and steeled myself to inspect the body. I'd never seen a murder victim before, not even for the previous murders I'd investigated. Those bodies had all been removed before my services were engaged. I tried to separate myself from the dead woman lying on the floor, but it was impossible. All I could think about was how spirited she'd been yesterday morning, how full of life. Now she was just an empty vessel, her life cruelly stolen.

Fortunately someone had closed her eyes so she no longer stared vacantly up at the ceiling, but nothing could be done about the lips swollen in death, or the crooked angle of her leg, half bent. I shuddered at the sight of the strangulation marks at her throat. The fabric had loosened enough to reveal the bruised flesh. It was clearly the murder weapon.

Harmony's no-nonsense voice came into my head, ordering me to notice every detail in case it was important. I wasn't sure how we could turn this into a case worth investigating—we would need a client for that—but there would be time to consider it later when I could think a little more clearly.

I inspected Madame Poitiers' throat but didn't touch her. The white lace had been wrapped around her neck just the once. The rest of it was bunched up behind her head. The killer had probably come up behind her, looped the fabric around her throat and pulled tight until she died. That required strength. From the awkward position of her leg, I suspected she hadn't been moved *post mortem*, which meant she'd died on this spot, facing away from the change room and the back room where the seamstresses worked.

The murder weapon was a bright white length of lace embroidered with seed pearls and silver thread. The lace looked delicate but it must have been strong not to tear under the force required to strangle Madame Poitiers.

I inspected the rest of the body and noted the blood under the fingernails and the scratch marks on her throat where she'd tried to pull the fabric away. She'd fought hard, the poor woman.

I glanced up to see the shoemaker comforting Miss Newland and the seamstresses clustered together, crying. No one took any notice of me. All seemed to be avoiding looking directly at the body.

I removed my glove and touched Madame Poitiers' cheek. It was cool but not cold. She hadn't been dead long. If she'd died after closing up yesterday, or early in the night, the body would feel much colder.

The door opened and a woman entered, only to stop and stare at all of us. She did not notice the body, thank goodness, but must have suspected something was amiss.

Miss Newland jumped up. "I'm afraid we're closed."

"I've come to pick up the veil for Lady Margaret Colclough's debut outfit," the woman said with an imperial stiffness that spoke of her displeasure at being turned away. "It was being shortened. I'm Lady Colclough's maid and—"

"Please, come back tomorrow. We're closed."

The maid drew herself up to her full height. "My mistress won't be pleased if her daughter's veil isn't ready."

Miss Newland started to cry.

I joined her at the door and addressed the maid. "There has been a distressing incident. If you'd be so good as to wait a day or two, it would be appreciated."

The maid looked around at the tear-stained faces of the seamstresses and promptly left. I closed the door and asked Miss Newland to lock it until the police arrived.

"I assume the veil she came to collect is…" I rubbed my throat.

Miss Newland closed her eyes. "I can't look."

"It is," one of the seamstresses confirmed.

There were seven of them and she appeared to be the eldest. Her gray hair was secured with pins and combs in a simple yet modern, loosely upswept style. Like all the seamstresses, she wore a white apron over a black shapeless uniform, the pockets stuffed with fabric and a pair of scissors.

One of the younger girls sobbed. "Now we'll have to make another one."

"We might be able to salvage it," one of the other seamstresses said.

The rest looked at her in horror. Realizing what she'd said, she burst into tears. The older woman put her arms around her and drew her to her chest.

The only one who didn't look upset by the murder of her employer was a tall woman with black hair, not much older than me. She leaned back against the counter, arms crossed, a thoughtful expression on her face as she stared at nothing in particular.

She suddenly roused, pushing off from the counter. "We should get back to work."

"Why?" whined one of the girls. "What's the point now?" She indicated the body without looking at it.

"There are orders to fulfill," said the older woman. She had an accent but I couldn't place it. "We must complete them."

"Who'll pay us?"

The dark-haired woman at the counter looked at her as though she was stupid. "Her husband, of course. Everything belongs to him now."

The seamstresses exchanged blank looks. "But we've never met him," said one.

"Will he keep us on?" asked another.

"Depends if he wants to continue to run the business," said a third.

"It can't survive without Madame. Can it?"

One of the girls sighed heavily. "I don't see how it can."

The youngest girl, who'd been sobbing into the arms of the oldest just moments ago, clicked her tongue. "I'll have to find employment elsewhere."

It would seem they'd got over the shock of seeing their employer lying dead on the floor and their thoughts had turned to more practical matters. It was rather telling that their tears dried so quickly.

I glanced at Miss Newland. She too seemed to have rallied as talk turned to the future of the salon without Madame Poitiers. She pocketed her handkerchief and suggested the seamstresses do as the dark-haired woman suggested and return to work.

"If nothing else, it will get them out of the way for when the police arrive," she said to the shoemaker and me once they'd gone.

He also excused himself to return to his unattended shop, leaving Miss Newland and me alone.

"I am sorry about all this," she said. "What is it you say you came for?"

I told her about Aunt Lilian's tonic and she set about looking for it in the sofa. "Do you know anyone who'd want to kill Madame Poitiers?" I asked.

She stilled. After a moment, she resumed her search amongst the cushions. "No."

"She was well liked?"

"Is this it?" She held up a small bottle.

"Yes, thank you." I accepted the bottle and tucked it into my bag.

We stood about awkwardly until Miss Newland said, "I'm sure you'd like to leave, but perhaps you should wait to speak to the police. Is that all right?"

"It's perfectly fine."

"Would you prefer to wait outside?"

"It's much too cold." I nodded at the counter where the order book in which Miss Newland had written the details of our dresses yesterday sat prominently in the center. "Is that always left out overnight?"

She followed my gaze. "Sometimes." She rounded the counter and I followed.

Below the counter were drawers and open shelves filled with more order books, measuring tapes, hand mirrors, scissors, and baskets of pins, threads, and samples of buttons, feathers, beads, ribbons and fabric swatches.

Miss Newland opened one of the drawers and slipped the order book inside, on top of a magnifying glass and a business card with a name printed on it that I recognized. It wasn't a name I expected to associate with a high-end dressmaker's salon.

"Why is there a card for a private investigator here?" I asked.

Miss Newland removed the order book to study Harry's card before returning it. "I don't know."

"Did Madame Poitiers hire him?"

"As I said, I don't know." She gave me a pointed glare. "Would you mind returning to the other side of the counter, please? Thank you, Miss Fox. I wouldn't want anything disturbed before the police arrived." For someone in quite a bit of distress earlier, she was now very composed.

I rounded the counter and followed its length, careful to avoid the dead body mere feet away. I traced my fingers along the polished edge only to stop at a small notch in the wood. A dark thread the length of my finger had been caught there. I would have ignored it except that it was out of place in the salon. It was thick and coarse, not fine like those which would be used on Madame Poitiers' gowns.

"What's this from?" I asked, holding it up.

Miss Newland glanced up from the ledger she was looking through. A frown scored her forehead, but not because of the thread. "I don't know. A dress, I suppose."

I didn't pursue it as she returned to study the ledger again. "Is there something important in there?" I asked.

She opened her mouth to say something then closed it. She shut the book too. "It's nothing."

Someone tried to open the door from the outside. Finding

it locked, they knocked. Being closer to the door, I opened it, and greeted Detective Inspector Hobart.

"Miss Fox!" He peered past me. "What are you doing here?"

"I happened to arrive at the same time as Miss Newland." I indicated the assistant, now standing behind me. "We discovered the body. That was about ten to nine."

I'd met the Scotland Yard detective several times. As Harry's father, he'd assisted us on occasion. He'd also overseen the hotel murder investigation, proving himself to be very thorough and methodical but somewhat slow to act. He was a good man and would make sure the right person was arrested for killing Madame Poitiers. I was glad to see him.

He led two constables and a sergeant inside and crouched beside the body. He ordered the sergeant to take notes.

"Has anything been touched?" He glanced up at Miss Newland, brows arched.

"No, nothing," she said.

"The body hasn't been moved," I said. "But Miss Newland placed the order book into the top drawer. We also searched through the sofa cushions to find my aunt's tonic." I opened my bag and showed him the bottle. "That's why I returned here this morning. Aunt Lilian left it here yesterday during our fitting."

Miss Newland folded her arms over her chest. "Yes, that's right. I thought you were asking if the body had been touched." She gave a slight shudder.

"There are also seven seamstresses through there." I indicated the door to the back workroom. "They came out when they heard Miss Newland scream. The shoemaker next door came in then too. I didn't see them touch anything."

Detective Inspector Hobart stood, grunting a little with the effort. He wasn't a large man, but he wasn't young. Harry said he was in his sixties and considering retirement. He regarded me with his blue eyes that could be friendly at times but were now steely.

After a few questions about my dealings with Madame Poitiers, he dismissed me as unimportant. He turned to Miss Newland and asked her about the shop's morning routine.

"You arrived at ten to nine," he said. "Is that your usual arrival time?"

"Yes," Miss Newland said.

The sergeant scribbled her answer in his notebook.

"The door was locked?"

"Yes."

"Is that unusual if Madame Poitiers is already in?"

She shook her head. "She keeps it locked until we open at nine. She doesn't want people wandering in off the street if they don't have an appointment." She glanced at the book on the counter.

"And what time does Madame Poitiers usually get in of a morning?"

Miss Newland removed the tear-soaked handkerchief she'd tucked into her sleeve. "It depends. Sometimes she comes in before me to speak with the seamstresses. They begin work at eight. Sometimes she might meet an important client before opening, but that's rare." She glanced at the book on the counter again. "I think that was why she was here this morning before me. The appointment book mentions Lady Bunbury was due at eight-fifteen."

I'd heard the name before but couldn't place it.

Detective Inspector Hobart reached across the counter and picked up the book. "You were not aware of this appointment, Miss Newland?"

She frowned. "No. I noticed it just now. Usually, I write the appointments in the book, but not that one. You can see it's in a different hand."

The inspector made sure his sergeant wrote that information down then returned the book to the counter.

"I'm sure it doesn't mean anything," Miss Newland said quickly. "Lady Bunbury is a very good customer."

"Does she usually come so early?"

"No. She has her fittings during the day, just like everyone else. Any private appointments with Madame made before opening or after closing are usually of a financial matter."

"You mean that's when the customers pay her?"

"No-o." She teased out her handkerchief before bunching it up again. "Accounts are sent to the client's home and usually settled by the head of the household or his man of business. Private appointments in the salon are made when the client either doesn't want her husband to know how much she has spent and settles the account in person, or if she needs to make other arrangements."

He arched one bushy gray eyebrow. "Other arrangements?"

"A payment schedule is agreed upon, for those clients who are in financial difficulty."

"Which do you think is the case for Lady Bunbury?"

She glanced at me. "I couldn't possibly say."

Detective Inspector Hobart also looked at me. Then he nodded at one of the constables who opened the front door. "Thank you, Miss Fox. I know where to find you if I have further questions."

I had more to tell him, but they were mostly theories and he would come up with the same ones after he spent some time looking around. The only thing he might overlook was the coarse thread which I still held.

I handed it to him. "I found this caught on a notch on the counter's edge."

"And?"

"And it might have come off the killer's clothes. It doesn't belong in a shop that sells gowns made of expensive fabric."

He removed a pair of spectacles from his inside jacket pocket and peered through them at the thread. Then he handed it to one of the constables. "Thank you for your observation."

I left, wondering how long it would take him to find Harry's business card and whether he'd do anything about it.

I returned to the hotel and asked one of the footmen to take the bottle of tonic up to my aunt. I immediately left again before anyone from my family saw me and asked where I was going. I would think of a suitable lie later, depending on how long I was absent.

I headed to Harry's office in Soho, stopping at the café next door and ordering two coffees from Luigi. He chatted amiably as he made the coffees, his thick Cockney accent broken by the occasional Italian word. The two elderly regulars with the complexions of aged leather didn't look up from their cups when I entered or when I wished them a pleasant day as I left.

I balanced the small cups in one hand as I pushed open the door at the base of the steps and then the second door at the top. Harry looked up from his desk, his lips parting in a silent gasp before closing again.

"Still haven't learned to knock?" he asked.

"My hands are full." I set the cups down on his desk and removed my hat and coat.

"You managed to work the doorknob."

I hung up my coat alongside his on the stand near the door and returned to the desk. I sat without being invited and greeted him with a smile. "It's good to see you too, Harry."

He picked up one of the cups and sipped. Another cup from Luigi's café sat empty on the side of the desk. He'd been in for some time. He watched me over the rim of the cup, trying to hide his scrutiny. It failed rather spectacularly. I felt the heat rise in my cheeks.

I arched my brows to let him know that I knew he was watching me. It was better to acknowledge it instead of pretending it wasn't happening. Better, but not easier.

"You look well," he said, setting down the cup.

"As do you." It was true. He was a very healthy looking specimen of masculinity. Very healthy indeed, with his dark hair combed neatly back and the strong angles of his face defining a firm and cleanly shaved jaw. He had wide shoulders and was more athletic than slim, despite being tall.

"How are you, Cleo?" he asked, all polite formality. At least he used my first name.

"Fine, thanks. And you?"

"Busy." He indicated the paperwork spread across his desk. He'd been reading a file when I walked in, but he now closed it.

"You have a lot of cases?"

He smirked. "Not enough to put on an assistant, if that's what you're thinking."

"I'm thinking that I would be an associate, not an assistant, but I'll overlook your mistake this time."

The smirk turned to a genuine look of amusement. It quickly faded, however. He sipped his coffee again and I sipped mine. The silence turned awkward, and I knew I should break it, but I didn't want to launch into the nasty business of Madame Poitiers' death just yet. The problem was, I didn't know what else to say.

"Are your family well?" he asked.

"Yes, thank you."

"I see the renovations have started for the new restaurant."

"You've been past the hotel?"

"It's not far from here. I can't avoid it." He shifted in the chair, the unspoken reason for him not stopping to call on me hanging between us. "It's a busy time at the Mayfair, but it will get busier."

"Indeed. Mrs. Hessing and her daughter checked in yesterday. She made a fuss when her room wasn't available and you weren't there to smooth things over."

"She'd find something else to complain about if it was ready."

"She remembers you fondly. Both she and her daughter do."

He pressed his lips together in a non-committal smile. "Forgive my bluntness, Cleo, but are you here for a particular reason? It's just that I have an important client who's rather demanding."

"Madame Poitiers?"

His eyes flared with surprise. He set the cup down. "No. Her husband. Why did you mention her?"

"She's dead. I found her murdered this morning in her salon."

His jaw slackened. He shook his head as if trying to shake loose a myriad of tangled thoughts. "Murdered? And *you* found her?"

"Along with her assistant." I gave him an account of my morning, beginning with why I'd called at the salon in the first place and finishing with the arrival of his father. "I found your card in a drawer. Why did she have it if she's not your client?"

He shrugged. "Perhaps she found it amongst her husband's things and took it."

"What did he hire you for?"

"That's confidential."

I tilted my head to the side and regarded him. "It was something to do with her, wasn't it? Did he need evidence of a lover to divorce her?"

He leaned back in the chair and crossed his arms. He looked like he had no intention of telling me anything. "I told you, I don't take on those sorts of cases." From the way he didn't quite meet my gaze, I suspected that wasn't entirely the truth.

I knew he had strong opinions about divorce cases, although his objection specifically pertained to seducing wives to trap them into committing adultery, not divorce itself.

My mind raced through the possible reasons he could have been hired. "Madame Poitiers would only have your card if she intended to confront you, and she wouldn't do that if the reason her husband hired you had nothing to do with her. Which means your investigation does have something to do with her." He simply blinked back at me, neither confirming nor denying if I was heading in the right direction. "With her gone, there's no need to be so secretive anymore, Harry. Your investigation will be ended by Monsieur Poitiers as soon as he finds out about her death."

"Mr. Lindsey."

"Pardon?"

"His name is Bertrand Lindsey, not Poitiers. Her married name is Gertrude Lindsey. Her maiden name was Russell. She was born and bred in England, although she resided in France many years ago, so he told me."

That was one mystery solved. It was hardly a revelatory one, however. Even Flossy assumed the dressmaker wasn't French, so I doubted many others believed the act.

"You're really not going to tell me, are you?" I asked.

He smiled in the most irritating way. "As I said, it's confidential." He leaned forward, clasping his hands on the desk. "My client wouldn't like me blurting out his business to all and sundry."

I leaned forward too, clasping my hands in an identical manner. I regarded him from beneath heavy lids and lowered my voice. "I'm not just anyone, Harry."

My tactic to unsettle him worked. He suddenly sat back, stroking a hand through his hair and looking everywhere but at me. "Yes. Well."

"We're friends now. Aren't we?"

He cleared his throat. "Why do you want to know? You're not investigating the murder. Scotland Yard is. My father will get to the bottom of it, if he hasn't already."

So much for my attempt to get answers. I really wasn't very good at persuasion. Or perhaps I wasn't very good at persuading *him*. "Very well. You win. I'm leaving." I picked up my bag and the cups and headed for the door. "Oh, one more thing. Do you know Lady Bunbury?"

He removed my coat from the stand and assisted me into it. "The name is familiar, but I've never met her. She wasn't a guest at the hotel when I worked there. Why?"

I simply smiled, earning a scowl in response.

He reached for the doorknob just as the door opened suddenly. Harry stepped out of the way, bumping into me. I lost my balance and dropped the cups.

Harry grabbed hold of my arms, although I was in no danger of falling. He let the cups drop. The dregs of our coffees dribbled onto the floorboards.

I blinked up at him. He stood so close I could see the dark speckles in his eyes and smell the subtle scent of his cologne. "Thank you," I murmured.

He swallowed heavily.

"You again, Miss Fox!" The booming voice of Harry's father had us both pulling away. I felt guilty, but I wasn't sure why. "I should have known you'd seen his card." His grunt was filled with amusement, not censure.

"Harry was just about to tell me what he knows about Lady Bunbury," I said on a rush of breath.

"Is that so? Was he going to shout it at your back as you descended the stairs?"

I bit my lip. It really wasn't a good idea to lie to a man who'd spent forty years trying to detect them.

Inspector Hobart closed the door and indicated we should both return to the desk. Harry hesitated, but I didn't. I sat on one of the guest chairs while Inspector Hobart took the other.

After a moment, Harry resumed his seat. "I don't know

anything about Lady Bunbury," he said. "Why do you want to know?" This question he directed to his father, not me. He'd guessed there was a connection between her and the murder.

"According to Miss Newland, the assistant, Lady Bunbury owed Madame Poitiers money," Inspector Hobart said. "She had an appointment early this morning, most likely to discuss a payment plan for an outstanding debt. She's possibly the last person to see the victim alive."

"Or she could be the killer," Harry pointed out. "Or perhaps she wasn't let into the salon at the scheduled time because the victim was already dead and the killer gone."

His father nodded in approval. "Did Harry tell you why he's working for the victim's husband, Miss Fox?"

"No. He told you?" I arched my brows at Harry. "What happened to not blurting it out to all and sundry?"

Harry clamped his mouth shut but glared at his father.

"He wanted to talk it through with someone," Inspector Hobart said.

"So seeing his card in the drawer at the salon came as no shock to you."

"It did a little, since it was the husband who hired him to find out about her background."

"Father," Harry ground out.

His father waved his hand. "You might as well tell her. She's smart. She might be able to help."

"I don't need help."

"I didn't mean you."

"Shouldn't you be at the crime scene?" Harry asked.

"My sergeant is there, taking down witness statements. I'll go through them later, but I wanted to speak to you first." He withdrew Harry's card from his pocket and slid it across the desk. "Begin by telling Miss Fox why you were hired, then tell us both what you've discovered."

$\mathcal{H}$ arry sighed, sounding very much like he'd been shepherded into a corner. At least it wasn't me who'd cornered him, that way he couldn't get angry with me. "I was hired by Mr. Lindsey to find out more about the woman he married. After twenty-one and a half years of marriage, he started to wonder if she was lying to him. Not about being French—he knew she wasn't—but other things. She wouldn't tell him anything about her past from before they met, for example, and he began to notice holes in her stories that went beyond colorful embellishment. She would claim she was in a particular city at a particular time and then would say she'd never visited it at all or was there in another year entirely."

"He only started wondering that now," I said, "*twenty-one years* after they married?"

Harry shrugged. "According to him, he was in love and overlooked her lies."

"What changed?"

"He planned on filing for divorce. I know, I know, I said I wouldn't take on those kinds of cases, but needs must."

"This one is different," I assured him. "No one is asking you to find a lover or make one up."

He looked pleased with my response. My opinion mattered to him, I realized with surprise.

"Why did he plan on divorcing her?" Inspector Hobart asked.

"A man came to their flat when she was at the shop three days ago. He said he was a friend of Gertrude's and knew her by her maiden name, Russell. He wanted to speak to her. Mr. Lindsey told him nothing and the man went away but came back that evening. His wife was home by then and spoke to the man in private. They spoke in harsh tones, but Mr. Lindsey couldn't make out what they talked about. His wife refused to tell him anything after the man left."

"I don't see the connection between an old friend turning up and Mr. Lindsey wanting a divorce now," I said.

"The stranger told Mr. Lindsey that the Gertrude Russell he knew was a singer, not in the opera as she claimed, but for a performing troupe that traveled through Europe putting on shows, playing at country fairs. That's how they met. He was a pianist in the troupe. Since she has been telling everyone for years that she was an opera singer who could have sung with Nellie Melba if she hadn't got a disease of the throat, Mr. Lindsey wondered what else she lied about. He hoped I could find something in her past that would give him just cause to divorce her. If she'd misrepresented herself to him before they married, it might be enough for a judge to end it."

I could see why he'd assume there were other skeletons in her closet. Where there was one, there were possibly more.

It also made Mr. Lindsey a suspect in her murder. He might have confronted her about the lies and the stranger, perhaps accusing him of being a former lover. The argument could have escalated into physical violence. He picked up the closest thing at hand, the veil, and in a fit of anger he strangled her.

But surely he'd confront her in the privacy of their own home, not at the salon early in the morning. Also, why confront her *after* hiring Harry?

"Have you discovered anything about her past yet?" Detective Inspector Hobart asked.

Harry shook his head. "I want to speak to the pianist, but he left no name or address with Mr. Lindsey. According to my client, he was dressed somewhat shabbily and had a foreign accent, so I assume he's staying in a cheap hotel until his business with Madame Poitiers was concluded. I searched some hotels yesterday and was about to resume my search again today. But now that she's dead, he'll probably leave."

"Particularly if he murdered her," the detective said darkly.

There might be a faster way of finding him. In two out of three of my previous investigations, attending funerals had proven quite helpful. "He might show up at her funeral."

Detective Inspector Hobart rose. "I'll be sure to attend. Thanks, Son. You should call on Mr. Lindsey soon and collect your fee."

"I can't ask him to pay me. I haven't accomplished anything."

"You should be paid for yesterday's efforts."

Harry shook his head.

The detective looked thoughtful then headed for the door. He stopped before he reached it. "Are you dining with us this evening?"

"Not tonight. I'm dining out."

The detective's brows rose. "Who with?"

"No one you know." Harry's gaze flicked to me then to his business card on the desk. He picked it up and placed it with the stack of others. "You'll be on your way now too, Cleo."

I nodded, somewhat absently. Something had been bothering me, and I just realized what it was. "Why do you think Madame Poitiers took your card to her shop?"

Harry shrugged. "Perhaps she planned to approach me and ask why her husband hired me but was killed before she had the opportunity."

It sounded plausible, and yet it didn't quite make sense. "Why did her husband leave it lying about where she could easily find it? Surely he knew it would raise her suspicions if she saw it. Why not try to keep it more secretive?"

"Perhaps he wanted her to know," the detective pointed out. "I'll ask him when I speak to him. First, I'd best get back to the crime scene and see how my sergeant fared with the witnesses. May I walk you out, Miss Fox, or are you planning on staying longer to speak to Harry?"

"Cleo and I have nothing more to say to one another," Harry said without meeting anyone's gaze.

His dismissal stung. He might be trying to keep me at arms' length for my sake, but did he have to go about it like a marauding Viking wielding a hammer?

"Good day to you too, Harry," I couldn't resist saying as I followed Detective Inspector Hobart down the stairs.

Harry's father held the café door open for me as I balanced the coffee cups in my hands. "I'm sorry about that. He's not himself lately. Ever since he left the hotel, he's been out of sorts."

I bit the inside of my cheek as the familiar swell of guilt for my role in his dismissal returned with a vengeance. I thought I'd put it behind me, but it seemed I hadn't. Perhaps I never would, particularly if I continued to see Harry again from time to time.

"Out of sorts in what way?" I asked.

"Sometimes very happy, the most cheerful I've seen him. And sometimes, he behaves like that. And why not tell me who he's dining with tonight? It's not like him."

"Perhaps he's having dinner with a woman and doesn't wish you to get your hopes up if the relationship is very new."

"Our hopes are rarely raised. We know what he's like."

I was going to wonder what he meant by that for the rest of the day and probably beyond.

* * *

FRANK HAD NEVER HEARD of Lady Bunbury. Nor had Goliath, the porter, or Peter. I thought I might have better luck with Mr. Hobart. Like his nephew, he knew everyone who had ever graced the hotel's opulent foyer, even if they'd simply attended one of the balls held throughout the year and had never actually stayed overnight. I was in luck.

"She stayed here years ago, before she married Lord Bunbury," Mr. Hobart told me. I'd found him in his office with wads of cotton stuffed in his ears to block out the sound of hammering coming from next door. The senior staff offices were closest to the new restaurant's location, and the constant noise of construction must grate on the nerves after a while. It wasn't too loud, but it was incessant. He removed both the cotton and his spectacles to speak to me. "It was before Harry's time, some fifteen years ago."

"Her family were guests here?"

He nodded. "They came to London to present their daughter and find her a husband. It worked remarkably well. She married Lord Bunbury within the year."

"Does my aunt know her?"

"She isn't one of Lady Bainbridge's close circle, and she has never joined her for afternoon tea here." This seemed to baffle rather than annoy him. He was of a mind that the Mayfair served one of the best afternoon teas in London, if not *the* best, so surely she *should* come. "But Lady Bunbury invited your family to a ball last year, so they certainly know her. Why are you inquiring about her?"

I could trust Mr. Hobart and I knew his brother the detective did too, so I had no qualms telling him about Madame Poitiers' murder and Lady Bunbury's appointment scheduled prior to opening. I didn't mention Harry's involvement, however, or that I'd seen him that morning.

If he thought I held something back, he didn't show it. He was speechless with shock. Mr. Hobart's blue eyes were the same color as his brother's. But where the detective's could be stormy or bright, and everything in between, according to his mood, the hotel manager's were always the blue of a summer sky in the countryside. He now blinked those eyes back at me, quite stunned.

"This will upset your aunt," he said.

"I know." Aunt Lilian wasn't friendly with the dressmaker, but the murder of an acquaintance would unsettle her. With her delicate nature, the news could darken her even further and have her reaching for her tonic. "I think she should hear about it from one of us rather than a guest or acquaintance."

"Quite right, quite right."

"I'll go to her shortly. Is there anything else you can tell me about Lady Bunbury?"

"Didn't you say my brother is investigating the murder?"

I stroked my fingernail along the edge of his desk, much as I had done to the counter in the salon. But there were no stray threads here. "He's busy sifting through witness statements. I thought I could help by gathering information about Lady Bunbury."

His eyes crinkled at the corners. "I understand perfectly." He knew I needed something to occupy my mind as well as my time and that investigating appealed to my inquisitive nature. "But Stephen might not if he feels you're getting in his way."

I put up my hands in surrender. "I promise not to get involved where I'm not wanted. I just thought I could help gather a clearer picture of Lady Bunbury for him, since my aunt may be acquainted with her."

I thanked him and headed out, wondering how long I ought to wait before I informed my aunt of the tragic demise of her dressmaker. I was saved from making the decision when Goliath informed me that Harmony wanted to see me. He didn't know where to find her now, so I started in the staff parlor. She wasn't there, so I made my way down to the basement.

If the foyer was the luxurious first-class berth of the hotel, the basement was its engine. It was where the staff jostled one another as they hurried along corridors, arms laden with fresh towels and sheets, or pushed trolleys to the service lift. They sweated in the steam room as they pressed the guests' garments. Their hands became red and chapped from being constantly immersed in hot water in the laundry or received cuts and burns in the kitchen. Their work was hard, sometimes tedious, and not well rewarded. Coming down to the basement always served to remind me of how fortunate I was that I'd been born into a family that didn't need to do such back-breaking work to put food on the table.

I didn't need to be down here. Harmony wouldn't have come this way. She would be somewhere upstairs, still cleaning rooms. I told myself she might visit the laundry for fresh supplies or call in at the kitchen to see Victor, whom I suspected she secretly held a torch for, despite her rudeness towards him. In truth, I had another motive.

I wanted to spy on the new *chef de cuisine* in the kitchen. Under the previous chef, the kitchen was a frightening place for both staff and outsiders. He ruled absolutely. His word was law. His voice should be the only voice heard. Anyone caught being idle or talking was dismissed or threatened with either dismissal or the loss of a finger. As far as I was aware, he'd never followed through on the latter threat, although there were several cooks missing a fingertip or two.

He might have been a temperamental madman with violent tendencies, who'd cheated the hotel over several years, but he had also revolutionized the kitchen and the menu. For starters, he stopped the cooks getting drunk. The hot atmosphere bred a constant thirst, so the cooks drank beer to quench it. Consequently they were often well-oiled before dinnertime. He replaced the beer with water. He was also a stickler for cleanliness. He made sure the cooks arrived for the day in clean white aprons, not stained from the previous days' spills. He restructured the processes, ensuring there was more communication between each section so there was no duplication of work for the basic stocks and sauces used across stations. He introduced new and unique dishes of his own creation, ensuring the Mayfair's restaurant rivaled those of other luxury hotels. The guests didn't want to dine out. They wanted to enjoy the delights on offer in the dining room here.

My uncle would have gladly kept him on to head up the new, larger restaurant designed to feed the well-heeled public as well as hotel guests. If only the chef hadn't defrauded him.

All of the gains won by the previous chef could so easily have been lost if his replacement was not of the same caliber. The new restaurant could fail spectacularly if the discerning public were disappointed with the dishes. It still could; Mrs. Poole would leave as soon as a permanent *chef de cuisine* was appointed, something she had made clear to my uncle. That hadn't stopped him from repeatedly asking her to rethink and stay on.

That's what he appeared to be doing now. Their heads were bent together as they looked over paperwork at one of the empty cooking stations. Cooks worked around them, mostly cleaning up after the luncheon rush had ended. In the far corner, cooks piped soft white cream through a bag onto the top of several cakes, and tart cases were being filled with a red substance and topped with strawberries at another station. They would be taken upstairs to the larger of the two sitting rooms later, ready for afternoon tea. At the back, steam rose from the large pots of stock that simmered for hours. None of the cooks avoided my uncle and the chef or looked worried or harried. They went about their work calmly and efficiently. Mrs. Poole had quite a different style to her predecessor.

Victor looked up from the counter he was wiping and spotted me. He arched an eyebrow in question. I mouthed, "Harmony." He shrugged.

I returned upstairs before my uncle saw me. I checked the staff parlor again as I passed it but only two footmen sat there, talking quietly as they drank cups of tea and ate biscuits that weren't quite stale but were no longer fresh enough to serve to guests. Out in the foyer, the lift door opened and Floyd emerged, yawning.

"Have you just risen?" I asked.

He glanced around to check we were alone. Despite a few guests leaving the dining room and another taking a seat on one of the burgundy leather armchairs with a newspaper in hand, no one was about. "I got in very late this morning."

"Were you at your club?"

Floyd often stayed out until all hours at one of the gentlemen's clubs he and his friends belonged to. If not there, then they adjourned to a private party which he only ever alluded to in conversation. These parties were not the genteel kind like the sort my uncle and aunt attended at their friends' houses. If they were, he wouldn't close up when I asked questions. The only reason I discovered these parties were of a disreputable kind was because I'd once caught Floyd and Jonathon entering the hotel at eight in the morning dressed in formal evening wear. Floyd sheepishly claimed he'd lost track of time as they'd been engrossed in a discussion on the merit of the art nouveau movement. Jonathon blushed fiercely and hadn't been able to meet my gaze. My cousin was an adequate liar, but not superb. Even if he'd been a thoroughly convincing actor, I would have been suspicious. For one thing, when I'd tried to have a serious discussion with him about art once, he'd not known a Turner from a Cézanne. Also, both men smelled of women's perfume.

He now looked at me like I'd been the one to drag him out

of bed before he was completely rested. "Enough questions, Cleo! It's bad enough I have to put up with it from my parents, but I didn't think you'd badger me too." He slunk away, head down like a cat caught sniffing around the bird cage.

John the lift operator had waited for me. "Going up, Miss Fox?"

I stepped into his ascending room, as some of the older guests called it. As we passed the second floor, I remembered why I preferred the stairs. I would have reached the fourth floor by now. After we passed the third, John eased the lever into the stop position so that the lift's floor was perfectly aligned with the corridor. It was the pride of John's profession that he could gauge precisely when to pull the lever to have it stop completely level.

I knocked on Flossy's door but there was no answer. I almost moved to the next door, belonging to my aunt and uncle's suite, but decided against it. I wasn't ready to tell my aunt that her dressmaker was murdered. I'd prefer to have Flossy with me.

I returned to my own room, planning to order something to eat through the speaking tube. Inside, I stopped short upon seeing both Flossy and Harmony in my sitting room. Harmony was pretending to be dusting but her feather duster hardly touched any surfaces, and I knew they were clean anyway. She'd dusted only yesterday. She looked relieved upon seeing me.

"There you are," Flossy said without getting up. She sat on the sofa, magazine in hand, her legs stretched out along the length of it. Her shoes were tucked under the table next to her. She'd never sit like that in the presence of her mother or father, but she felt comfortable enough with me.

I eyed her and then Harmony. Clearly they hadn't been whiling away the time with idle chat. Indeed, what would they talk about? They had very little in common. Not only were they from different stations but they were nothing alike. Harmony was quite serious whereas my cousin was all froth and little substance. I suspected Harmony had been waiting for me and when Flossy showed up, she had to pretend she was working.

"Is something the matter?"

Although I asked the question to both of them, it was my cousin who answered. "Yes! There is quite a to-do at Madame Poitiers' salon. Mrs. Hessing and her daughter have just returned from there, rather annoyed they weren't allowed in for their appointment. Apparently the police turned them away. I know you went this morning so I wondered if you knew what happened."

"I do."

Flossy swung her legs off the sofa and patted the cushion beside her. "Oh good. I knew you would. You always seem to ferret out trouble."

Over by the desk, Harmony made a small huffing sound through her nose.

"It's something rather horrible, I'm afraid," I said. "Madame Poitiers was murdered in her salon."

Flossy gasped and her peaches and cream complexion paled. "Oh, the poor woman. How horrible."

Harmony stopped pretending to dust and sat down on one of the armchairs. I had her full attention too. I could see she was bursting with questions, but felt compelled to remain silent in Flossy's presence. I told them how I'd discovered the body with Miss Newland and spoken to Detective Inspector Hobart when he arrived. I did not mention any clues, including finding Harry's business card. I would tell Harmony later. Although my cousin knew I'd been hired as a private detective from time to time and solved murders, I had not been hired to solve this one. She wouldn't understand why I wanted to poke my nose in.

Not that I would. Mr. Hobart was right; his brother had it in hand. I would simply ask my family about Lady Bunbury and pass on what I knew before stepping back.

"Does the detective have any ideas who may have done it?" Flossy asked, still looking wan. "I do hope it wasn't the assistant. Imagine if we were in the presence of a murderess, Cleo! She could have done us all in." She shuddered.

"She would have no reason to kill us. Besides, while she strangled one of us, the other two would fight her off and scream at the top of our lungs, bringing in the seven seamstresses working in the back room. I think we were quite safe at all times, Flossy."

"That is a relief."

"What do you know about Lady Bunbury?"

She blinked rapidly at the sudden change in topic. "She's the queen of society. Why?"

"She may have been the last person to see Madame Poitiers alive." I didn't want to give away too much so left it at that.

Harmony's eyes narrowed. She knew there was more.

So did Flossy. "Is she a suspect?"

"Everyone connected to Madame Poitiers is a suspect. Even us."

She scoffed. "Don't be ridiculous. Everyone knows we're lovely people without a violent bone in our bodies. Well, everyone knows Mother and I are. You're an unknown quantity." Realizing what she was implying, she flushed. "I don't mean you are violent, Cleo! Just that our friends are not familiar with you, yet. They don't know you like we do. *We* know you're not a murderess. You have no reason to murder Madame Poitiers."

I gave her a wry smile but I suspect it was lost in her fluster. "Thank you, Flossy."

"Nor does Lady Bunbury. I can't imagine her strangling a dressmaker with a wedding veil. Her husband, perhaps." She pulled a face. "Dull old goat, so I hear. She might want to remove him so she could remarry."

"She has no financial problems?"

"I don't think so. She buys a lot of new gowns every year. She usually wears a new outfit to each occasion and she attends a lot of events."

"That would be enough to bankrupt some."

"Not the Bunburys. He has a house here in London and an estate in the country somewhere. They're wealthy. They must be."

"Why?"

She shrugged one shoulder. "Because she's the queen of society! She hosts the first, largest and most prestigious ball of the season. If you receive an invitation to the Bunbury Ball, you're guaranteed to be invited to more social events than someone who missed out. If you miss out, you might as well pack your bags and leave London. It means you'll only be invited to the second and third tier parties. Your season is effectively over."

"It sounds to me as though she has too much power."

"Oh, she does. Everyone hates it, but there's nothing we can do. Not only does she control who society will accept, she effectively decides who will be the year's favorite debutantes. She will declare one girl to be the most beautiful, another the most graceful, another as the most accomplished. If a girl manages to score on all three counts, her star will rise indeed. Of course, it's utterly corrupt. She has been known to bestow an honor or two on her own nieces or a friend's daughter."

"She sounds thoroughly horrid."

"And yet everyone wishes to be her friend, including Mother. Last year, she pushed me into Lady Bunbury's path so that she noticed me. I got her attention, that's for certain," she said wryly. "I stood on her toe."

Harmony covered her mouth with her hand. I suspected she was trying not to laugh, proving she wasn't so serious after all.

"So you don't know her very well," I said.

"Not at all. So I suppose she could be poor. Wouldn't that be something to set the tongues wagging if it got out!" The wicked gleam in her eye was unexpected and somewhat unnatural on my sheltered cousin.

"Would your mother be privy to more gossip about her?"

"Probably. Girls my age only care about Lady Bunbury up until the point of her ball. After that, she's just another woman past her prime." Lady Bunbury couldn't have been more than thirty-three. Mr. Hobart said she'd found a husband in her first season in London, and that was fifteen years ago when she'd stayed at the hotel. Most girls were eighteen when they debuted, give or take a year. "Mother might have heard rumors that the Bunburys are struggling."

I bit the inside of my lip. It was time. It had to be done. "We should tell her about the murder before she finds out from someone else. Will you come with me?"

Flossy led the way outside while I hung back long enough to whisper to Harmony that I had more to tell her. When I joined Flossy in the corridor, my cousin looked troubled. I thought she was worried about Lady Bunbury being a murderess, but apparently her thoughts were more selfish.

"What will become of our dresses now?"

"Hopefully our order will be fulfilled on time," I said. "It's up to her husband to decide if he wants to keep the business going or not. He'd be mad not to, at least until the season has ended."

"Madame Poitiers was married? I didn't know. She never spoke about a husband, and she spoke about *everything*."

She did indeed. Or, rather, she spoke about the things she wanted others to know about her—the famous people she'd met, her singing career, who'd worn her gowns at which events. At least some of it wasn't true, if the stranger appearing at her flat could be believed.

Aunt Lilian was in bed, propped up on pillows, an open magazine beside her. Her eyes were closed, but her hair had been arranged so her maid must have come this morning. Despite the closed eyes, she wasn't asleep. Her hands trembled and her feet moved restlessly beneath the covers.

Flossy sat on the edge of the bed. "Mother?"

Aunt Lilian's eyelids cracked open before closing again. "What do you want?"

Flossy glanced at the bottle of tonic on the table beside the bed. "I know it's hard, but it's good that you haven't taken anything today."

"My head feels like it's going to explode." Aunt Lilian pressed her trembling fingers into her temples as if she would gouge out the offending part of her brain if she could.

"Try to withstand it a little longer."

Aunt Lilian's lips thinned but she refrained from snapping at her daughter. She lowered her hands and Flossy took one in her own.

"Mother, we have some bad news. Madame Poitiers is dead."

Aunt Lilian's eyes sprang open and she blinked as if it were too bright for her, even though it was quite dull in the bedroom. The only light came through the adjoining sitting room windows. "That's dreadful. Just dreadful. The poor woman." Her entire body began to shake and she pressed a hand to her chest, patting it as if trying to steady her heartbeat.

Flossy reached for a neatly folded handkerchief on the table and handed it to her mother. "She was murdered. Cleo found her this morning when she returned to fetch your tonic."

Aunt Lilian smothered her gasp with her handkerchief and stared at me. Tears filled her eyes. "You poor thing, Cleo! It must have been quite a shock."

I sat on the bed too. "It was, but I'm fine. Don't worry about me." I told her very briefly how Miss Newland and I discovered the body, downplaying the awfulness of the situation as much as possible. But the truth was, now that I'd had time to think, the situation was truly awful. The sight of Madame Poitiers' dead eyes staring up at the ceiling was going to haunt me for some time.

Aunt Lilian didn't cry. In fact, she seemed to rally as I spoke. Perhaps she wasn't as delicate as we all thought. Like Flossy, she wondered if our outfits would be completed. I gave her the same response I'd given my cousin: that it was up to the widower.

"Mr. Hobart's brother is investigating," Flossy told her. "I'm sure he'll find out who did it soon. But he has asked Cleo to help him." I wasn't sure if she made an innocent mistake or deliberately changed my story for her mother's sake. Aunt Lilian would probably be more willing to answer my questions if she thought I was asking them in an official capacity, and I wouldn't be surprised if Flossy knew that.

I quickly assured Aunt Lilian I was only helping him in a minor way and only because she moved in the same circles as Lady Bunbury. "She's not a suspect, you understand. But he wants to know why she was there early this morning, if only so he can rule her out." The last thing I wanted was for her to think Lady Bunbury was a killer.

"How extraordinary," she murmured.

"In what way?"

"Lady Bunbury is a woman of leisure. For her to be up and about so early, it must have been important." Her judgmental tone implied she didn't place herself in the same category, yet here she was, still in bed. "I assume the early appointment was so no one would see her come and go."

"Madame Poitiers' assistant said she may have been in financial difficulty and the appointment was to set up an arrangement for paying her debt. Given the delicate nature of the discussion, the appointment was made when no one could walk in on them and overhear. Do you know if Lady Bunbury is economizing?"

"I doubt it. Her husband is wealthy. They lead a lavish lifestyle. They host the Bunbury Ball, of course, but also several dinners and luncheons throughout the season. They have some marvelous artwork in their townhouse, and she always wears the most exquisite jewelry. She'll be weighed down by diamonds and other gemstones at this year's ball, just wait and see. There are the new clothes every year, too, and they have a box at the opera. I've never been to their country estate but I believe it's vast, and the house is just as beautifully furnished as their London residence."

"Perhaps she simply doesn't want Lord Bunbury to know how much she spends on gowns," I said. "Even wealthy men can be miserly."

"It's possible. I don't know him well." She thought for a moment. Her feet increased their restlessness, swishing back and forth beneath the covers, and her fingers took up a rapid beat as they drummed against her thigh. She seemed unaware of her movements. "He participates in all the social events with her, so unless he's completely oblivious to the cost of women's clothing, he must have at least an inkling of how much she spends."

"There could be another reason for her early appointment," Flossy said, but she didn't offer any suggestions for what the reason might be.

"What is Lady Bunbury like as a person?" I asked.

My aunt opened her mouth to speak, paused, then said, "Would you like to meet her and judge for yourself?"

Detective Inspector Hobart wouldn't want me to follow up this line of inquiry. He would be most insistent that I decline the offer. Nevertheless, I eagerly accepted. In fairness, I wasn't going to interrogate Lady Bunbury. I was simply going to gauge her character and the likelihood that she would lose her temper and strangle someone with the closest thing at hand.

"I'll invite her to afternoon tea the day after tomorrow." Aunt Lilian sounded pleased. "I'll tell her I want to introduce you to some influential ladies prior to your first season."

Flossy huffed a soft laugh. "If you truly want to flatter her, tell her she's *the* most influential lady in London."

"I believe I will. It is true, after all. Do be punctual, both of you, and do wear something fashionable as well as appropriate. Oh, and Cleo, perhaps don't mention the lectures you attended in Cambridge, and steer clear of any talk of women's suffrage, class inequality, and the importance of a university education for girls."

This had quickly changed from being a murder investigation to a social event that could either ruin or elevate me before the season had even begun. I must question Lady Bunbury delicately. I wouldn't want to offend her and cause Flossy and my aunt problems. If Flossy didn't receive an invitation to Lady Bunbury's ball, she'd be devastated.

I wasn't sure I could be diplomatic enough, but I would try—for their sake.

CHAPTER 5

"*W*hy were you waiting to see me?" I asked Harmony when I returned to my suite. She was still there with her feet up on the sofa beside her, a magazine in hand.

She put it down and sat up straight. "The same reason as Miss Bainbridge. I overheard two guests mentioning the police were at Maison de Poitiers this morning, and I knew you'd gone there. So what more can you tell me?"

I told her about finding the coarse thread, and about the seamstresses working out the back when we'd found the body. I described how she'd been strangled with a veil that was waiting to be picked up by a lady's maid. Then I mentioned finding Harry's business card in the drawer behind the counter.

Harmony's brows rose. "Is he a suspect?"

"No! Good lord, Harmony, is your opinion of him that low?"

"Not at all. I quite like Mr. Armitage now that he's no longer my superior and telling me what to do."

"It was his job to tell you what to do," I pointed out with some amusement.

She bristled. "Anyway, I know you like him and you're a good judge of character."

I felt the heat rise to my cheeks and quickly tried to school my features. "He's nice, I suppose, if you like overly charming men who are far too aware of how handsome they are."

"I'm sure he likes you too," she quipped.

I made a scoffing sound. "He was rather keen for me to leave his office this morning, and he made it quite clear that we need not see one another again."

"You've spoken to him already? What did he say? Why was his card in the salon?"

I told her how Harry had been employed by Mr. Lindsey after a stranger called at their flat and asked after his wife. "Not only was she not French, not named Poitiers, and was never on the verge of singing opera with the great sopranos of the stage, but she traveled with a carnival troupe before she returned to England and met her husband. He hoped Harry could find out what else she lied about so he could have enough reason to divorce her."

Harmony placed the magazine she'd been reading on the top of a pile on the table. "I hope Mr. Armitage doesn't take over the case and push you out altogether. If he was a gentleman, he'd ask you to join him." She made it sound as though she hadn't decided if he behaved enough like a gentleman to be called one.

"There is no case, Harmony. Not for him or me. The police are handling it."

"What if Mr. Lindsey decides the police aren't moving quickly enough? What if he employs Mr. Armitage to investigate on his behalf? It's his right to hire whomever he wants, of course, but *you* found the body. You should be involved too."

"Mr. Lindsey is free of his wife. He doesn't need a divorce and won't need to employ anyone now."

Harmony gave me a grim smile. "You'd better check his alibi for the time of the murder, and double check it."

"You mean Detective Inspector Hobart must."

The door burst open and Flossy breezed in. Harmony sprang to her feet and pretended to straighten the pile of magazines. She needn't have bothered. Flossy didn't look at her. Sometimes, my cousin—and people like her—could be quite oblivious when it came to the staff.

"I almost forgot," she said. "I have friends coming for afternoon tea. Would you like to join us, Cleo?"

"I can think of nothing better," I said. "Thank you."

Satisfied, she left as quickly as she'd entered. She was like a puff of smoke, here one moment then blown away by the wind the next, leaving behind the faint scent of her perfume.

"Nothing better to do?" Harmony echoed, a mischievous look on her face.

"Unfortunately, I couldn't think of anything in time. Besides, I'm starving. I missed lunch."

* * *

THE FOLLOWING afternoon I received a summons from Detective Inspector Hobart to meet at Harry's office. It was Saturday, a busy day for the hotel with guests coming to London for the weekend, but there was little for me to do. I was more than happy to see what he wanted.

The day was sunny and had warmed up after a crisp morning. People were out enjoying the first fine day in months. Piccadilly Circus was organized chaos, as usual. Loaded carts jostled for position with private carriages, hackneys, and omnibuses. Pedestrians took their lives in their hands trying to cross against the police constable's signal. Youths sat on stools on the pavement surrounding the central fountain, offering to shine shoes for a ha'penny. A man had hopped off his bicycle and was inspecting one of the wheels, while three women with baskets over their arms had stopped to chat.

London was growing on me. I felt settled. There was an energy here that I'd not experienced in Cambridge. Perhaps it was living with elderly grandparents for so many years, or perhaps it was the academic culture there, but I finally felt as though I'd shrugged off a thick blanket. The sunshine certainly helped. With spring upon us, the city seemed to be blooming.

I did not collect coffees from Luigi this time. Roma Café was filled with people, mostly men, chatting in Italian, smoking cigarettes and drinking from small cups. I headed upstairs and opened the door. Harry and his father were talking quietly but stopped and stood upon my entry.

I hung up my coat and took the vacant seat. "Do you need to question me again, Detective? Am I a suspect?" It was said half-jokingly, but as one of the people who'd been at the salon early yesterday morning, I ought to be considered a suspect. Any detective of quality should put me on his list.

"Not yet, but I like to keep an open mind." The corners of his eyes crinkled like his brother's did when he smiled.

I looked to Harry, partly because I wanted to see if he knew why I'd been asked to come, but also because I simply liked looking at him. What woman wouldn't?

"He won't tell me why he's here either," he said, accurately guessing half of my reason for turning to him.

"It's to ask for your help," D.I. Hobart said.

"Mine?" both Harry and I asked.

"Yes," Inspector Hobart answered, not clarifying. "Let me begin with what I learned from the assistant and seamstresses yesterday." It would seem he had no qualms sharing his notes with us. Again, I suspected another detective wouldn't have been quite so trusting. It wouldn't surprise me if this was against Scotland Yard policy. I wasn't about to mention it, however. I wanted him to tell me everything.

"None of the seven seamstresses saw or heard anything before Miss Newland's scream moments after your arrival at the salon, Miss Fox. They all arrived at eight, which is their usual start time. Mrs. Zieliński, the senior seamstress, is the only one with a key to the door that leads directly to the workshop from the laneway." He paused to check his notes. "Madame Poitiers always enters the shop through the front door via New Bond Street, so the seamstresses don't see her arrive. She doesn't often greet them of a morning and can stay in the salon all day without coming into the back room."

"So she could have been dead before they even arrived," I said.

"What time does Madame Poitiers get to the salon?" Harry asked.

"Sometimes she comes in early, but usually it was later, sometimes as late as nine, according to Miss Newland. All agreed she wasn't predictable. She never told anyone what time to expect her. When I mentioned an appointment had been listed for eight-fifteen in the appointment book, the seamstresses claimed they didn't know about it, but the assistant did because she saw it. If Lady Bunbury had arrived at the appointed time and spoken to Madame Poitiers, the seamstresses wouldn't have heard anything anyway. The work room is noisy once the sewing machines start, and there is always at least one going at all times."

"It's also well insulated," I added. "We couldn't hear the sewing machines until the door between the salon and work-room opened."

"Was there any sign of a break-in?" Harry asked.

"None. The windows and doors hadn't been forced. There are three keys to the front door. One is in Miss Newland's possession, one belonged to Madame Poitiers, and the third is a spare, kept at her flat. There are another three keys for the back door that leads from the lane directly to the workshop. Mrs. Zieliński, the head seamstress, has one key, Madame Poitiers another, and the third is a spare, which is also kept at the flat. We found both of Madame Poitiers' keys in her bag behind the counter. Miss Newland used her key to let herself and you in through the front door on the morning of the murder, Miss Fox. Mrs. Zieliński also had her key on her, but claims it went missing for a day and a half about a week ago."

"Long enough for a copy to be made," Harry pointed out. "Where did Mrs. Zieliński find it when it reappeared?"

"On the floor, under one of the tables. Some discarded material hid it from view, but she was convinced she'd looked there and everywhere else in search of it."

"And the spare set of keys?" I asked.

"Missing. Mr. Lindsey couldn't find them when I questioned him yesterday. He claims he hadn't seen them for some time, perhaps months. They used to hang inside a cupboard door in the kitchen, but they weren't there when he looked. Of course, he was quite flustered by the news of his wife's death and probably not thinking clearly. They may have already turned up by now."

"So the killer either took those keys or the one belonging to Mrs. Zieliński," Harry said. "If the latter, it's most likely one of the seamstresses, but there is a chance someone came in off the street while they weren't there and stole it."

"How did Mr. Lindsey seem?" I asked.

"Suitably upset," the detective said. "Neither too much nor too little, considering he wanted to divorce his wife. Indeed, he was shocked more than bereaved."

"Did he mention he wanted to divorce her?" Harry asked.

The detective scoffed. "No, and he'd be mad to. It would give him a motive. He didn't mention hiring you, and I didn't want to let him know that I knew. Not yet. He informed me about the stranger coming to the door and asking after his wife under her maiden name, and how he'd returned later when she was home and they'd argued. Unfortunately he was unable to tell me any more about the fellow than he told you."

"So he's not hiding anything, except the fact he hired me."

"So it appears, but I'm keeping an open mind."

I nodded. We couldn't rule anyone out yet. That brought me to my main question. "Why have you summoned me here? Why are you telling any of this to Harry and me?"

The detective inspector smiled. "I wish to hire you both as consultants."

My jaw dropped. Harry stared at his father, his mouth also ajar.

"I have cleared it with my superiors. They agree you can both achieve something the police cannot. In the first instance, you already have an acquaintance with Mr. Lindsey, Harry. I want you to question him, but do it subtly, as if he is still your client and you're simply curious about the murder. Find out why his wife took your card. Take Miss Fox."

"Why?" we both asked.

"Because it looks more professional to have an associate. Also, a woman's touch is helpful. People open up to women more."

"Usually only other women do," Harry said, irritably.

I bristled. "That's not true. Women can get answers from men just as well. People trust women. It's why we make good detectives. Not that the police commissioner realizes it yet."

Detective Inspector Hobart put up his hands. "There's no need to glare at me. I agree with you."

"I still don't think it's necessary to involve her," Harry said. "What if Lindsey is the killer? He could target Cleo." He was annoyed, and not necessarily with his father. Harry just didn't want to spend any time with me. That much was abundantly clear.

I wasn't going to let him talk his father into taking me off the case, however. "You'll just have to put up with my company. It won't be so bad. I think I can endure it. For the sake of justice, you understand."

He folded his arms over his chest and pressed his lips together, and presented me with stony silence. He was in no mood for light-hearted banter. He was taking my uncle's threats more seriously than me, and was determined we should not become friends so that I could maintain a good relationship with my family. Working closely was going to test his resolve. No wonder he was annoyed.

I still saw the amusing side, however, and couldn't quite wipe the smile off my face.

"There's a second thing I want you to do for me, Miss Fox," the detective said. "I questioned Lady Bunbury yesterday. She claimed her appointment was for a fitting and that Madame Poitiers was not there when she called on her at eight-fifteen. She went home without seeing her. I have an inkling she was lying about part or all of her story, however"

"Did you ask her coachman if she went inside?" Harry asked.

"She said she walked."

"That is odd," I said in all seriousness. Women like Lady Bunbury and my aunt didn't walk anywhere if they had a conveyance they could use.

"I checked with the shoemaker and other neighboring shopkeepers, but none can recall seeing her early in the morning. That doesn't mean she wasn't there, but it leaves me without proof."

"If she's telling the truth, it means Madame Poitiers was probably already dead by eight-fifteen," Harry pointed out.

"Indeed."

"What do you want Cleo to do about it?"

"I want her to speak to Lady Bunbury and see what she can learn. I suspect her ladyship will reveal more to a young woman than an old policeman. I found her to be somewhat difficult."

Harry scoffed. "Cleo can't call on someone she's never met. People like Lady Bunbury require an introduction from a trusted source first."

"I'm sure I'll manage it," I said to them both, adding a smile for Harry.

He frowned. He was suspicious.

I rose. "Shall we call on Mr. Lindsey now?"

It wasn't until we'd parted from his father and were on our way to Mr. Lindsey's flat that Harry challenged me. "You already had an arrangement to meet Lady Bunbury, didn't you?"

"We're having afternoon tea at the Mayfair. My aunt set it up."

"You spoke to her about Lady Bunbury?"

"Yes, and Flossy too. According to them, the Bunburys don't have any financial troubles, but I want to make sure. I'll take more notice of her clothing than they will. If her outfit isn't well made, for instance, or if her hair looks as though it was done by her own hand rather than a maid, we will have our answer without even needing to ask a question."

We walked on in silence. Harry still seemed to be simmering, although I couldn't imagine why. We were fortunate indeed to be hired as consultants. "Isn't it marvelous that your father has commissioned our help for this case?"

"It's so marvelous, I'm speechless."

"There's no need for sarcasm."

"There is when my own father doesn't think I can interview a suspect without a chaperone."

It was so absurd that I couldn't help laughing. "You honestly think that's the reason why he asked me to join you?"

His pace quickened and I had to race to keep up with his long strides.

It was time to confront the proverbial elephant in the room. "Would you truly rather believe he commissioned both of us as consultants because you're inept? Honestly, Harry, you do your father a disservice if you think that."

He hunched his shoulders, suitably chastised.

"He did it because he wants us to be friends again," I pointed out, in case he really couldn't see it for himself. "He knows we work better together and that you've decided to avoid me because you think it's in my best interests."

"It *is* in your best interests," he ground out.

"Can I be the judge of that?" My voice was harsh but so be it; I was angry. Angry at him, for assuming he knew what was best for me, and angry at my uncle, for dictating who I could be friends with. They'd each taken on the role of my guardian, and I'd asked neither of them to do so.

I expected an apology, rather foolishly as it turned out. The lack of one only made me angrier. We walked on in taut silence that grew more and more strained. It was a relief to finally reach the Lindsey residence.

Occupying the second floor with flats above and below, and a bookshop on the ground level, it was mere minutes from Maison de Poitiers on New Bond Street. Madame Poitiers would find it a very convenient location, but an expensive one. Handsome buildings in central locations didn't come cheaply, even if it was only a one or two bedroom flat.

Mr. Lindsey was at home and welcomed us inside. He was a short man in his mid-fifties with thinning gray hair and a paunch. He led us into a sitting room furnished in the same dusky pink shades as the salon. It had Madame Poitiers' style stamped all over it, from the cream wallpaper with pink roses, to the slender lamp base carved into the shape of a woman languidly and somewhat seductively reaching up to the shade. The rest of the furniture and knickknacks were of the same fine quality, each piece matching the others in some way yet somehow being unique and timeless. She had a good eye.

Harry was in the middle of introducing me when another man walked in, stopping short upon seeing us.

"This is my son, Gerald Lindsey," Mr. Lindsey said, a hint of weariness in his voice. He must be exhausted. There was a lot to do after the death of a family member. He might no longer have loved his wife, but there were still many things that required his attention now, big and small. He had the added pressure of her salon, too.

Gerald drew himself up to his full height as he shook Harry's hand. It had no effect. He was still considerably shorter. He eyed me up and down then simply gave me a nod before turning back to Harry. We sat, but neither father nor son offered us refreshments. Given that it was usually a woman's job to make the tea, neither would be used to playing host.

"You both have our deepest sympathies," Harry said. "We're very sorry to hear about the passing of Madame Poitiers."

"Lindsey," Gerald snapped. "Her name was Gertrude Lindsey."

Harry apologized. Gerald continued to scowl at him.

"Thank you," his father said to Harry. "I assume you saw it in the newspapers this morning."

"Actually the police visited my office yesterday afternoon. My card was found in the salon, and the detective in charge of the case wanted to know how it came to be there. I told him that you'd hired me." He didn't glance at Gerald, but I suspected he was worried the father didn't want his son to know he'd hired a private detective to investigate his mother

"Why would you tell them that?" Gerald's sneer was thick with contempt. "No wonder that Hobart plod grilled my father yesterday."

"He was just doing his job," his father said, placating. "Until I can be ruled out, I'm a suspect too." To Harry, he added, "I was here until eight yesterday morning, which is when I left for work. Gerald was here too, asleep, so I'm afraid no one can vouch for me."

"None of your neighbors saw you leave?"

"Not that I am aware."

The shop was only a few minutes away. If he left at eight, Mr. Lindsey could have gone to the salon, opened the front door with the spare key, killed his wife and left before Lady Bunbury's appointment at eight-fifteen. The time frame would have been tight, but it wasn't impossible if he walked quickly. Or he could be lying and have left home before eight. Without witnesses, we would never know.

"Mr. Lindsey, do you know how my business card came to be in your wife's shop?"

Mr. Lindsey frowned. "Now that I think of it, no. I'm sure I still have it. Will you excuse me a moment? I'll check."

He left the sitting room, leaving us with his son, still throwing scowls in Harry's direction. I decided any small talk was going to have to come from me. No matter what Harry said, Gerald would close up.

"What is it your father does for a living?"

"He's a teacher."

"And what do you do?"

"I finished school last year and I am considering my options. I might go on to university but I'd rather start earning."

"Will you go into teaching too? It's a noble profession."

He snorted. "My father teaches literature and history at a board school to children with no appreciation for education. He receives a pittance for his efforts and chalk thrown at his back when it's turned. There's nothing noble about it."

I would have liked to give him a lecture but doubted it would achieve anything. Instead, I gathered up every ounce of patience I could muster, determined to get as much information out of this spoiled youth as possible. "Then what sort of work are you looking for?"

"I haven't decided. Something in finance and banking. That's where the real money is. I'm only nineteen, so I've got time to wait for the right position to come up." He spoke with the same upper-class accent as Floyd and Jonathon. It was the sort of accent picked up in an exclusive school.

"I'm sure the perfect job will fall right into your lap."

He didn't detect my sarcasm which was probably just as well. "I know it will. The fathers of my old school chums are either in banking or have a business where they made their fortune. One of my closest friends is the heir to a canned goods empire. Those who aren't in trade are landed gentry, of course. I'm sure one of them will offer me something." If his nose tilted any further into the air it would touch the chandelier.

Mr. Lindsey returned, brandishing Harry's card. "I thought I still had it."

Harry checked it before handing it back.

Mr. Lindsey frowned. "I wonder why Gertie had one too. Did she call on you?"

"No," Harry said.

"Perhaps she used a different name."

Harry pointed to a wedding photograph of Mr. and Mrs. Lindsey. She wore a beautiful dress that would have been the height of fashion at the time. "I don't recognize her," he said.

"What a lovely gown," I said. "Mid-seventies, am I right?"

Mr. Lindsey picked up the photograph and studied it. "We married in '78. We had what they call a whirlwind courtship. I was dazzled by her beauty, her stories... She was the most interesting person I'd ever encountered. We met in March and were married in October." He spoke mechanically with a hint of bitterness. If he'd ever been in love with his wife, it had died long before she did.

"When did she open Maison de Poitiers?"

"The same year, June of '78. I had some savings and she used all of it to lease the shop, purchase equipment and fabric, and put on a seamstress. My wife was a remarkable businesswoman." It was spoken with a measure of awe but not an ounce of fondness.

"And it was an immediate success?"

"Not at all. The shop was in a different location to where it is now. It wasn't in the best district. The sort of clients she coveted didn't want to go there. She had to settle for second and third tier customers which meant her designs weren't getting seen by the right people. She tried to get invited to the events attended by more influential ladies, but doors simply wouldn't open for her. She was incredibly frustrated. Her clients were loyal and adored her designs, but they just weren't important enough to satisfy her ambitions. It wasn't until an actress wore one of Gertie's gowns during a performance that people took notice."

"Myrtle Langford," I said, recalling the framed magazine article in the salon.

Mr. Lindsey seemed pleased that I knew. "You have done your research."

"How did your wife convince a famous actress to wear one of her designs?"

"I don't know. She must have wandered into Gertie's shop

and fallen in love with it. Either that or they met at a party and Gertie talked her into wearing it." He studied the photograph again. "She could be incredibly convincing."

Gerald rolled his eyes, as if he didn't quite believe it. "She was ridiculous."

"Don't speak about your mother like that."

"Why not? She didn't care about me when she was alive so why should I care about her now she's dead?"

"Of course she cared about you."

"She packed me off to boarding school as soon as I was old enough," Gerald told us. "When I came home for holidays, she was too busy with the shop to spend any time with me. She was not a normal mother."

"That's enough, Gerald." There was no heat in Mr. Lindsey's chastisement, only resignation. "I know I only hired you on Wednesday, Mr. Armitage, and you had very little to go on, but did you find out anything about that fellow who came here and argued with Gertie?"

"I didn't, I'm afraid. I've visited several hotels in the area, but none recognized the man matching the description you gave me. Would you like me to continue the search?"

"I am curious," Mr. Lindsey hedged. "Why was he angry with her? Why search for her now, after all these years?"

"When did the man claim to know her?" I asked, trying to get the timing right in my head.

"I'm not entirely sure of the dates. She told me she was an opera singer before she met me. She returned to England for an operation on her throat, ending her career."

"Her career as a vaudevillian," Gerald muttered.

"I assume that was in '78 or '79, just before we met, but now…I'm no longer sure of anything she told me. According to that fellow, she didn't sing opera. What else did she lie about?"

"I can continue to search for him if you like," Harry said.

"Why bother?" Gerald said to his father. "It doesn't matter now. Anyway, you told the detective about the foreigner, so let the police find him. It won't cost you a thing." He turned to Harry. "My father won't be paying you."

"Gerald," his father chastised, without much effort. He

reached into his inside jacket pocket. "I owe you for the work you've already undertaken, Mr. Armitage."

Harry refused the money. "That's kind of you, but I don't want to be paid for a job I didn't do."

I thought he ought to be paid for the day's work, but I knew I wouldn't be able to convince him.

I was glad to leave Gerald behind in the sitting room as Mr. Lindsey showed us out. It made it easier to ask questions without him looking down his nose at us. "What are your plans for the salon now?"

Mr. Lindsey sighed, as if it was all too much to think about. "I'll keep it going for a while." He shrugged. "I don't know anything about fashion. Nor about operating a business. Her assistant and the seamstresses will have to carry on by themselves. Gertie had an accountant, too. I suppose he could help me."

"She didn't keep her own accounts?" Harry asked.

"Her eyesight was poor. She wouldn't want to squint at the books all night after a day in the salon."

"You didn't keep the books for her?" Harry asked.

Mr. Lindsey shook his head. "I never had anything to do with the business. It could be doing very well for all I know, or very badly."

We bade him farewell and headed downstairs to the street. "That was interesting," I said, glancing over my shoulder to make sure no one followed. I didn't want Gerald overhearing what I said next. "The son is a horrid, spoiled turd."

"He just lost his mother."

"A mother he didn't seem to like very much."

"That could just be his reaction to grief. He might be angry at her for dying on him, leaving him alone."

I was about to point out that he wasn't alone, he had his father, but going by Harry's stony-faced look, I suspected he wasn't thinking of Gerald Lindsey's situation. Harry's mother had died when he was eleven, leaving him very much alone. He'd had no father, no grandparents, aunts or uncles to turn to. It must have been a traumatic experience.

It was moments like this I wanted to loop my arm with his, but I knew it wouldn't be welcomed. I settled for walking a little closer to him. I was pleasantly surprised that he didn't widen the gap again.

"At least we solved the mystery of my card showing up in the salon," he said.

"We did?"

"If it wasn't the one I gave Mr. Lindsey, there's only one other explanation. It came from the stranger himself. On Thursday, I spent the entire day visiting hotels in the area. I handed my card to the clerks at each check-in desk in case they came across the man I described. I suspected at the time that he might stay at one of the hotels, but I knew the clerk wouldn't tell me. I hoped my card would be passed on to the fellow and he would approach me if he wanted. He didn't, but it seems he gave the card to Madame Poitiers—Mrs. Lindsey."

"Gertrude," I said, my mind racing. "That means the stranger saw her again *after* their argument outside the Lindseys' flat on Tuesday evening. Indeed, it must have been some time on Thursday."

"I'll send word to my father, along with a list of each of the hotels I visited."

"Or you could revisit them yourself and ask for your card back. The one that doesn't give it to you is the one who passed it on to the guest."

I thought he'd insist that Scotland Yard take over. When he turned to me with a sly smile, I couldn't help smiling in return. "I'll inform my father, but I'll offer to do the legwork. At his age, he'll probably appreciate it."

My smile widened. "And we are consultants now, after all."

$\mathcal{H}$arry and I split up and spent what was left of the day visiting the hotels he'd called on previously. We didn't get to them all, but by the time we met at his office at six, we'd done more than half. Unfortunately, neither of us had any luck. Every clerk at every check-in counter was able to produce Harry's card upon asking. We agreed to continue in the morning.

Back at the Mayfair, I checked with Mr. Chapman the steward about dinner. If anyone knew whether my family expected me to dine with them, he would. No one had mentioned their dinner arrangements to him, however. As always, the family table would remain available if there was a last-minute change.

The hotel was quiet at this time of day. Most guests were getting ready in their rooms for dinner or a show. The maids and valets who'd accompanied their mistresses and masters to London were coming and going, carrying mended or pressed outfits, hair curlers and accessories. Those guests who either couldn't afford their own maid or valet or hadn't brought them to London, hired the services of one of the hotel staff. Harmony was highly sought after, with her excellent hair styling skills. If she wasn't being used by Flossy or me, she was always busy with one of the other guests. I didn't see her on the fourth floor. I was about to head to my room when I noticed Uncle Ronald's office door was slightly ajar.

Laughter spilled out through the gap. I recognized his booming baritone, but not the tinkling female laugh.

I tiptoed to the door and peered in. My uncle sat on the edge of his desk, his crossed arms resting on his thick middle. He smiled at the woman standing in front of him dressed in white hat and apron with a chef's knife belt strapped to her waist. If he hadn't been so attentive to her, he would have seen me.

I quickly stepped back out of sight, but didn't move away. I should. I didn't want to intrude on his private conversation with Mrs. Poole. But given she ought to be in the kitchen at such an important time of the day, I felt compelled to find out what had brought her all the way up here.

"He was most insistent," Mrs. Poole was saying, her voice light and airy, like one of her delicious soufflés. "I tried telling him it wasn't the same, but he wouldn't listen."

My uncle chuckled. "Then it's his own fault."

"Oh, I quite agree. He won't try to swindle me again after that."

"You're marvelous, Elizabeth," my uncle said, softly. "Absolutely marvelous."

"You'd best call me Mrs. Poole, even in here. You don't know who's listening."

My heart jumped. I hurried away, only to stop when my uncle called my name.

I turned, smiling, pretending I'd not been eavesdropping, but no one would believe I was just passing by. My suite was to the left of the stairs and lift, and my uncle's office was to the right. Unless I needed to see him, I had no reason to head down that part of the corridor.

My uncle returned my smile and beckoned me closer. "Cleo, help me convince Mrs. Poole to stay on permanently as head chef."

"Oh." It was all I could manage. I'd been preparing excuses in my head, not expecting to be let off the hook.

"Tell her the hotel needs her."

Mrs. Poole's eyes warmed as she smiled at him. She wasn't a beautiful woman, but she was pleasing to look at, particularly when she smiled. Her brown eyes almost disappeared altogether when she laughed heartily, and her apple cheeks were always flushed. There was a heartiness about her, and an air of command that she even managed to maintain in the presence of my uncle, a man who could make staff cower with a mere look.

"It most certainly does," I said and meant it. "The food has never tasted better, and the cooks have never been happier."

"Oh? You've been in my kitchen?"

I swallowed and tried to look as innocent as possible.

"*Your* kitchen?" my uncle blurted out. "It's not yours yet, Elizabeth—but it can be."

Mrs. Poole gave him a teasing arch of her brow then turned to me. "Don't look so frightened, Miss Fox. As long as you don't cause an accident or get in the way, you're welcome to come into the kitchen at any time."

I released a breath. "I'm so used to the previous chef shouting at me every time I set a fingernail inside his domain; it's going to take some time to grow accustomed to this new, calmer regime."

She laughed. "It's taking the cooks some time to get used to it too, but I think they're starting to understand my ways. If you like the kitchen so much, why not have cooking lessons when it's quiet? I'd be happy to show you some simple skills you may need one day."

"She taught me how to boil an egg once, years ago," Uncle Ronald said.

"I can boil an egg," I said, "and make a number of other dishes. My grandmother taught me." After Grandpapa died, leaving Grandmama and me with nothing but fond memories and crippling debt, we'd moved into a smaller place and done most of the chores ourselves with the occasional help from a charwoman. Grandmama did most of the cooking until she could no longer manage it, and then I'd taken over. It wasn't my favorite chore, but I'd not set fire to anything, and every dish had been edible, if not always flavorsome.

Mrs. Poole looked at me as if seeing me for the first time. "I knew you didn't grow up here, but I assumed..." She shook her head. "Never mind."

"You assumed I was a pampered princess."

Her eyes twinkled.

Beside her, my uncle suddenly stiffened. I turned to see

what had caught his eye and spotted my aunt at the lift doors. She wore her Russian sable cloak over an evening gown of sage green with something sparkling threaded through her hair. From the erect way she held herself, I suspected she'd just taken a dose of her tonic. As if sensing us staring, she suddenly looked up and beamed. She looked as though she didn't have a care in the world. She waved. We all waved back. The lift doors opened and she stepped inside.

"She's dining at a friend's house tonight," Uncle Ronald said, even though no one had asked. "I'm going to my club." He cleared his throat. "Thank you for telling me about the change to the menu, Mrs. Poole. If the fishmonger causes you any problems again, do let me know."

"I can handle a supplier trying to pass off one thing for another. They quickly learn not to try it again."

"Indeed."

She watched him retreat into his office with a slight frown scoring her forehead.

I returned to my suite and decided to order my dinner through the speaking tube. I spent the evening reading and went to bed early, only to be woken up by someone knocking on my door. It was still dark and the knocking was urgent. That wasn't a good sign.

I threw on my dressing gown and turned on the lights in each room as I passed through to the front door, grateful for instant electric lighting. With my heart in my throat, I jerked the door open.

"Jonathon! My God, you look dreadful. What's happened?"

He blinked eyes mapped with red veins at me, the bright light clearly stinging them. The buttons of his dinner jacket were undone and his tie was askew. He wore no hat, nor did he carry one. He must have lost it somewhere. He sucked in deep breaths so I suspected he hadn't just come from Floyd's room down the hall. "Nothing happened to me. I'm fine. Why? How do I look?" He self-consciously patted his hair and, realizing it stuck out at angles, tried to flatten it.

"Like you had to fight your way out of a situation, although I see you don't have any bruises. Has something happened to Floyd?"

"That's the thing." He glanced along the corridor then lowered his voice. "I lost him."

"Lost him where?"

"I'd rather not say." He rubbed the back of his neck and regarded me through a curtain of blond hair. "You wouldn't approve."

I leaned against the doorframe, arms crossed over my chest. My heart had resumed a steadier beat now that I could see no one was ill. "He probably fell asleep there. He'll return when he wakes up." I smothered a yawn. "What time is it?"

He pulled out his watch by its gold chain and flipped open the cover. "Ten past four." He slipped it back into his pocket. "He didn't fall asleep there. When I was ready to leave, I looked everywhere for him. I thought he might have come back here, but I don't have a key to his room and I didn't want to knock on his door. If he's in a drunken slumber, he won't hear it, and I don't want to knock too loudly or I'll wake his parents."

"So you thought you'd wake me instead."

He gave me a sheepish grin. I wanted to slam the door on it. "I hoped you could convince the night porter to use the spare key to open Floyd's door. He won't do it for me, but he will for you."

I sighed. "Wait here while I put on slippers."

With slippers on and my finger hooked through the handle of the small oil lamp I kept beside the bed, I rejoined Jonathon.

"You look nice," he said.

I glared at him. He bit his lip and looked straight ahead.

We took the stairs down to the ground floor. Philip, the night porter, looked surprised to see me with Jonathon, even though he'd greeted Jonathon a few minutes earlier when he arrived. I quickly explained that we were worried about Floyd not having returned, then stopped myself.

"*Has* he returned to the hotel?" I asked. In my sleepy state, I hadn't been thinking clearly. Jonathon could have asked Philip the same question. There was no need to rouse me.

"No, Miss Fox," Philip said.

I gave Jonathon another glare.

He pretended not to notice. "Thank you. Carry on." After

Philip walked off, Jonathon turned to me, "Now I am worried. Where could he be?"

I tried to get his measure, but I couldn't quite manage it. I wasn't sure if he was too drunk to think clearly and had simply not thought about asking Philip, or if he was trying to endear himself to me somehow. Surely he must realize that waking someone up at four in the morning for no reason would not endear anyone to him. Perhaps he really was worried about Floyd.

Now I was worried too. "Where did you leave him?"

He dragged his hand through his hair. "Not at our usual club."

"A brothel?"

"No!" He looked shocked the word had touched my lips, let alone that I'd even considered it an option. "It's a private venue that caters for gentlemen gamblers. I didn't want to go, but Floyd met a fellow last week at another gambling den and he invited him. The man lost a fortune to Floyd but was good natured about it. He begged Floyd to give him the opportunity to win it back at this other place."

"That doesn't seem disreputable at all," I muttered.

"Yes, well, I tried to warn him the fellow might be a swindler, but he wouldn't listen."

"You should have kept a closer eye on him."

"I drank a little too much and lost track of time. I was in another room and when I went searching for him, I couldn't find him. I asked the guards at the door if they'd seen him leave, but they were no help. They're paid for their brawn, not their powers of observation."

"Or loose tongues. So where could he have gone? Out with another friend?"

"All the other patrons were strangers to us."

"Perhaps he made new friends and left with them. Or he met up with a woman. He has a mistress, doesn't he?"

Jonathon's eyes widened. He kept his mouth shut, but in my book, that was confirmation that my guess was right. I had no reason to suspect my cousin kept a mistress, but I knew many single young men of means had one. Some married ones, too. Often they were actresses or dancers, taking advantage of their pretty looks to earn as much as they could while they were still young.

The front door to the hotel opened and a surge of cold air swept into the foyer. Floyd stumbled through and fell to his knees on the tiles. Jonathon and Philip rushed to assist him to his feet. Outside, a carriage drove off. It was too dark to see who rode in it.

With the help of his friend and the night porter, my cousin lurched to his feet. "Jon'th'n? What're you doing here?"

"Looking for you." Jonathon caught Floyd around the waist and asked Philip to take his other side. "We need to get you upstairs. Does anyone know how to work the lift?"

The lift operator didn't work this late at night, and none of us knew how to make it go. We had to get Floyd up four flights of stairs, quietly, and without the night porter's help. Being the only one on duty, he couldn't leave the foyer. I took over from Philip at the base of the staircase. Thankfully Floyd was conscious enough to put one foot in front of the other—just—and Jonathon supported most of his weight.

"Your cousin and I were worried about you," Jonathon said, keeping his voice low.

Floyd peered at him from beneath eyelids lowered to half-mast. "Cousin?"

Jonathon nodded at me. Floyd followed his gaze, turning his head slowly as if sudden movement would cause pain.

"Cleo!" He circled his arm around my waist and gave me an awkward hug. "You're the best cousin in the world. You're even better than Flossy."

"Flossy is your sister, not your cousin," I said.

"S'actly."

We eventually made it to the fourth floor without making too much noise. Jonathon searched through Floyd's pockets for the key and we propped him against the wall while he unlocked the door. I couldn't keep holding him on my own, so he slid to the floor where his head fell forward. He let out a soft snore.

We managed to carry him the rest of the way to the bed. Jonathon began removing one of Floyd's shoes, but that was the end of my involvement. I bade him goodnight.

Jonathon took one look at the sleeping Floyd sprawled on

the bed and left him there, still wearing one shoe. "I think I've done enough tonight too."

We closed the door behind us. I made my way to my rooms, a shadow tailing me. I stopped at my door and turned to him. "Goodnight, Jonathon. Thank you for being a good friend to him. I'm not sure he deserves it."

"He's done that and more for me in the past." He gave me a flat smile, tilting his head a little so that his blond hair fell into his eyes. "But I've mended my ways and am a reformed rake now."

Some women liked reformed rakes. In my experience, they were only reformed for a brief time before they returned to their rakish ways. But I wouldn't say that to Jonathon in case there was a chance I was wrong.

One thing I felt sure about was that Jonathon was flirting with me and possibly hoped that it would lead to something more. That made two men in recent weeks who'd made advances towards me—Edward Caldicott and now Jonathon. I'd never had this much male attention, and I was under no illusions that I'd suddenly become prettier, or more charming or interesting. They were flirting with me because I was related to the Bainbridges and assumed I'd inherited half of my grandfather's fortune via my mother. Few were aware of the real story.

I was suddenly glad that the people who mattered knew I'd inherited nothing.

* * *

THE FOLLOWING MORNING, I didn't need to continue with my half of the list of hotels. One of the footmen delivered a message from Harry saying he'd started early and found the hotel where the stranger was staying. The check-in clerk had admitted to passing Harry's business card to the guest. The stranger was not presently there, but Harry would wait and watch for the man's return. He didn't tell me which hotel so I wasn't able to relieve him of his duties or just help him pass the time by talking.

I pushed aside the pinch of disappointment and spent most of the day with Flossy. Before it was time to meet Aunt

Lilian and Lady Bunbury, we went our separate ways. I headed to the staff parlor. As I suspected, Harmony was there with Victor, Goliath, Frank and Peter. Even though he was now assistant manager, Peter liked to have a short break with them in the afternoon and gossip over a cup of tea.

They could see I had news and directed me into the corner away from the other staff. With teacup in hand, I told them how Harry and I had been employed by the police to help catch Madame Poitiers' killer.

"How much are they paying?" Harmony asked.

"We didn't discuss a fee."

She pressed her lips together and shook her head. "Sometimes I despair of you."

Victor agreed with her, for once. "I'd expect Armitage to insist before beginning work. He was always a tough negotiator."

They all nodded in agreement.

"I can be a tough negotiator too," I said, sounding more hurt than I was.

Harmony gave me a sympathetic look. "You don't even know how much to ask for."

She had a point.

Goliath stretched out his long legs and crossed his arms over his massive chest. "So who're your suspects?"

I told them about the stranger with the accent who'd gone to the victim's flat to look for her then argued with her later that evening when he returned. I also told them how she had lied about her past which had led to her husband hiring Harry. If he inherited the salon, he was definitely a suspect too.

I almost didn't tell them about our third suspect, but I decided they ought to be given the full picture. They might offer some insights we hadn't considered. "And there's Lady Bunbury, too. She had an appointment with the victim before the salon opened. Apparently, only customers who need to make alternative financial arrangements meet Madame Poitiers at that hour. I'm having afternoon tea here at the hotel with her soon. Have any of you heard of her?"

They shook their heads. "Is she quality?" Frank asked.

"Everyone with a Lady in front of their name is quality," Goliath said.

"She ain't quality if she has to make alternative financial arrangements with the dressmaker," Victor pointed out.

Harmony's spine stiffened and she glared down her nose at him. "One's financial situation doesn't define whether a person is quality or not."

"Neither does having a title."

Harmony had no retort. I suspected that annoyed her more than his reply. She turned her shoulder to him.

Victor looked as though he regretted disagreeing with her.

"According to my aunt and cousin, Lady Bunbury is the queen of society," I told them. "Everyone wants to be her friend and attend her ball. The girls she chooses as the most accomplished, the most beautiful, the most charming, can expect to enjoy all the fruits of a bountiful season and will probably find themselves a husband within months of their debut. Alternatively, a snub from her is a major blow to a girl's aspirations. She'll be fortunate if she gets further invitations to top-tier society events."

Harmony pulled a face. "I've never been gladder not to be one of those women."

"Me too," I said.

They all looked at me.

"I'm not," I assured them. "I honestly don't care about balls and parties. I'd much rather solve a murder."

Frank leaned closer to Goliath. "I thought we were about to get another lecture on how she doesn't want to marry."

I gave him a withering glare. "Very amusing."

Harmony smacked his shoulder. "You're forgetting who you're speaking to."

Frank flushed and immediately straightened. "Sorry, Miss Fox. I overstepped."

I smiled. "No, you didn't. I'm glad you're comfortable enough with me to make such a joke."

He looked relieved.

Harmony turned her glare onto me. She rose and peered into my empty teacup. "If you're meeting the queen of society, you'd better let me do your hair."

I patted it. Finding a few stray strands had escaped, I

tucked them back into the arrangement. They immediately fell out again. "It's not that bad."

She plucked the teacup from my hand. "We'd best get started. It's going to take a while."

* * *

THE MAYFAIR'S main sitting room was always decorated prettily for its famous afternoon tea ritual. Silverware glinted against bright white tablecloths. Delicate china added a touch of color with subtle patterns in the hotel's colors of gold and burgundy with a hint of black. Voluminous flower arrangements filled large vases and tall palm trees added interest to otherwise drab corners. The gentle modulations of a string ensemble set a soothing mood for the ladies dressed in their best daytime outfits.

Aunt Lilian introduced me to the incomparable Lady Bunbury, a woman as beautiful and elegant as the Mayfair itself. There was no more suitable setting for her than the center of the sitting room, surrounded by feminine luxury. Her blonde hair was arranged in a sweeping style that framed her heart-shaped face. Sky-blue eyes were fringed with long lashes, darkened to add definition. She wore no other makeup that I could see. She didn't need it.

I was glad I'd changed into my dove-gray and white gown and had Harmony fix my hair, but next to Lady Bunbury, I felt plain. The high collar of her white blouse embroidered with foliage in shades of soft green complemented the sea-green of her silk dress with the central panel embroidered with the same pattern of foliage as the blouse collar. With her beauty, tiny waist and considerable bosom, she looked like she'd stepped off the page of the latest edition of *Les Modes*, the French fashion magazine Flossy subscribed to.

When Lady Bunbury spoke, her voice was soft and musical. I had to lean in to hear her over the string ensemble. I suspected that was the point. It made it appear to those watching on that we were hanging on Lady Bunbury's every word. "We were so disappointed to learn you're not doing your court presentation, Miss Fox."

I didn't know who she meant by "we." Perhaps it was in the royal sense, and she was simply referring to herself. She was a queen, of sorts, after all. "I'll attend the occasional event, if I'm fortunate enough to receive an invitation, of course."

Lady Bunbury smiled benignly. "I'm sure a girl such as yourself will receive many invitations."

It was almost an assurance that I would receive one to her ball. The vague promise was enough to bring a broad smile to Flossy's face and have my aunt breathe a noticeable sigh of relief.

"Cleo is already proving herself to be very popular," Aunt Lilian said.

I refrained from glaring at her and simply smiled demurely.

Lady Bunbury sized me up. "It's her maturity. Some gentlemen prefer sensible conversation over giggling imbeciles." She made it sound as though sensible was a synonym for dull. I wasn't sure who was more offended, me, to be called boring, or Flossy, who'd just been labeled an imbecile due to her youth.

It would seem Lady Bunbury had a cutting tongue to go with her queenly crown. I started to hope she was the killer, simply to see her endure public censure the way she censured others. But the more we talked over finger sandwiches, strawberry and vanilla tarts, meringues, pastries, and sponge cake, the more I doubted she was our murderess. She was too genteel to lift a finger and do her own dirty work. She also struck me as too cold to fire up with the sort of passionate anger that had caused the killer to strangle Madame Poitiers with the veil. Lady Bunbury's murder weapon of choice would be poison.

Directing the conversation towards the murder was easy enough. Madame Poitiers was a popular dressmaker for London society, and her murder was the most interesting thing to have happened in the city, as far as many were concerned.

Inevitably, our talk turned to who could have done it. Lady Bunbury seemed keen to tell us her theory. "It must be someone from her past, someone who knows her true identity." What an odd assumption to leap to first.

"What makes you say that?" Aunt Lilian asked.

"She's not really French. Anyone with a half a brain knows that."

"Oh, yes, we knew," Flossy said quickly. "We even talked about her dreadful accent on the way home from the salon."

Lady Bunbury turned her penetrating gaze onto me. "I heard you discovered the body, Miss Fox."

"I did, along with her assistant, Miss Newland."

My aunt looked as though she'd be sick. She swallowed hard then clasped her throat. "A dreadful business. Poor Cleo received quite a fright."

Lady Bunbury managed to convey frowning without a single crease wrinkling her forehead. It was as if she'd learned to blink in such a way that she didn't need to actually frown, so that she could preserve her flawlessly smooth complexion for longer. "How awful it must have been for you. Did you happen to see any clues that could point to the identity of the killer?"

I gave her the full force of my frown. "No."

"Did the police confide anything to you? Perhaps there was a particular customer they wished to speak to."

I'd already suspected this woman did and said nothing spontaneously. Every word steered the conversation in the direction she wanted, every smile and flutter of her lashes was designed to project a certain image of herself. Now I realized her very presence here wasn't simply to partake in gossip and delicious morsels that she barely touched. She'd accepted Aunt Lilian's invitation to join us for afternoon tea at short notice not because she had no other offers, but because she wanted to find out what I knew about the police's suspicions.

I played innocent and gave her a blank look.

"Why would the police wish to speak to one of her customers?" Flossy asked, without guile.

"Perhaps the customer was unhappy with one of Madame's designs and was overheard arguing with her about it." Lady Bunbury lifted a hand in a dismissive wave, drawing attention to the diamond and moonstone ring she wore. It matched the pale blue enamel, diamond and moonstone flower brooch pinned to her dress. "Perhaps she met someone before opening the salon that day." She plucked up her teacup, as if she were just making conversation. The gaze that held mine over the rim of the cup was at odds with her gossipy tone.

"If so, then you might have seen them when you met with her," I said. "I believe you had an early appointment at the salon."

My aunt and cousin both went very still. I held my breath, hoping I hadn't made a dreadful error. I wanted to know the reason for her early appointment and see her face while she gave it.

Lady Bunbury momentarily forgot to keep her forehead clear to stave off future wrinkles and frowned at me. She quickly schooled her features again and regarded me coolly. "It was the only time I could arrange my final fitting." If it was a lie, she hid it well. "Anyway, I never saw her. My knock went unanswered. Tell me, Miss Fox, is it true you have the ear of the police?"

It was my turn to go very still. Was she guessing or did she know? Only Harry, his father, his Scotland Yard colleagues and superiors, Harmony and some of the other staff knew. All were trustworthy.

While I was scrambling to think of a response, my aunt came to my rescue. "Cleo would never stoop so low." A muscle in her jaw twitched and she fidgeted in her seat, restless. Lady Bunbury eyed her as if those were signs of a lying conscience. I knew it was because my aunt's tonic gave her excess energy and she couldn't sit still. She'd been trying to contain her restlessness ever since sitting down. "What a lovely brooch, Lady Bunbury. I've been admiring it all afternoon. Is it Lalique?"

Lady Bunbury gave her a stiff nod then rose. "I'm afraid I must go."

"But I haven't had a chance to ask you about the ball yet," Flossy whined.

"The decorations are a secret. If all and sundry knew my plans beforehand, they'd be copied."

"Quite right," Aunt Lilian said. "Thank you for coming, Ruth. It's been a pleasure."

Lady Bunbury bestowed half-hearted smiles on us and saw herself out. Once she was gone, Aunt Lilian asked us to sit again. I'd expected her to leave straight away to rest, as her hands had begun to shake. She asked Flossy to pour another tea for each of us and bestowed a sly smile on me.

"So, what do you think of the remarkable Lady Bunbury, Cleo?"

"I think she suspects that I suspect her of the murder."

"Don't you?"

I didn't expect my aunt to be direct. I expected her to beat around the bush, never quite saying what was on her mind, and being well mannered and bland as she did it. I liked being proved wrong. She was sharper than she let on.

"It doesn't matter what I think," I said, accepting the teacup from Flossy. "It's up to Detective Inspector Hobart."

My aunt regarded me levelly until Flossy handed her the teacup and saucer. I didn't assume her silence meant I'd fooled her. Thankfully she chose not to press me.

My aunt sipped thoughtfully. "If you do happen to see the detective again, perhaps you can pass on a piece of information that might interest him."

"I don't understand."

Her shaking hand made the teacup rattle in the saucer so she set them down on the table. "I happen to own a Lalique brooch."

Flossy nodded. "The dragonfly. It's lovely."

"It is, and it is beautifully made. It's not so much the jewels that make it beautiful but the craftsmanship. It's quite complex. Each segment of the dragonfly is well defined, the stones chosen to fit perfectly into the body and wings. The enamel is finely worked too, and it adds to the overall arrangement. Lady Bunbury's brooch wasn't a Lalique. I'd stake my reputation on it."

Flossy gasped. "The diamonds are paste?"

"I'm not entirely sure. They were too small, and I wasn't close enough. It could be that some are real and others not. But I can be sure the brooch isn't a genuine Lalique. What flower do you think it was supposed to be?"

Flossy and I exchanged glances. "Dahlia?" she asked.

"I think it was a chrysanthemum, but that's the point. It was impossible to tell. If it were a genuine Lalique, we would know what the flower was supposed to be even if we were sitting at the next table. The jeweler who made her brooch lacked Lalique's skill."

"Mother, you are clever! So Lady Bunbury couldn't afford a real Lalique."

"Or she could, at one point," I said, thinking out loud. "But needed money so sold it and had a copy made."

Flossy's eyes gleamed with this new, scandalous information. "You were right, Cleo. The Bunburys *are* poor."

"Do not tell a soul," her mother warned. "We are not in the business of ruining the reputation of good families."

Flossy agreed.

When I didn't, they both arched their brows at me. "I'll have to tell Detective Inspector Hobart. It'll be up to him to use the information in any way he sees fit. If she turns out to be the murderer, it will all come out anyway."

Flossy rolled her eyes. "She's not a murderer, Cleo. She's the queen of society. She was the most favored debutante of her day. She's Lady Bunbury."

She looked to her mother for support, but Aunt Lilian had gone pale, her hand pressed to her temple. She looked as though she wanted to throw up everything she'd eaten at afternoon tea. Despite earlier eyeing off the food as though she could devour every tartlet, sandwich and slice of cake on her own, she'd restrained herself, not wanting to appear gluttonous. But now, one glance at the leftovers turned her face green.

She excused herself and asked Flossy to escort her to her rooms.

I watched them go then headed to Mr. Hobart's office. I had to make a telephone call to his brother and let him know what I'd learned about Lady Bunbury. Although I couldn't imagine her strangling Madame Poitiers after an argument over money, I knew it was foolish to rely on instinct. Instincts could be wrong. Only evidence mattered.

And the evidence against Lady Bunbury was mounting.

CHAPTER 7

*D*etective Inspector Hobart thanked me for passing on the information about Lady Bunbury's Lalique brooch but gave nothing away. If he thought it any more than mildly interesting, I was none the wiser. He also wasn't surprised when I mentioned she seemed to know I was working for Scotland Yard. After D.I. Hobart questioned her, Lord Bunbury spoke to the commissioner, warning him not to bother his wife again. The police commissioner probably let it slip then. I thought it unprofessional of him to mention my name at all. The inspector claimed the commissioner probably thought it would shoe horn him into Lord Bunbury's good graces. I got the impression Inspector Hobart had little respect for his superior.

I wanted to see Harry and find out if he'd had any success speaking to the stranger, but I decided not to seek him out. He would send a message if he had any news.

At a loss for what to do next, I loitered in the hotel foyer, hoping for inspiration. I sat on one of the comfortable armchairs and watched the guests coming and going. Some were of Lady Bunbury's ilk, but their families no longer had London residences. Others were not of noble birth but were wealthy and stayed here when they came to the city. A good number were from overseas. I wondered how many wore a Poitiers' outfit or owned one. Probably quite a few. While the House of Worth in Paris still reigned supreme, Maison de

Poitiers had an excellent reputation here in London, particularly for those ladies who preferred a bespoke shopping experience.

Until now, I'd never taken a keen interest in fashion. I liked well-made clothes, but I kept outfits for a few years, altering them to suit my own tastes and the changing times. I didn't need new ones every year. Nor did I like changing outfits during the day, unless absolutely necessary. I'd once counted the number of ensembles Flossy had worn in a single day. It was five. And the social season had not yet fully begun.

Mrs. and Miss Hessing, the American mother and daughter duo, entered the hotel. Goliath and another porter trailed behind them, balancing boxes and parcels of all shapes and sizes. They needed no instruction as they carried them towards the service lift, but Mrs. Hessing bellowed after them to take everything up to their suite.

She headed for the guest lift, nodding a greeting to me as she passed. Despite her purposeful strides, she looked tired. It must have been a long day of shopping. "Come along, Joan. You may draw me a bath. I'm much too exhausted to do it myself."

Miss Hessing's shoulders, already slumped, stooped even further. She tucked the magazine she was holding under her arm and, with a heavy sigh, followed her mother.

"Mrs. Hessing, one moment, please," I called out. "I couldn't help overhearing... May I have one of the maids draw your bath for you? It's just that I wish to speak to Miss Hessing."

Mrs. Hessing screwed up her face to peer at me. "What could you possibly have to speak to Joan about?"

"The magazine she's holding. There was a lovely dress I saw in that very edition, but I wanted another woman's opinion on it. A woman of my own age," I said quickly lest she decide to stay behind.

"I suppose..."

"Let me arrange it for you." I gave Miss Hessing a wink when I turned away. After a quick word with Peter, I returned to them. "Peter will see that someone comes to your room immediately, Mrs. Hessing."

She gave me a quizzical look but didn't insist her daughter return to the room with her. Miss Hessing and I watched her disappear into the lift. Neither of us sat until the doors were closed and we knew the lift had risen with her in it.

Miss Hessing settled into one of the armchairs with another deep sigh. "Thank you, Miss Fox. It's been a trying day."

"You don't like shopping?"

"I don't mind it, but not all day. And my mother is never satisfied, nor do I like anything she chooses for me." As if she suddenly remembered, she handed me the magazine. "I'm not sure I'll be of much assistance, but I can offer an opinion if you show me the dress. Although I do think Miss Bainbridge's opinion would be of more worth. She has style."

"My cousin has a style, it's true. I'm just not sure it's *my* style."

Miss Hessing seemed quite shocked that I would disparage Flossy like that, but she giggled when I smiled and winked. She covered her mouth with her hand to stifle it and looked around guiltily.

I didn't admit that I'd made up the story about the dress to give her a reprieve from her mother, so we looked through the magazine together. We both pointed out clothes we liked. Miss Hessing's taste was quiet, like her. She preferred muted colors, high collars, and few frills. She turned the page and pointed to the caption below a series of pictures of different ball gowns. They were designs by Madame Poitiers.

"Such a tragedy," Miss Hessing murmured.

"Indeed."

We sat in silence as we studied the beautiful gowns and considered the awful demise of an icon of the London fashion scene.

"My mother thinks her dresses are as good as any you can get from Worth," Miss Hessing said. "She did once make a snide comment that they were a little close to Worth's in structure, but I pointed out that Madame Poitiers probably studied Worth when she was younger. Did she work there before she set up on her own here?"

The question took me by surprise. In fact, it was such a

good question that it set my mind racing. "I don't know." I flipped through the pages of the magazine, taking note of all the names of the different fashion houses. There were too many to remember. I needed to write them down.

I couldn't abandon Miss Hessing too soon, so we talked some more. Mr. Hobart approached me to say that he was leaving for the day and that Peter was in charge until the night porter started.

"Do you have any messages for me, Miss Fox?" he asked.

"No. Goodnight, Mr. Hobart."

He hesitated. "I'm dining with my brother, sister-in-law and nephew this evening."

Ah. He was asking if I had any messages for Harry or the inspector. Before I could respond, Miss Hessing spoke up. "Are you talking about Mr. Armitage? Do give him my regards," she said, lashes fluttering. "Tell him the Mayfair is not the same without him, and my mother and I hope he'll be back here where he belongs next year."

Mr. Hobart bowed his head. "That's very kind of you to say, Miss Hessing. I will pass on the message. My nephew will be pleased that he hasn't been forgotten by you or Mrs. Hessing."

She gave him a serious look. "Oh, we could never forget Mr. Armitage. Never."

Mr. Hobart smiled at her then glanced at me, brows arched.

"I'll see you in the morning," I told him. "I'm heading out early. I have an appointment with a friend in Broadwick Street."

His eyes brightened at the mention of the address for Harry's office. He understood I wanted to see Harry in the morning and would pass the message on. He bade us good evening.

"You are fond of Mr. Armitage," I said idly to my companion.

Miss Hessing smiled. "Oh yes. Such a kind man. And so handsome. It's a wonder he's not married."

I flipped through the pages vigorously, tearing the corner of one. "Isn't it."

Miss Hessing didn't seem to notice my distraction. She

spent the next five minutes dreamily staring at Peter, but I suspected he was Harry in her mind.

Goliath entered the foyer from the direction of the service lift and said something to Peter. They both glanced at me.

"I should change for dinner," I said, rising. "It's been a pleasure, Miss Hessing."

"Thank you for your company, Miss Fox."

"May I borrow your magazine for the evening?"

She handed it over and made to leave but hesitated. "I hope we can do this again. I enjoyed it." With a shy smile, she dipped her head then made her way to the lift.

I joined Peter. Goliath had loped off outside. "Did he have a message for me?" I asked.

"Harmony is waiting for you in your rooms," Peter said.

"Oh? But I don't need her help dressing tonight."

He leaned in. "I think she just wants the company."

"Doesn't she have company back at the residence hall?"

"She can't talk about murder there. Not without the other maids fainting in horror." He grinned. "How did your afternoon tea with Lady Bunbury go?"

I told him about her fake Lalique brooch and indicated the magazine. "I've got work to do tonight. In fact, I'm glad Harmony's available. I need her help."

As I headed up to the fourth floor, I realized I was going to need the help of someone else, too. Someone who could speak fluent French.

But first things first.

I found Harmony napping on the sofa in my sitting room, an open magazine on her lap. At first, I thought she'd had the same thought as me, then I noticed it was a cookbook written by our very own chef, Mrs. Poole.

I sat at the writing desk by the window and settled in to make notes.

Harmony yawned loudly. "Cleo? What are you doing?"

"Listing the name of every fashion house in this magazine I borrowed from Miss Hessing."

She padded up behind me in her stockinged feet and peered over my shoulder. "Why?"

"Because Gertrude Lindsey—Madame Poitiers—must have learned her craft at one of the great fashion houses.

Doucet and Worth... Paquin," I added upon seeing the name associated with a coral colored muslin day dress with blue embroidery and tucking.

"Are they all French?"

"Most." I flipped through the pages. "There must be more."

"I'll fetch some magazines from Miss Bainbridge's room," she said, already pulling on her shoes.

She returned a few minutes later with an armful of magazines and Flossy. "Will one of you tell me what this is about?" my cousin demanded.

I explained my theory and we three set about listing every name of every fashion house we came across, big and small. Flossy knew some without needing to stumble across them in the magazines. She seemed unconcerned that one of the hotel maids sat beside her on the sofa and helped. She was too interested in our task to care that we'd set aside propriety.

After an hour, we had twenty-eight names. It was too many for what I had planned.

"Not all of these would have been around in the Seventies," I said. "We need to speak to someone who will know which ones, and follow up only those."

"Who?" Harmony asked.

Flossy and I exchanged glances then rose from our chairs at the same time.

"Harmony, will you take a message to Mr. Bainbridge's room," I said. "Ask him to meet us here in fifteen minutes. If he asks why, tell him we need his French."

Flossy eyed the carriage clock. "He won't come now. He's about to head out."

"He'll come." To Harmony, I added, "If he refuses, tell him he owes me after last night."

Flossy frowned. "What happened last night?"

"Jonathon and I put him to bed when he rolled in drunk." I waved off her concern. "Don't worry. He was fine."

"And what about you and your reputation? It could have been ruined if someone saw you with a man in the middle of the night." That was not my cousin speaking but my maid and friend. Flossy merely looked disapproving. Harmony was the one who voiced it.

"It wasn't the middle of the night, it was almost dawn. And my nightdress was fully covered by my dressing gown. It was all very respectable."

Harmony made a miffed sound through her nose.

Flossy merely stared at me. It wasn't until we reached the door that she said, "Do not let my father find out."

"I don't intend to."

Aunt Lilian rested on the sofa, her eyes covered with cucumber slices to cool them. She was not asleep, but she didn't rise when we announced ourselves.

"Don't talk so loudly," she whispered. "My head is pounding."

"Sorry," Flossy whispered back. "Mother, we need your help."

"I can't. My head…"

"I know it hurts, but this won't take long."

"Come back later after I've taken my tonic. I'll be more use to you then."

Flossy frowned down at her mother but it was lost on Aunt Lilian. The cucumber slices remained in place. "You shouldn't take it again so soon after the last time. I know you're suffering, but it'll be worse in the long run if you take another dose now."

"I have to. Your father and I are dining out. If I don't take the tonic soon, I won't be able to get ready let alone endure an entire evening." She sat up and swung her feet to the floor. The cucumber slices fell onto her lap as she went to catch her head in her hands. "It feels like my skull is cracking open."

Flossy sat beside her and took her hand. I retrieved a face cloth from the bathroom, dampened it in cold water, and passed it to my aunt to press against her forehead and neck.

She smiled gratefully. "Why do two bright girls like yourselves need the help of an old thing like me?"

Flossy hugged her mother. "Don't say that. You're not old."

Aunt Lilian sighed. "Right now I feel ancient. But my tonic will fix that." She gazed longingly at the door to her bedroom. The bottle must be on her bedside table where she kept it handy.

"Aunt, if we tell you some names of fashion houses, do

you think you can tell us which ones were around in the Seventies?"

"Oh. Yes, I can certainly do that. Your mother and I wore some of the loveliest gowns when we were younger. Everyone said we both had a good eye." She smiled wistfully. "Of course, the styles were different then. The colors were bolder, the skirts fuller, and the waistlines a little more forgiving than what they are now. And the bustles!" She chuckled only to stop suddenly and wince.

I read names off the list we'd made and Aunt Lilian said yes or no for the ones that were in business in the Seventies. She had an excellent memory, only needing to stop and think three or four times. For every other name, she answered instantly. Most were too new and didn't exist back then. Only six did, and she added another two to our list who'd since gone out of business. I had no way of contacting those. Of the six still operating, all were based in Paris. According to Mr. Lindsey, his wife had returned to England for her throat operation and he'd met her soon afterwards. Before that, according to the stranger, she'd traveled around Europe singing in the troupe. We didn't know how long she'd been with the troupe, but it was certainly feasible that she learned to create high fashion in the years before joining it and becoming a singer. After the operation, with her throat too damaged to return to her prior career, she'd taken up sewing and designing again.

Of course, there was the possibility she was self-taught, in which case all of this work would be for nothing.

Flossy and I returned to my suite where Harmony was waiting. Floyd arrived a few minutes later. With arms crossed over his chest, he demanded to know why I'd threatened him.

"It wasn't a threat," I said. "I was merely counting on your guilty conscience. You do owe me, by the way. Jonathon saw me in my dressing gown. Luckily I don't sleep in hair curlers or my humiliation would have been complete."

His brow cleared and his arms lowered. He watched me with an odd look on his face.

I quickly focused on what we needed him to do. "You would have learned French like every upper class schoolboy. Can you write it fluently?"

"Yes."

"Good. I need you to write a telegram for me, in French."

"Why?"

"Because I'm trying to find Madame Poitiers' killer, and to do that, I need to know more about her background. She must have learned her craft somewhere. I hope it was at one of these fashion houses. I'll send telegrams to each of them tomorrow morning, asking if they remember her."

Floyd scoffed. "That's quite a long bow to draw."

"At least I'm drawing it, or trying to. We need to find out more about her past. It's somewhat murky right now."

"We?" He glanced between Flossy, Harmony and me. "Are you all investigating?"

"Mother approves," Flossy bit back.

"Mother knows?"

"Don't tell Father."

"If you do," I warned him, "I'll have to tell him how you disappeared from a notorious gambling house, leaving Jonathon with no alternative but to wake me at dawn dressed in nothing but my nightgown."

"I thought you said you wore a dressing gown over it."

"That depends on the version I tell your father."

He groaned. "You win. Give me some paper and dictate what you want translated."

I did, using our victim's maiden name of Gertrude Russell. In truth, I didn't have much hope that we'd fill in some of the gaps of her background. Floyd was right; this was a long bow to draw. But it made me feel useful.

I suspected Flossy and Harmony felt the same.

When Floyd finished, he bade Flossy and me goodnight, completely ignoring Harmony, who'd disappeared into the bedroom at some point. I walked him to the door and when we reached it, he glanced behind me to make sure his sister hadn't followed.

He leaned down to my level. "Are you sweet on Jonathon?" he whispered.

"No."

He blinked rapidly as he straightened. "Did you want to think about that?"

"No need. If he gives you reason to think he's sweet on

me, do set him straight. It would be kinder coming from you."

He nodded thoughtfully. "I will." He opened the door but didn't exit. "What's wrong with Jonathon?"

"I don't know him well enough to answer that."

"He's wealthy and he'll inherit a title."

"If that's important to you then *you* should marry him."

He ignored my jibe. "He's something of a ladies' man. It's probably just as well you're not interested. Men like that can't be tamed." He was suddenly all cheeky smiles and twinkling eyes. He slapped his hat on his head. "Nor should we be."

"You?" I laughed, teasing him. "You and Jonathon are cut from different cloths. You're crying out to be tamed by the right woman."

"Ha! I'll forgive you that, since you're new and haven't seen me in my element yet. All in good time, Little Cousin." He chucked me under the chin then sauntered off down the corridor.

I didn't necessarily believe what I said, nor did I entirely believe him, either. But it was fun bantering with him.

Harmony came up behind me before I closed the door. "Do you think we can trust him not to say anything to Sir Ronald?" she asked, keeping her voice low.

"We can."

She left, but not before giving me strict orders to let her know the responses from the fashion houses as soon as I received them.

* * *

THE CLERK at the telegraph office sent all my telegrams to the same central Paris office. The clerk there would ensure they were delivered to the correct fashion houses.

I continued on to Harry's office, stopping in at Luigi's café for coffee. Harry was there, perched on a stool next to the two regulars. He looked as comfortable at the counter beside the old men as he did sitting behind his desk or surveying the guests in the hotel foyer, or...well, Harry looked comfortable wherever he went. It was part of his charm.

It was no wonder Miss Hessing missed him. I would too, I realized with a start.

He turned before I greeted him. "Good morning, Cleo."

"Good morning, Harry," I said, matching his bland tone. "Have you ordered me a coffee?"

As I said it, Luigi set a cup down on the counter before me. "This is for you, *Bella*."

Harry arched his brows at the café owner. "That was supposed to be mine."

Luigi's entire body lurched with his shrug. "She has a prettier smile."

I slid the cup to Harry. "I wouldn't dare deprive you."

He slid it back. "Take it. I've already had one." He scrubbed a hand through his hair. He wore no hat and his hair already looked as though it had been tugged and teased several times. Did something trouble him? On closer inspection, I realized it wasn't worry. He was exhausted. "Uncle Alfred said you wanted to see me this morning."

"Straight to business, I see."

"Would you like to discuss the weather first?" He glanced at the window. From this angle and with the taller buildings opposite, he couldn't possibly see the sky, but he pronounced, "It looks like rain."

"Of course it does. It's March."

I sipped my coffee, aware of the tight silence between us. I missed the comfortable silences, the friendly banter, the little jokes and flirtations. There was an edge to our conversation this morning, even though we'd parted on good terms the day before yesterday. Harry was brooding. Exhaustion could do that to anyone.

Luigi set a coffee cup on the counter for Harry. Harry paid him and we took our coffees upstairs to his office.

"Is it all right with you if we start discussing the case now?" he asked as he sat.

I studied him, but he wasn't looking at me. He studied the coffee in his cup. "Of course."

"You wanted to tell me something."

"You first. Did you find the stranger?"

He shook his head. "He didn't return to the hotel. His

things are still there and he hasn't checked out yet, but…" He shrugged. "I gave up waiting."

"Would that be around dawn this morning?"

He looked up sharply. "I returned to the hotel after dining with my parents, uncle and aunt. I watched all night."

"Harry," I gently scolded. "Have you slept at all?"

He glanced at the brown leather armchair. "I got a couple of hours."

"Have you eaten breakfast?"

"I ate at Luigi's." He picked up his cup and studied its contents again, avoiding eye contact. "So what did you want to tell me?"

He seemed very keen to get this meeting over with. I would have teased him about having something better to rush off to, but I doubted my attempt at lightness would go down well. The strain between us reminded me of the time I'd cost him his job at the hotel.

Those days had been among some of the worst in my life.

I told him my theory that Gertrude had learned to design and sew high fashion outfits from one of the top French houses. He thought it a good theory and leaned forward, keen to hear more.

"I sent telegrams to six designers in Paris this morning, inquiring about Gertrude Russell, but I don't expect a reply for some time, if at all."

He nodded. "It's worth a try. So you know all about French fashion?"

"I know probably about as much as you. Perhaps less, considering you worked amongst ladies who always wore designer dresses. Flossy, Harmony and I scoured magazines for names then asked my aunt which ones were operating in the Seventies."

"You asked your aunt? Cleo, are you mad?"

"She won't tell my uncle, if that's what you're worried about."

He leaned further forward. "If he gets wind of this, he'll have more than enough reasons to cut you off and force you to leave the hotel. Not only are you working as an investigator, but you're working with me. In his book, that's two of the worst things his niece could do."

"Let me worry about my uncle."

He sat back, arms crossed over his chest. "Since this is my fault, I'll worry too."

"Don't be absurd. It is not your fault. You're being..."

He thrust his chin forward. "I'm being what?"

I shook my head, suddenly deflated. I felt like my aunt looked when she lay on the sofa with cucumber slices on her eyes. "Never mind. I don't want to argue with you. I don't like it. I hate it, in fact."

He passed a hand over his face. When it came away, the exhaustion was clear where before there'd been mere hints. "I hate it too. I'm sorry, Cleo. I'm aware of how bullish I'm being." He heaved a sigh. "I find I can't stop myself saying things I'll regret."

"You're tired. You're not yourself."

"It's no excuse for my temper."

"Everyone at the hotel would be surprised to learn you have one. Particularly Miss Hessing."

He put up his hands in surrender. "In my defense, it only comes out when I'm frustrated beyond measure."

"You're frustrated?"

His cheeks flushed. "Please accept my apology, and know that I'm still coming to terms with this arrangement." He pointed at me then himself. "But I *will* come to terms with it."

"Take heart that it's only temporary."

A small vein pulsed in his throat above his collar. He gave me a long look, but I couldn't read it. I got the feeling he was trying to work out if I was referring to our working relationship or something more. In truth, I didn't know what I meant either.

He turned away and stared at the photograph of his parents. Then his gaze shifted to the photograph of the pretty dark-haired woman sitting alone in the photographer's studio. He rarely spoke about his natural parents, or about his life before he was adopted by the Hobarts. It was curious that he focused on his birth mother now.

"She looks young there," I said.

"She was nineteen."

"Before she married your father?"

His chest rose and fell with his deep breath. "Her mother was a seamstress."

His avoidance of my question wasn't lost on me, but I didn't push him. According to the file from the orphanage, where he'd spent two years of his childhood, his parents were deceased. It had not listed their names. It was possible they'd never married.

"Was your mother a seamstress too?"

"She taught needlepoint in a school for privileged girls. Needlepoint and painting. She enjoyed it, but she used to tell me she was frustrated the parents didn't give their girls the same educations as their sons."

"She sounds like a woman after my own heart."

He smiled at that. "She was intelligent but her own formal education was basic. She left school at twelve and went to work. Later, she learned as much as she could by reading. She read books on travel, history, science, whatever she could get her hands on. The school's library was well stocked, even though the girls weren't taught half of the topics covered by the books. My mother made me read them too. I think she just wanted to discuss them with someone."

I blinked in surprise. I thought his mother would have given up her profession when she had Harry. "You were brought up in the school?"

"I lived there with her until she died, but I was educated at a local school during the day."

"No wonder you know how to charm the female sex. You were surrounded by women from a young age."

"And yet some women remain impervious to my charms." His arched look was a sure sign that he meant me. I decided not to set him straight.

This openness about his past was rare. I couldn't let it slip by without pressing for a little more. "How old were you when your father died?"

His face suddenly shuttered, his features tightening. "All this talk about fashion and designers made me think of my maternal grandmother. I hardly remember her, but I do recall she worked in a small attic room with three other seamstresses. It was stifling in summer. They would talk all day as they sewed, gossiping like harpies, as my mother would say. I wonder if Gertrude's staff gossiped while they worked too."

I finally latched onto his point. "Perhaps gossiping about their employer?" I drained my coffee cup then stood. "Let's speak to them now."

"My father has already interviewed them."

"He won't mind if we do it again."

"We should work with him, not parallel." Even as he spoke, he gathered up the coffee cups and removed his coat from the stand by the door. He might be saying one thing, but he wanted to interview the seamstresses as much as I did.

"You can telephone him after we're done and compare notes."

I took the cups from him so he could lock the door. I watched him closely, his fine chiseled jaw and high cheeks, his dark hair and intense, almost black eyes. He might take his coloring from his mother, but his striking features must have been inherited from his father. The face of the woman in the photograph was softer.

So why didn't Harry want to discuss his real father? If he'd died when Harry was young and he didn't remember him, why not just say so? Why did he change the subject every time?

It was a mystery. One I planned to solve.

CHAPTER 8

$\mathcal{W}$e found Maison de Poitiers open for appointments. It was Monday. The body had been discovered Friday morning so they'd had the weekend to discuss how to proceed. I wondered if Mr. Lindsey had spoken to the staff about the future or if he was too busy with funeral arrangements.

Miss Newland the assistant greeted me warmly and eyed Harry with curiosity. She quickly forgot about us, however, as she dealt with her clients, a woman and her two daughters.

Harry and I quietly slipped into the adjoining workroom. The whir of sewing machines and the hum of voices suddenly stopped. All seven pairs of eyes stared at us.

Even though I'd seen them on the day of the murder, I hadn't formally been introduced. I did so now, calling myself a client who also happened to be a detective consulting on the case for Scotland Yard, alongside Harry. He didn't correct me. It would seem he was satisfied to be called my associate and not my employer—this time.

"We have some questions to ask you about Madame Poitiers," I said. "We know you're busy, but can you spare a few minutes?"

Although Mrs. Zieliński was the eldest seamstress and the longest employee, according to D.I. Hobart, it was the dark-haired woman, Miss Keane, who took charge. "We've already spoken to the police. I don't want the girls reliving that morning for no good reason. It was a traumatic experience."

"Our questions aren't about what you saw or heard that morning, or where you were or who had a key. We want to know more about Madame Poitiers."

She emerged from behind the dress form where she'd been pinning a skirt and thrust a hand on her hip. She looked me up and down, then turned her attention to Harry. She met his direct gaze without flinching, blushing or dipping her head. In my experience, that took some nerve.

He extended his hand. "Harry Armitage. A pleasure to meet you, Miss Keane."

She looked at his hand with appreciation then shook it. "What do you want to know, Mr. Armitage?"

Harry indicated I should ask the questions. I wasn't sure that was wise since he already had Miss Keane's attention.

Nevertheless, I asked the first question we'd agreed upon on the way to the salon. "Did you know Madame Poitiers wasn't really French?"

Some of the younger women looked surprised and exchanged glances. The older women and Miss Keane didn't. "I assumed she wasn't," Miss Keane admitted. "But we never discussed it among us. It didn't matter. Most English designers pretend they're French or studied in France. It's something they have to do to impress the clients."

"Did she talk about Paris or any particular designer she may have studied under?" I addressed my question to Miss Keane, but watched Mrs. Zieliński out of the corner of my eye.

The older seamstress sat passively at one of the sewing machine tables, unconcerned.

"She spoke about designers all the time," Miss Keane said with a slight sneer. "She was always seeing them at parties, shows, dinners and balls in Paris. She claims she was invited everywhere."

"You sound as though you don't believe her."

She lifted a shoulder. "Her stories were sometimes outlandish. Once you suspect she's lying about being French you find it hard to believe anything she says. I think some of her stories were true and some not."

"We'll never know now," said one of the young women on a sigh. She looked close to tears.

"I reckon it was all lies," said another, much harsher. She was older, perhaps in her late thirties. "You can't trust a thing that woman said."

The younger women stared wide-eyed at her. They looked around, nervous. But no one admonished the speaker for her disparaging comments.

"Do you know where Madame Poitiers learned her craft?" I asked.

They all shrugged or shook their heads.

"Mrs. Zieliński? You've known her the longest. You've been with her since the shop first opened. What do you know of her background?"

The older woman rolled her shoulders back, as if they were stiff. She was quite stooped. No wonder, if she'd spent a lifetime bending over her sewing. She couldn't even rest against a chair back. They'd only been provided with stools. "I knew she was not French. When we first met, she was Miss Russell; she soon married and became Mrs. Lindsey. She did not have an accent then." She spoke with a thick accent herself.

"Tell me how you two met."

"My husband and I came to England from Poland." She counted in her head. "Twenty-four years ago. I found work as a seamstress here and there. Sometimes I did piece work at home, sometimes I sew for shops. When I see Mrs. Lindsey's advertisement, I applied. After a trial, she employed me. That was not here. Her shop was in Earl's Court then. After she opened it, she became Madame Poitiers to the public."

"Surely you two talked. Did she tell you anything about her past?"

"Only what she tells everyone else all these years. She used to be a singer. Opera. But she had a bad throat and needed an operation, but it stopped her singing career. She was sad when she spoke about it. But the sadness became less as the years pass until she could speak about it without tears in her eyes."

"Do you remember the names of other staff from those early days?"

"There were no others in the beginning. Just the two of us for many months. We worked hard, but it was good work."

"She sewed herself?"

"Yes. Designed and sewed."

Miss Keane exchanged skeptical glances with two of the other women.

"Sometimes she sent embroidery out," Mrs. Zieliński went on. "But all of the sewing was done by us. We worked long hours to fulfill orders. Very long."

"Still do," muttered one of the seamstresses.

Mrs. Zieliński's eyes flashed. "You do not know what hard work is. We worked until our fingers bled and we could no longer see the needle because our eyes water from lack of light. Sometimes we worked through the night, sleeping an hour or two at our tables."

"Why did you do it?" I asked. "Why did you work so hard for a woman you'd just met?"

"I needed the money. Maybe I would not have worked so hard if she was not working hard too. But she did."

"Well, it was *her* business," one of the girls muttered.

Again, Miss Keane exchanged glances with some of the other women.

"So in all the time you two worked together, alone, you didn't find out where she learned to design ballgowns?"

Mrs. Zieliński shook her head. "She talked much, but not about that. She talked about her singing, the famous people she met, actresses and opera stars. You must have noticed, Miss Fox. She was the same then. She always had stories of a wonderful life, but I could not say if they were true or not."

"Did you get along?"

"We did. She was kind to me although she was not interested in Poland or my past. But she was good. Even before she had paying customers, she paid me on time. In those early years, it was a struggle, I think. There was some customers, but not many, and not the sort she has now. They were not rich ladies. But they were not poor either."

"Did she continue to pay your wages on time?" I asked the question to all the women.

They nodded, but I got the feeling they held something back. At least, some of them did.

"Did she pay well?" Harry asked.

"As good as anywhere else," Miss Keane said.

One of the older women snickered. "You mean as bad as anywhere else."

That produced a round of nods, but not from Mrs. Zieliński.

"Did she still do any of the sewing?" I asked.

Miss Keane snorted. "Lord, no. She only ever came in here to tell us to work harder, stop dawdling or chatting. She never picked up a needle and thread or sat at a machine."

"When did you talk about the designs with her?"

Mrs. Zieliński answered. "She brings me her new styles late in the year. We discuss where to change it, if it needed to be changed, then I would make patterns for the girls to use. It is a long process so we start the year before the social season."

Miss Keane leaned back against one of the workbenches, her arms crossed. She studied Mrs. Zieliński with a frown.

"It is our busiest time now," Mrs. Zieliński went on. "There are many gowns to create and small adjustments to make so no two debutantes are dressed the same. We only sew here. Our work is specialized, difficult work. I only hire experienced girls. After the gown is made to fit the client, we send it off to piece workers who add applique, embroidery, ribbons or other embellishments. That work is easy. In here, we do the complicated tasks."

All the girls lifted their chins or puffed out their chests a little. They were proud of their skill. They knew not every seamstress was good enough to work for a popular designer like Madame Poitiers.

"Did you like her?" Harry suddenly asked.

They all stared at him, unsure how to answer. Only Miss Keane had the courage to admit she didn't. "She was a snob. She acted like she was born a lady but she was no better than us. She worked as a seamstress all them years ago when she first got started."

"She was a designer," Mrs. Zieliński said sternly. "Yes, she did sew too, at the beginning, but she had a good eye for design and knew what high class ladies wanted. That is what made her better than us. That is what made her gowns popular and you should not forget that. She was hard on us, it is true, but she was fair. She just wanted to see women wearing beautiful clothes. She succeeded when so many failed."

The other seamstresses shifted uncomfortably, chastised. But not Miss Keane.

"Madame wouldn't be anywhere without us, yet she hardly deigned to speak to us. If she wanted to communicate something, she went through Mrs. Zieliński. She made us work long hours and the pay is low. Shop girls earn more. A little appreciation would be nice."

"We are not shop girls," Mrs. Zieliński pointed out. "We are seamstresses. We earn the same as others in our profession."

Miss Keane lowered her head and rested her hands on the bench behind her. "I don't want to speak ill of the dead, but there's no point in pretending we liked her. We didn't. None of us did." She looked to Mrs. Zieliński who simply turned away.

Not liking their employer wasn't enough motive to kill her. But had dislike led to hate? Had one of them argued with her? According to D.I. Hobart, Mrs. Zieliński was the only one of the seven seamstresses with a key. Her key unlocked the back door that led to the lane behind the premises. But he'd also told us that the key had gone missing recently, turning up in a place Mrs. Zieliński was certain she'd already looked. Any one of the other women could have taken it, had a duplicate made, then returned it without being seen.

Harry must have been thinking along the same path as me. He opened the back door and disappeared into the lane.

The door to the salon suddenly burst open, making all the women jump. All except Miss Keane and me. The young girls visibly relaxed when Miss Newland entered and apologized for the interruption.

"I'm available now if you want to question me." She looked around the workroom, frowning. When Harry returned, she smiled. "There you are, Mr. Armitage. Would you and Miss Fox like to follow me? We can talk in the salon."

I didn't have the heart to tell her we didn't come to speak to her. Besides, interviewing her couldn't hurt.

Harry and I followed her out of the workroom.

Miss Newland sat on one of the sofas and Harry remained standing, waiting for me to take a seat.

"Do you mind if I look around the salon while you two talk?" I didn't give Miss Newland a chance to reply. I simply smiled my thanks and rounded the counter. "Don't mind me."

Harry seated himself on the sofa. "What do you know about Gertrude Lindsey's past?"

"Ah. So you know she wasn't Madame Poitiers," Miss Newland said.

"Did you?"

"I found out when her husband came here yesterday and introduced himself. I only came to see that we were ready to open this morning. I wasn't expecting him."

As they talked, I read the framed article from *The Queen* magazine about Myrtle Langford wearing a Poitiers gown. Dated 1883, it was written a few years after Gertrude opened the first shop in Earl's Court and before it moved to New Bond Street. The actress gushed about the dress, saying it made her feel sophisticated, beautiful, and desirable.

I rifled through drawers, scanned ledgers and appointment books, and searched for anything that might be relevant. Lady Bunbury's only early appointment was scheduled for the day of Gertrude's death. Her other appointments were all during regular shop hours. I couldn't find any accounts, but there were bills ready to be issued. It would seem Gertrude asked for payments to be sent directly to her accountant. There was no way for me to know if the shop was struggling financially.

According to her husband, Gertrude didn't do her own accounts because her eyesight was poor and she'd find it tiring after being in the salon all day. I returned to the drawers. The top one contained a magnifying glass. Harry's business card had been under it on the day of her murder. I found another two magnifying glasses on shelves under the counter.

I tuned out of Harry's conversation with Miss Newland. She wasn't telling him anything we didn't already know. I thought back to our appointment. Miss Newland had taken our measurements and written them down. Looking through the book now, I could see everything was written in the same neat hand. Gertrude had also squinted at the embroidery on one of the dresses. In fact, she'd squinted a lot. I searched behind the counter again, but found nothing written in a different hand.

I picked up the leather-bound catalog filled with the watercolors of Madame Poitiers' designs and rejoined Harry and Miss Newland. He finished up his questions and looked at me, brows arched, asking if I had anything to add.

I did. "Miss Newland, in your opinion, did Madame Poitiers design the gowns?"

Miss Newland's breath hitched. "What are you suggesting?"

"Her eyesight was so poor that she couldn't write down measurements or keep her own accounts, let alone do fine needlework or sketch designs." I opened the catalog. "Did she do these?"

"Of course."

"Did you see her do them?"

"No, but she worked on her designs after hours."

"Who told you that?"

"She did. Miss Fox, I can see you don't know much about fashion design." She took the book and pointed at the open page with the images of flowing gowns on pretty models. "An artist doesn't need to be able to see perfectly to design an outfit. It's all broad strokes and implied detail, not actual detail. With the aid of a magnifying glass, she did these in her spare time. She then took them to Mrs. Zieliński to make the patterns and the girls worked from those. It's true Madame would have needed good eyes to sew or embroider, but she didn't do those tasks. Others did. She was the one with the ideas and the creative flair. She knew what ladies liked and how they wanted to feel attending a ball or party." She tapped at the page. "Madame designed these. I'm sure of it."

I returned the catalog to the counter. We thanked her for her time and left as her next appointment arrived. Miss Newland welcomed the newcomers with a sad smile and accepted their condolences gracefully. She spoke with confidence. There was none of the temerity I'd seen in evidence during our dress fitting.

Harry and I walked off. I was about to ask him for his

thoughts when he stopped. "I want to go back to the work-shop via the lane entrance."

"You don't want Miss Newland to see us?" I suspected I knew why but waited for him to confirm.

"The seamstresses were holding something back earlier. I think they think as you do—that Gertrude didn't design anything. Someone else did. They just didn't want to say. They didn't want to get anyone into trouble."

"Because if that person was jealous of Gertrude receiving all the attention as the designer, it's a motive to kill her."

Our gazes connected and I knew he thought the same as me—that Mrs. Zieliński must be the real designer. If it was any of the seamstresses, it must be her. She was the longest employee. She had also been desperate for work when she first arrived in England all those years ago. It would have been easy for a manipulative person to take advantage of that desperation.

Harry's eyes were bright with the enthusiasm of our breakthrough. I suspected mine were the same. He led the way towards the lane entrance. "Good work in there, Cleo."

"The theory may be wrong. Miss Newland is adamant that Gertrude designed everything."

"But you don't believe it and nor do I. Not if her eyesight was so poor."

"It's not just that. I found no notes, no half-finished sketches, no scraps of ideas lying about."

"And no one but Mrs. Zieliński sees her to discuss the designs. Convenient."

We entered a small courtyard at the back of the workshop. It was mostly empty except for some boxes and a broken stool.

"You ask the questions," I whispered to Harry as he pushed open the door.

The seamstresses stopped what they were doing and turned to us. Some of them exchanged glances. Miss Keane stood. Mrs. Zieliński bent to work again, feeding fabric through her sewing machine. I remained by the door and watched Harry go to work.

He apologized for intruding and said we'd thought of one more question to ask. He nodded at the door that led to the shop on the other side of the room. "We've just learned that Mrs. Lindsey had poor eyesight. She never took the measurements or other notes, and there are numerous magnifying glasses lying about. So how could she design ballgowns and beautiful dresses?"

Mrs. Zieliński stopped her sewing machine. The workshop fell silent. Some of the seamstresses blinked back at us, mouths ajar. His accusation had stunned them. But not all of them.

Miss Keane studied the floor. I'd expected her to be the first to say something, but she was clearly not interested in confirming or denying our theory. She didn't even dare look at anyone.

"You've known her the longest, Mrs. Zieliński," Harry said gently. "Do you think she designed the Poitiers' clothes? Or did someone else? Someone with great skill and excellent taste."

Nice touch, Harry.

"It's true that her eyes got worse," Mrs. Zieliński said. "But it did not stop her. She used a glass, as you see out there." She made a circle with her thumb and forefinger and put it up to her eye. "So no, I do not believe what you say. Madame designed everything herself."

"Then why are there no half-done sketches or notes?"

She shrugged. "The current designs were done months ago. She has tidied up since then."

"So you don't think another person was the real designer?" he pressed.

"No."

"Not her long-term employee, for example?"

One of the younger girls gasped.

"No!" Mrs. Zieliński cried. "I am just a seamstress. I could never do what Madame did."

"You're an excellent seamstress." Harry couldn't possibly know that. "You've been with her since the beginning. No one ever saw Gertrude making sketches or notes. No one ever saw her bring them to you in the mornings before the others arrived. We only have your word for it."

"It is true that no one saw her, but I did not design anything. I do not have the eye for it, or the...the..." She clicked her tongue in frustration as she searched for the right word. "I cannot say what it is that made her a great designer. She had it in here." She tapped her chest. "It is a sense, like smelling, hearing...but it is not like that too." She spoke quickly, her accent thickening. She was flustered.

"I think Mrs. Zieliński means she isn't creative enough," Miss Keane said.

"Yes! Creative. I am not creative. Madame, she knew fabric. How it sits when the girl is still, how it floats when she dances, how to pair it with other fabric. She knew color too. What suits a girl's skin, what color goes with another, when to add more color or take it away. But most, she knew how to make clothes flatter. How to draw the eye to a girl's best feature, or away from her worst. I could not do that." Mrs. Zieliński withdrew a handkerchief tucked into her sleeve and dabbed her nose with it. "I could not do what she did," she added in a murmur.

Miss Keane put her arm around the older woman's shoulders. "None of us could. Madame was as unique as her designs. That's what made her so successful."

Harry and I left. As soon as we were out of earshot, he said, "Convinced?"

"Not entirely. You?"

"I'm not sure. I wonder if Mrs. Zieliński's last comment was telling."

"'I could not do what she did,'" I echoed.

"Perhaps she was referring to being the face of the business rather than the actual designing."

"You think they had a mutual agreement? Mrs. Zieliński designed the clothes, but Gertrude sold them?" I'd been assuming Gertrude took advantage of Mrs. Zieliński as a newly arrived immigrant, but perhaps Mrs. Zieliński never wanted to be acknowledged as the designer.

"Gertrude was a vibrant person," he said. "She had charm and wit."

"Of sorts," I cut in. "She was somewhat irritating."

"She had the gift of the gab, like most good salespeople. She could talk easily with customers. Mrs. Zieliński was shy and preferred to stay in the workshop and not speak to clients. The arrangement suited her. It suited them both and took advantage of their different strengths."

"But something went wrong recently," I said, following along. "The business arrangement turned sour. They argued and Mrs. Zieliński killed Gertrude."

"It's a good theory."

"It's an excellent theory."

He grinned. "We work well together."

"I know," I quipped. "But I'm glad you've finally realized it too."

We decided to call on his father at Scotland Yard. For one thing, we ought to update the detective leading the case. For another, we needed information to move forward with our theory.

We took an omnibus to the Victoria Embankment. The handsome red-brick building housing London's Metropolitan police headquarters was humming with activity. Although arrested offenders were taken through a different entrance to the holding cells, uniformed policemen sat at desks or stood chatting behind the front counter. The officers in plain clothes were sometimes indistinguishable from the members of the public waiting to be seen.

Harry and I joined them as a constable fetched D.I. Hobart. He soon returned and asked us to follow him.

D.I. Hobart shared an office with another detective who didn't even look up upon our entry. He bent over his paperwork, scribbling furiously, his tongue poking into the inside of his cheek as he concentrated on his task. His desk was untidy whereas D.I. Hobart's was orderly.

I started the discussion by repeating what I'd learned about Lady Bunbury at afternoon tea. He'd been noncommittal when I first mentioned it and I wanted his opinion. "She seems to be in some financial difficulty," I finished. "But we'd need to gather more information to know for certain."

"Agreed," he said. "I'll see what I can find out."

"As will I."

"Leave the Bunburys to me, Miss Fox. Is there anything else?"

Harry told him about our morning and what we'd learned, as well as our theory about Gertrude not designing the clothes. As he spoke, his father leaned forward, listening intently. The theory interested D.I. Hobart more than Lady Bunbury's brooch.

"I'll find out more about Mrs. Zieliński from the accountant," D.I. Hobart said as he wrote in his notebook. "Whether she was getting paid more than the others, or was receiving a share of the profits. If they had an arrangement, he'll know."

"We also want to see where Mrs. Zieliński lives," Harry said. "To get a feel for her life and financial situation."

His father flipped through the file and wrote down Mrs. Zieliński's address on a piece of paper. He handed it over but did not immediately let go. "If no one is home, you must leave. No breaking and entering, Harry. Understood?"

Harry gave his father one of his charming smiles. "I'd never do anything illegal."

His father scowled, but let go. Harry read the address then passed the paper to me.

"I suggest you don't take Miss Fox with you."

Harry huffed. "You don't know her very well if you think I have any sway over what Cleo does and doesn't do."

His father clasped his hands on the desk and addressed me with a very serious air. "You're a newcomer to London, Miss Fox, so you won't be aware of all the different characteristics of its areas. But Whitechapel is not a place a well brought up young lady should frequent."

"I remember the Ripper murders," I said.

News of the gruesome crimes had reached Cambridge and, although I'd been young at the time, it had made an impression on me. Whitechapel had been etched in my mind ever since. I pictured crumbling buildings packed close together on dirty streets, drunkards sleeping in recessed doorways, shoeless children and scrawny dogs scavenging for scraps. And crime.

"I'll be fine. It's the middle of the day and I have a manly escort. Also, I'm not dressed conspicuously."

They both studied me critically. The inspector huffed. "That outfit is conspicuous by Whitechapel standards. Can I say anything to change your mind?"

"No."

"I'll take care of her," Harry assured his father.

Ordinarily I'd roll my eyes at such masculine chest beating, but a wise person took note of local knowledge. Besides, I knew neither Harry nor his father were prone to exaggeration. The looks on their faces were quite serious.

I removed my leather gloves in the hansom and the small pin holding the edges of my collar together. My hat was understated by modern standards, but was probably still too nice for Whitechapel. Even so, a woman never went hatless out of doors. I'd be even more conspicuous if I removed it. With no alternative, I left it on.

Harry slid the panel in the roof aside and asked the driver to let us out on Whitechapel Road. After we alighted, Harry led the way through streets that were not too different from what I imagined. The rows of houses were indeed small, crumbling, and squashed together on streets where the gutters were filled with stinking mud. Paint on the doors had long since faded or peeled off. Windows were covered in a sooty film, making it impossible to see through. The rooms inside must be dark all the time.

There were no drunkards lolling in recessed doorways, however, no beggars holding out their caps, or prostitutes soliciting us. There were some children playing in the street, their faces dirty, their toes poking through shoes too small for them. But they didn't look as though they were starving or miserable.

After ten minutes, I realized we were going in a rather circuitous route to reach our destination. Harry was keeping to the better streets.

"Is this the most direct way?" I asked.

"I'm avoiding the markets. Too many pickpockets."

"You're familiar with Whitechapel, aren't you?"

After a beat, he said, "It's one of my old haunts." He'd briefly lived on the streets before being arrested when he was thirteen. Whitechapel would have been a hard place for a child. He would have been one of the shoeless children scavenging for food, picking pockets in the crowded market and stealing food off a distracted stall holder's cart. If he hadn't been arrested then adopted by the Hobarts, he could very well still be living here, trying to eke out a living as a laborer, drowning his misery in cheap beer.

If he thought about what his life might have been like, it didn't show on his face. He was focused on the task at hand.

We turned a corner onto a street lined with shops on one side and tenement buildings on the other. Unlike Whitechapel Road, the street was narrow but two carriages could still fit down it side-by-side as long as neither was too large. The shops and tenements were only two stories high, their condition as deplorable as the others we'd passed. Some shopkeepers had made attempts to clean their windows, but most had only managed to smear the sooty film rather than remove it.

There were more people here. Women strolled in and out of shops, baskets over their arm, small children clinging to their skirts or balancing on their hip. They stared at me and I tried not to stare back, but temptation got the better of me on occasion. The women were of different ages, but all looked worn out, their faces with only marginally more color than the corpse of Gertrude Lindsey. Their eyes were dull and bleary, their dresses ragged, yet there was a defiant set to their jaws. I overheard some haggling inside the shops. They were loud, determined, and desperate to drag the price down as far as the shopkeeper could go.

Most of the meat in the butcher's shop window had a grey-green tinge. There was very little of it, and most of what was there was fatty or the parts that were only good for adding flavor to broth.

A woman emerged from the greengrocer and bumped into me. "Watch it," she snapped.

I apologized. After thoroughly scrutinizing me, she spat on the pavement near my feet. I was not welcome here. I was not one of them.

Harry took my arm and dragged me away, stopping outside a shop that seemed to sell anything and everything. Dented pots and pans, odd spoons and forks, balls of yarn that looked as though they'd been pulled out of the gutter. Broken pieces of mirrors had been positioned together on a table to show the shopper that one complete mirror could be made from them, almost. There were odd buttons, chipped teacups, and mismatched gloves. An apron that had probably once been white but was now yellow had been placed on a dress form with red glass beads draped around the neck. A mob cap had been slapped on top of the neck stump, completing the bizarre combination.

Mrs. Zieliński lived directly opposite. According to her downstairs neighbor, no one was home in the upstairs rooms rented by the Zielińskis.

"Who else lives there?" Harry asked.

The neighbor placed a hand on her hip and looked him up and down. "Why should I tell you?"

Harry passed her some coins. She squirreled them away into the pocket of her apron, glancing past us to make sure no one saw. "Mrs. Zieliński and her son."

"Can we have a look around?"

She straightened. "No! This ain't a freak show. The Zielińskis are good people, and folk like you should leave 'em be."

Harry seemed unfazed by her rant. I wondered if he planned to enter when her back was turned.

He removed his hat and placed it against his chest, reverent. "I apologize. It's just that I used to live around here, many years ago, and remember these shops, these houses. Mrs. Zieliński was kind to me once."

The woman's spirits lifted, and she appraised Harry anew. "Well, well. Ain't you come up in the world since then? Good for you. What's your name again?"

"Harry. Tell me, I recall the Zielińskis had a large place up there. But I may have seen it through a boy's eyes and could be misremembering."

"They've got two rooms. They're small, just enough for a bed in each and a desk or table. But this building's solid, not like some others. The roof don't leak, except when it's coming down real heavy. We're lucky to live here."

"Do you know what time Mrs. Zieliński left for work on Friday morning?"

Her gaze narrowed, once again skeptical and cautious. "I don't spy on my neighbors."

He thanked her for her time. She folded her arms and remained on the doorstep until we walked off.

We questioned the shopkeepers opposite, starting with the greengrocer standing in the doorway of his shop, leaning against the doorframe. Behind him, wilting vegetables and shriveling fruit in boxes looked as appetizing as a muddy puddle. Sprouted potatoes had rolled onto the floor from a sack. Some looked as though they'd been nibbled by creatures with small sharp teeth.

Harry jangled the coins in his pocket, catching the bored greengrocer's attention. "Do you know Mrs. Zieliński? The Polish woman who lives there." He indicated the first floor window of the tenement.

"Aye."

"What's she like?"

"Quiet, causes no trouble. Hard working woman." He nodded at the window. No curtain hung across it. We could see right inside, but because of the angle, only the ceiling was visible and the top of a wardrobe. "I start early and I see her there, bent over her sewing most mornings. She'll often work for an hour or two before heading out to that fancy dressmaker's."

"Isn't it dark?" I asked.

"She works by lamplight. Don't know how she does it at her age." The little hair he had was thin and gray, and his skin sported all the signs of middle-age. He couldn't be much younger than Mrs. Zieliński, although a hard life may have aged him prematurely.

"Do you know her employer was murdered?" Harry asked.

The grocer nodded without emotion. He didn't care about the death of someone he didn't know. Violent death probably happened in Whitechapel more frequently than anywhere, even after the Ripper stopped.

"Did you see her working at home last Friday morning?"

The grocer arched his brows, suddenly interested. "You reckon she did it?"

Harry handed over some money. "Just answer the question."

The grocer rubbed the back of his neck as he looked up at Mrs. Zieliński's window. "She was there, same as always, sewing before she left for work."

"What time was that?"

"About seven-fifteen. That's when I get in."

"She must have left soon after that to catch an omnibus," Harry said. "If she walked, she wouldn't get to work by eight."

"Did you see her leave?" I asked the grocer.

"No. I've got work to do. Can't stand around here spying on the neighbors, can I?"

We thanked him and moved on to the other shopkeepers along the street, asking the same questions. The butcher also claimed he saw Mrs. Zieliński working early on Friday morning. None of the others noticed a thing.

"The body was cool, not cold," I pointed out. "The murder must have happened shortly before I arrived."

"The coroner puts the time of death between seven-thirty and eight-fifteen, based on the time Gertrude left home that morning and the state of the body when you found it. If Mrs. Zieliński was still here at seven-fifteen, she'd only just make it to work by eight which is when the other seamstresses were arriving too. It's not enough time to commit murder."

I looked up at Mrs. Zieliński's window. "It's a wonder she can afford to take an omnibus every day. They may not cost a lot, but it adds up." Mrs. Zieliński lived amid desperate poverty. Her rooms might be one of the better ones, according to her neighbor, but they were located in the worst area of London. She lived very differently to her employer in the large flat located in one of the better streets.

We walked in silence until we reached Whitechapel Road, both of us lost in thought. "So what now?" I asked as we climbed into a hansom cab.

"Now we return to the hotel to see if we can find the stranger who called on Gertrude."

I agreed it was the best course of action. It was too much of a coincidence that shortly after the man showed up, Gertrude was murdered. I didn't believe in coincidences.

CHAPTER 9

$\mathcal{W}$e still didn't know the stranger's name. The check-in clerk at the Duke Hotel refused to give it to Harry when he'd confronted him about the card yesterday. He refused again today, so Harry told me when he rejoined me outside.

I'd remained out of sight in case we needed to enact our second plan. If Harry couldn't get the stranger's room number from the clerk, it was my turn to swing into action. But entering too soon would look suspicious, so we stood outside and watched the hotel's entrance to pass time.

Harry yawned. A few minutes later, he yawned again.

"Go home and rest," I said. "I can do the next part alone."

He crossed his arms. The stern look he gave me was at odds with his casual pose, leaning against the lamp post. "I'm staying."

"Very well. Let's talk to keep you alert. I'll begin. How did you survive on the streets of Whitechapel all those years ago?"

He adjusted his crossed arms and turned away, presenting me with his profile. "You're nosey."

"Only about things that interest me."

A flicker of his lashes and a twitch of his cheek were the only indications my admission intrigued him. He continued to stare straight ahead.

"I like to know about my friends' lives," I added.

"You already know all there is to know. My mother died when I was eleven. I lived at the Dean Street orphanage for two years, then was employed at the factory as an apprentice bookkeeper. When that didn't work out, I left, lived on the streets and was arrested for theft by the man who later took me in. I went to work at the Mayfair Hotel. That's my story in a nutshell. There's nothing more to know."

"You've sketched the plot, but a story is more than its outline." I turned to look at the hotel entrance too. "I understand if you don't want to speak about it. But if you change your mind, I'll listen without judgement."

"You can't know that," he said softly.

I glanced sharply at him. His rigid profile was uncompromising. "I judge people on who they are now and how they treat people, not their past. It doesn't matter to me what you did to survive as a child." I gentled my voice, suspecting my next words would trouble him more. "I don't care who your father was either. Or whether you knew him."

His throat moved with his swallow, but he remained staring at the hotel entrance. If I'd angered him, he kept his temper under control. I suspected he was more shocked that I'd guessed the truth, or something close to it.

"You should go now," he said.

"It's too soon. You're just trying to get rid of me so I stop asking awkward questions."

"We can stand here in awkward silence instead."

"Or we can talk. You may ask me anything you like. I'll try to make my life sound as interesting as possible."

"Cleo…" He huffed out a breath. "It's best we don't get to know each other too much."

Right. Yes. Of course. He didn't plan on becoming friends. After this investigation was over, he'd once again attempt to put distance between us because he thought that was best for me and my relationship with my uncle.

His words stung, even though I knew the place they came from—concern for me. "Since you're tired, I'll forgive you for that."

I didn't wait for his response. I crossed the road and marched into the hotel as if I owned it.

Despite its lofty name, the Duke Hotel was little better

than the hovels in Whitechapel. The foyer was only big enough to fit a desk, behind which sat the clerk on a chair that looked too flimsy for his size. He wore no jacket and his waistcoat was unfastened. It wasn't large enough for the buttons to meet their buttonholes. His girth pushed it apart and spilled over the waistband of his trousers. His shirt collar was stained with sweat and the remnants of his last meal clung to his mustache.

He watched me from beneath protuberant eyelids. When I reached the desk, he hauled himself out of the chair. He wiped his mouth and mustache with the back of his hand. "Can I help you?"

"I'm looking for a friend of mine. He's a foreigner with a strong accent." I described the stranger as he'd been described to Harry by Mr. Lindsey. "I won't tell you his name because he would have checked in under an assumed one, and I don't know all the names he uses. He's hiding from a nasty fellow who's been looking for him, you see—tall, handsome and as wicked as they come." I shivered for good measure.

The clerk nodded knowingly. "He was just here."

"Can you tell me what room my friend is in?"

"He ain't there. He went out early."

"I didn't ask if he was in. I asked for his room number."

The clerk hesitated. "I can't do that, ma'am"

I bristled. With a toss of my head, I said, "Do I look dangerous to you? Or like a thief?"

The clerk eyed me up and down. He licked his lips.

This time I shivered involuntarily. "My friend told me he was staying here and to call on him at my convenience. It is *not* convenient for me to stand about down here and wait for him. I would like to wait in his room."

The clerk didn't look in the least bothered by my haughtiness. He merely shrugged and resumed his seat. The chair creaked under his weight.

"Look at this place." I ran my gloved finger along the counter. It came away dirty. "It's filthy. I wouldn't let a dog stay here. Perhaps I ought to notify the authorities. I have a cousin who works in the Department of Health and Sanitation." I had no idea if such a department existed, but it sounded official and

I suspected the clerk didn't know any better. "I'm sure he'd be interested in poking around back there." I indicated the door behind the clerk. "I'd wager he'd find evidence of rodents, not to mention unwashed sheets, blankets full of lice…"

The man snatched a set of keys from a hook inside a cupboard and slapped them on the counter. The tag on the keys said room number three-oh-four. I thanked him and headed up the stairs to the third floor.

Room three-oh-four was little larger than a storeroom. The narrow bed was pushed up against the wall. I had to kneel on it to open the window. Signaling to Harry below, I held up fingers so he would know which room to look for. A few minutes later, he entered.

"How did you get past the clerk?" I asked.

"His back was turned. How did *you* convince him to give you the spare key?"

"I hen-pecked him until he lost the will to resist."

Harry chuckled. I was more relieved than I cared to admit to see his good humor return. I was worried I'd overstepped earlier and driven a wedge between us with my questions.

I waved the travel documents I'd found among the man's belongings. "His name is Emmanuel Durant. He's French and is scheduled to leave the day after tomorrow on board a ferry to Calais."

Harry looked over the papers then placed them beside the dirty plate and cup on the small table. There was only one chair which he indicated I should sit on while we waited. He eyed the bed then decided to remain standing. I probably wasn't wrong when I accused the clerk of having blankets that harbored lice. The room was as filthy as the foyer.

I worried about awkward silences again, but we didn't have to wait more than a few minutes before the door opened. Emmanuel Durant must have been warned by the clerk that he had a visitor, but he had not been expecting two. He blurted out something in French.

"Don't be alarmed," Harry said. He introduced us as private detectives working for Mr. Lindsey, employed to learn more about Gertrude's past. He didn't mention our connection to the police or our involvement in investigating the murder. "I believe you would have known her as Gertrude Russell."

"She is dead," Mr. Durant said, without emotion.

"Sadly, yes. But our investigation is ongoing. Mr. Lindsey still wants to know more about his wife. She rarely spoke about her past and he is curious."

Mr. Durant glanced back through the doorway to the corridor. Considering his escape route? "She was ashamed."

"I think her husband wouldn't have cared what she did or what happened to her before they met," I said, not daring to look at Harry. "He would understand that sometimes a person doesn't always have the luxury of choice."

Mr. Durant again glanced through the open door.

"Why did you come to London?" Harry asked.

"I like to travel."

"Why did you seek out Gertrude after all these years?"

Mr. Durant rubbed the thumb on his right hand over his knuckles. He wore no gloves and his coat was threadbare with patches on the elbows. "We are old friends."

"Yet you didn't give your name to her husband or tell him where she could find you," Harry pointed out. "Why, when you say you were merely friends with Gertrude?"

Mr. Durant shrugged.

"Did you come to London specifically to speak to her?"

Mr. Durant's gaze darted to the door again. Then he ran.

Harry ran after him. With his long legs and athletic pace, he easily caught him. He hauled him back into the room, closed the door with a kick, and shoved Mr. Durant on the bed.

Harry looked unruffled whereas Mr. Durant breathed heavily. He was in his fifties, with the slender frame of a younger man, or one who ate irregular meals. I'd already guessed him to be poor based on my investigation of his meager belongings. This hotel was probably more than he could afford. Indeed, the entire journey would be a financial stretch. The decision to come to London wouldn't have been made lightly. He'd had a very good reason; something that involved Gertrude.

And now she was dead.

"Did you know where Gertrude lived before you arrived in London?" I asked.

He considered his answer carefully before shaking his head.

"Then how did you find her?"

His thumb furiously rubbed over his knuckles again. His gaze darted between us and the closed door. "I do not have to answer you."

"Why did you give my card to Gertrude?" Harry asked.

Again, Mr. Durant thought about his answer for several moments. "The clerk gave it to me when I returned to the hotel that day. He told me you came looking for me." He nodded at Harry. "Your card says you are an investigator. The only person who would hire you would be Mr. Lindsey, wanting to know who I am and what I want with his wife. So I told Gertrude so she would speak to her husband. She should know he is suspicious about her. She should know he is spying on her."

"When did you give her the card?" I asked.

There was another pause before answering. "Thursday, late." That was the night before she was killed.

Harry frowned. "So you saw her on Thursday as well as Tuesday when you returned to the Lindseys' flat a few hours after your first visit."

"Yes. On Tuesday she told me about her shop, so on Thursday, I met her there after it closes."

"What did you speak about when you saw her?" I asked.

Mr. Durant didn't hesitate this time. "I do not have to answer. You want to know about her past in France? I will tell you that. For Mr. Lindsey. He is her husband and deserves to know. She is gone now so there is no need to keep it secret."

A scandalous past could ruin Madame Poitiers' professional reputation, but I happened to agree that her husband should know. From what I'd seen of Mr. Lindsey, I didn't think he could learn anything that would change his opinion of his wife. He'd wanted a divorce. He'd stopped loving her and could not be hurt by any revelations.

"I met Gertrude Russell in Paris in '72. She joined our troupe when one of the singers left. I played the piano. We also had a violinist and dancers."

"Was she a good singer?" I asked.

"She could sing well enough with the others, but only if the audience is distracted by the dancers in their tight costumes." He arched his brows at Harry, as if sharing a joke with him.

Harry ignored him and exchanged a glance with me. It was the confirmation we needed that the story of Madame's talent had been just that—a story she concocted as part of the Madame Poitiers illusion.

"We were just an ordinary troupe playing at fairs. We took our traveling show all around France. They were good years. We all got along. It ended in 1875. Gertrude became ill, a cancer of the throat. She could no longer sing."

So that part was true. "Did she leave for England immediately?"

He nodded. "She came back for an operation. She said she would write when she was better, but she did not. We never heard from her again. None of us did. The troupe broke up soon after and I have not seen any of them since."

"So why have you come looking for her now?" Harry asked again.

Mr. Durant answered smoothly this time. "To see a friendly face in a foreign city. Perhaps she can show me the sights, yes? The Tower of London, the palace... Very interesting."

I didn't believe him. "How did you get her address if you'd not heard from her in twenty-five years?"

He wiped his palms down his thighs. "I did not kill her! We were friends."

"No one accused you."

Harry signaled to me that we should leave. We weren't going to get any more answers from Emmanuel Durant today.

"You should not trust her husband," Mr. Durant said as we opened the door.

"Why not?" Harry asked.

Mr. Durant scrubbed a hand over a jawline in need of a shave. "She told me something on Thursday night. Something that makes him a suspect."

Harry closed the door. "Go on."

"She said she was going to leave her husband. Now that her son was older, she wanted a divorce. She said she was going to leave him...and would cut him out of her will." He made a scissoring motion with his fingers.

"Thank you for the information," I said.

"You will tell the police this?" Mr. Durant asked. "About the will?"

"You can tell them yourself," Harry said. "They will want to speak to you."

Mr. Durant simply nodded. I wasn't convinced he'd take himself off to Scotland Yard.

I led the way downstairs, ignoring the clerk sprawled in the chair. Harry touched the brim of his hat as we passed.

"You!" He pointed a stubby finger at Harry. "How did you get in?"

"I walked. Don't get up."

The clerk struggled to rise, his face growing redder and redder with each heave. He gave up with a grunt as we exited.

"What do you think of Mr. Durant's revelation about the will?" Harry asked me.

"I think it's worth finding out who benefited financially from her death."

"We'll telephone my father." He trudged on, head bowed, his shoulders rounded. I was about to suggest he go home and rest when he said, "I think he was telling the truth about her leaving the troupe for throat cancer."

"But there's definitely a story behind why he came to look for her now."

"Agreed. He's not here to sightsee. So why did he come? How did he find her? And what did they talk about on Thursday night?" As he talked, Harry straightened. He looked more alert. He found investigating invigorating.

He knew of a silence cabinet inside a large pharmacy where, for a few pennies, the public could make telephone calls from within an enclosed booth that blocked out the surrounding noise. I waited outside the booth and browsed the display of face creams as he telephoned Scotland Yard. After his allotted three minutes, Harry emerged looking thoughtful.

"Lindsey inherited the lot," he said as we headed outside. "The salon and everything in it goes to him."

"So if Durant was telling the truth, Gertrude never got around to changing her will."

"My father just returned from visiting Gertrude's accountant. Apparently Mrs. Zieliński received a similar hourly wage as the other seamstresses. In fact, she received a little less, as can happen for long-term employees who don't renegotiate their wages regularly. According to the accountant, every penny coming in and going out was accounted for. If Mrs. Zieliński was blackmailing Gertrude and demanding payment for her silence and continued cooperation, it was done off the books, but the accountant didn't think Gertrude was clever enough to hide it without his knowledge."

"So Mrs. Zieliński isn't the true creative mind behind Maison de Poitiers."

"Do you think someone else is the real designer?" Harry asked.

"Perhaps. But who?"

He blinked up at the mid-afternoon sky. We'd stopped on the pavement outside the pharmacy, unsure of our next destination. It was getting close to afternoon tea time at the hotel. I would be missed, even though I had no plans to meet my family.

Despite that, I would continue with our investigation if we had another lead. We did not. What I needed to do was sit and think, perhaps write down what we knew about Gertrude's past, both recent and long-gone. I would have suggested we return to Harry's office to mull it over together, but he was tiring again. With almost no sleep the night before, he was exhausted. Being a man, he wouldn't admit it.

"I think we should call it a day," I said. "We'll reconvene at your office tomorrow morning."

He stifled a yawn, nodding.

"Let me walk you home," I said.

He smirked. "Worried about safety?"

"Worried about you falling asleep on the omnibus and missing your stop."

"I can walk from here."

"Then you definitely need an escort. I can't have you falling down manholes or wandering into traffic."

He walked on without ordering me not to follow, which I took as a signal that he accepted my offer of an escort. "Is this your attempt to find out where I live?"

"You think I can't find out where you live unless you tell me?" I barked a laugh. "I am an investigator, Harry."

"And a very good one. So how would you go about finding me in this great city of ours without my knowledge?"

"I'd follow you from your office."

"I'd spot you immediately."

"You would not! I'd blend into the crowd. London is very busy." I indicated the steady stream of pedestrians passing us, and the vehicles clogging the street, driving slowly because there was too much traffic to go faster.

"You could never blend in, Cleo," he muttered.

We walked on side by side, with me trying to decide if his comment was a compliment or not.

"How did Durant know where Gertrude lived?" he asked, proving his thoughts had already moved on. "He didn't follow her. He had no idea where to start."

It was a question neither of us could answer.

When he worked at the Mayfair Hotel, Harry had lived in a room off the senior staff corridor. The steward and the housekeeper also lived on the premises. Mr. Hobart lived with his wife, a train ride away, and the temporary chef lived elsewhere too. When he was dismissed from the hotel, Harry had to find new accommodation as well as new employment. He moved back in with his parents briefly, but being a man in his late twenties, he didn't want to stay there permanently. I'd never learned where he moved to.

Until now.

If I'd put my mind to it, I would have realized he lived near his Soho office. It was convenient and he always seemed to be in early and stay late. If he had a long journey, he would be in the office less.

Soho was a vibrant, eclectic area, filled with theaters and eateries that stayed open well into the night. Even in cooler weather, the streets hummed with activity every evening. It wasn't just the wealthy of nearby Mayfair who frequented the

West End shows, but people from all walks of life enjoyed the productions and came for a night out. There was an energy in this part of London that I'd not experienced elsewhere.

Harry lived in one of the quieter streets in a flat above a row of shops and behind a theater. The handsome brick building with white window frames was accessed through a black door positioned between a confectioner and a tobacconist. Aside from the shopkeepers, both premises were empty. A sign on the large door opposite read STAFF and must lead to the backstage area of the theater. Two musicians carrying violin cases approached it. They nodded at Harry in recognition before entering.

"This is as far as you go," Harry said to me.

"Of course." I gave him a cynical smile. "I wouldn't want to risk my reputation by being seen entering a block of flats with a man. There are far too many witnesses." The closest pedestrians were some distance away and took no notice of us.

"It's not a joke, Cleo."

I bade him good day and walked off, heading home. Frank greeted me at the hotel's front door with a dour expression and a complaint. To the guests and other members of my family, the doorman was polite and friendly. To the staff and me, he found something to grumble about. It might be a rude guest who'd ignored him, or a passing child who'd stuck his tongue out. Or it could be something as mundane as the weather. Today, as it had been every day this week, it was the builders next door.

"I've told them time and again to quieten down." He shook his head at the builder wheeling an empty barrow inside after dumping the rubble into the waiting cart. "But they still shout. And the banging! It goes on and on."

"They have to remove the walls between the shops that used to be there, Frank. They need to open up the space. If it's any comfort, I think the walls are almost all down now, so it won't be like this much longer."

"And then what?"

I gave him a blank look.

"And then it'll be hammering, that's what."

Two guests emerged from the hotel and Frank smiled and

asked if they required a cab. I took the opportunity to slip inside before he was free again.

With four o'clock approaching, the foyer was filled with elegantly dressed ladies preparing to head into the sitting room to indulge in the Mayfair's famous afternoon tea. Indulge wasn't quite the right word. Keeping a strict eye on their waistlines meant there was always plenty of food left-over for the staff to enjoy later. It was one of the advantages of working at a luxury hotel.

I stopped at the post desk, but Terry had no messages or telegrams for me. The Parisian designers hadn't responded to my requests for information yet. I'd only sent them this morning, so it wasn't surprising.

Mr. Hobart and Peter were both mingling with guests milling in the foyer, waiting for the sitting room doors to open. I looked around for my cousin and aunt, but they weren't there. I was pleased Aunt Lilian didn't have company today. She needed to rest. Another afternoon tea would require her to take a dose of tonic and the less she took of it, the better, in my opinion. Her doctor's opinion differed, but he never saw her after the effects of the tonic wore off. Her family were the ones who suffered when she did.

Miss Hessing broke away from a group of women that contained her mother and two others, all speaking with American accents. "Miss Fox! Miss Fox, a moment of your time if you can spare it."

"Your magazine! I am sorry for not returning it earlier. I'll fetch it now."

"Oh that. Keep it. I can buy another." She eyed her mother then turned away from her to speak to me. "Do you see those ladies with my mother?"

"Yes. Are they guests here?"

She shook her head. "They're staying elsewhere but are joining us for afternoon tea."

"I do hope they enjoy it. Are they friends of yours from home?"

"No. We met them only yesterday. They're sisters. One of them has a son." She pulled a face. "He's horrid. So full of himself. He couldn't stop talking about his family business, his hobbies, his life in Chicago. He didn't show any interest in me. I know I'm not the most exciting companion, but he didn't even try to get to know me."

"I loathe men like that."

"I think my mother is courting his mother in the hopes of forming a union between the son and me."

"I thought you were here to find an English...husband?" I'd almost said "lord," but that would be much too familiar. I liked Miss Hessing but we were not friends yet.

She sighed deeply. "This is my third year here. I don't think Englishmen are interested in me."

"Englishmen are reserved compared to Americans. Give them an opportunity to get to know you."

She pouted. "That's precisely what Mother says we *shouldn't* do. She says I ought to keep my mouth shut so they don't discover how dull I am."

What sort of mother said that to her daughter? I might not be friends with Miss Hessing, but she desperately needed some sane advice. Because I was neither a friend nor a complete stranger, I felt I could say things to her I wouldn't usually say to others. "Perhaps your mother is the reason the Englishmen are staying away. Men in general do not want a cloying mother-in-law, and the English in particular are put off by brashness."

She nibbled on her lower lip, considering my words carefully.

Relieved that she wasn't offended, I pushed on. "Would it be so awful if you did marry an American? Not that woman's son, but another?"

"My mother lives in America and plans on staying there."

I pressed my lips together to smother my smile.

"She won't move here permanently. She already told me that. It's why I agree to come every year. Indeed, I'm the one who encourages the journey." She sighed. "But I don't think she'd agree to another year if I fail to secure a husband this time. She complains about the voyage, the weather, the food, the shops...everything!"

I lowered my voice so that she had to tilt her head down to hear me. "Then you ought to make it known to the gentlemen that she will live in America. And if you do find a fellow you like, try to speak to him out of earshot of your mother. I'm sure she means well, but you will have a better chance of charming him on your own."

"Charm?" she scoffed. "I'll be doing well if I don't trip over my own enormous feet on the dance floor. Or if *he* doesn't trip over them."

I laughed. "If you let him see that sense of humor, you will be just fine."

Floyd and Jonathon entered the hotel and spotted me. Floyd nodded a greeting while Jonathon approached. My cousin reluctantly followed and greeted Miss Hessing.

Jonathon gave her a cursory glance before turning his attention to me. Miss Hessing continued to smile, but it wilted a little. Floyd scowled at his friend for his rudeness, but Jonathon didn't notice.

"How has your day been, Miss Fox?" Jonathon asked.

"Pleasant, thank you. I've just come in. Miss Hessing and I were passing the time until she goes in for afternoon tea with her mother. They've come all the way from America to sample some of our English hospitality." By mentioning she was American, I hoped Jonathon would show a little more interest.

He did not.

Mr. Chapman opened the double doors to the sitting room and the waiting ladies moved towards him as if on a tide. Mrs. Hessing signaled to her daughter to join her. I was reminded of a dog owner calling her pet to heel.

Floyd offered Miss Hessing his arm. "May I escort you in?"

She blinked rapidly. "Oh! Yes. Thank you, Mr. Bainbridge." She took his arm and smiled shyly. She bade Jonathon and me good day.

"Your cousin is a boot-licker," Jonathon said with a shake of his head as they walked towards the sitting room.

I glared at him. "Floyd has a kind heart."

Jonathon wasn't as insensitive as I thought. He detected the note of irritation in my voice and realized he'd miss-stepped. "You're right. He's a good man, and I was impolite to your friend just now. My only defense is that I was distracted."

I was about to ask what had distracted him when I realized he was attempting to flatter me. Yet another miss-step on his behalf.

Not that he knew it, going by the hopeful smile he gave me.

"If you'll excuse me, I have friends to meet." I headed to the service area behind the lift, aware that Jonathon was watching me and probably wondering why I was going to the staff rooms to meet friends. I didn't care. His opinion didn't matter to me.

As I hoped, Harmony was in the staff parlor along with Victor and Goliath. She'd finished her housekeeping duties and wouldn't be required again until later when the ladies were getting ready for an evening out. Goliath was finished for the day and Victor hadn't yet started duty in the kitchen for the evening shift.

All three looked up from their teacups upon my entry, as did the other staff members seated there. Goliath got up and offered me his chair before dragging over another for himself. Victor poured me a cup of tea and Harmony handed me a slice of fruit cake.

They waited patiently for me to sip and take a few bites. Or, rather, the men waited patiently. Harmony fidgeted in her chair and tapped her finger against the side of her teacup until Victor placed his hand over it to still it.

She scowled at him. "Don't be so familiar."

"Don't be so agitated," he shot back. "Miss Fox will tell you what she learned today when she's ready."

"I know that. I simply don't like sitting still. I've been in the parlor too long already."

"What else do you need to do this afternoon?"

She sniffed. "My business is none of your affair, Victor."

"You're just going to read in your room, aren't you?"

"What if I am?"

He shrugged. "It doesn't bother me what you do in your spare time. In fact, I like well-read women. It makes them more interesting."

"It's a novel."

"Even better. Perhaps I can borrow it after you."

"It's a gothic romance. You won't like it."

"I love a good romance. The more gothic, the better."

She stared at him, trying to get his measure and decide if he was teasing her or not. It wasn't always easy to tell with Victor.

Goliath rolled his eyes. "If you two are finished, can we get on? I want to know what Miss Fox has been up to."

Throughout the spiky exchange, Victor's hand had remained over the top of Harmony's, against the teacup. She had not jerked away or asked him to remove it. He did so now and sat back, not smiling but somehow conveying amusement anyway.

Harmony's fingers tightened around the teacup.

I told them about my day, beginning with sending the telegrams to the Paris designers and ending with speaking to Emmanuel Durant. All three listened intently and asked questions, many of which I couldn't answer. Too many. There was still so much we didn't know.

Victor was clearly thinking the same thing, as he said, "We need to find out more about Gertrude's past. What's true and what's a lie?"

Goliath nodded. "Can we even believe what Durant said? What if he was lying?"

"Do you have paper and a pencil?" Harmony asked me.

I dug through my bag and pulled out the pencil and notepad I kept inside. I handed them to her and she flipped to a clean page.

"Let's start at the beginning," she said. "How old was Gertrude?"

"Fifty," I said.

"Born in 1850," Harmony murmured as she wrote the date. "What happened next in her life?"

"We don't know anything until the age of twenty-two. According to Durant, they met in Paris in '72. She joined his troupe as a singer and they traveled around France for the next three years. In '75, she developed cancer in her throat and returned to England to consult with doctors."

Harmony wrote it all down.

"We don't know what she did before she met Durant," Goliath pointed out. "Where did she live? Who did she live with? What did her parents do? Did she leave home and head to Paris straight away, or did she work somewhere in between? Is that when she learned to sew?"

"If so, who did she work for?" Victor added. "Did she work as a seamstress or in another profession altogether?"

"Or none at all? Maybe she didn't need to work."

Harmony wrote all these questions down. "What happened to her after 1875?"

I took up the story. "She met her future husband in March of '78. She was twenty-eight at that point. With his money, she opens her first salon in Earl's Court. She places an advertisement for a seamstress and hires Mrs. Zieliński. In October, Gertrude marries."

"Busy year," Victor said in his typical understated way.

"Their son was born in '81, making him nineteen. He went to a good school. Mr. Lindsey couldn't afford the fees on a teacher's salary so we can assume the shop was doing well enough to pay for the school fees as well as their nice flat by the time the son is school-aged in '85 or '86."

"When did the shop move to New Bond Street?" Harmony asked.

I thought back to the conversations with Mrs. Zieliński and Mr. Lindsey. "In '83 or '84. In '83, the actress Myrtle Langford wore a Poitiers gown. The business did very well from the publicity and soon moved to its current New Bond Street address. It has continued to do well, according to her accountant."

"Did her husband or staff point to any lengthy absences after '78?" Harmony asked.

"No. I assume she was in London the entire time, working to make her business a success."

Victor leaned close to Harmony to read her notes. She did not move away, nor did she look up. She seemed intent on the notes too.

It was Goliath who spoke. He didn't need to read the notes to notice the gaps in the timeline. "There are two periods of time when no one can account for her. Before she moved to Paris in '72, and after she left in '75 and before meeting her future husband in '78. We need to find out where she was in those years."

"That's assuming the murder is related to her past at all. It could be something else entirely."

Harmony nodded. "Like the real talent behind Poitiers' designs becoming frustrated with the lack of attention."

Victor suddenly looked up. The movement was quick, jerky. For a man who always seems so calm, it was unlike him and got our attention. "Myrtle Langford is performing in London at the moment."

Goliath shrugged. "So?"

"So I should speak to her," I said, my spirits lifting.

Victor agreed. "Maybe she knew the victim, that's why she wore her design."

"And if she didn't know her, why wear her gown at all? Why not wear something from a well-known designer at the time? Miss Langford was at the height of her career then. Designers would have been begging her to wear their dresses."

"Where is she performing?" Goliath asked.

"The Regency Theater," Victor said.

"I haven't seen posters with her face on them and I go past there every day."

"She's not the lead. She's got a supporting role only."

"That's what happens when actresses age," Harmony muttered. "They're no longer wanted for the main roles. It's different for men. They can tread the boards with creaking bones and no hair."

Goliath stretched out one of his long legs and nudged Victor with his boot. "How do you know Myrtle Langford's in a show at the Regency? You follow her career that closely?"

"I've got a friend who works backstage."

Goliath nodded in admiration. "You know everyone."

"Can your friend get me in to see Miss Langford?" I asked.

"I'll speak to him after my shift finishes tonight and find out when she's expected in tomorrow."

The more I thought about it, the more I liked Victor's idea. Myrtle Langford had worn a Poitiers design for a reason. If she knew Gertrude, she might be able to fill in some of the gaps of Gertrude's life.

"Why wait for tomorrow?" I said. "Could your friend let us in tonight?"

Victor shrugged. "We can try after the show."

"You can't go tonight!" Harmony cried. "What will your family think if you leave the hotel without their permission in the middle of the night?"

"For one thing, I don't need their permission," I said. "I am a grown woman and can make my own decisions." We both knew that wasn't entirely accurate. My aunt would be horrified to know I was out in the city at night and my uncle would be furious. "And for another, they won't know. I'll sneak out. Victor can accompany me."

Harmony clicked her tongue. "I'd better come too, to maintain a level of respectability."

"Your company would be welcome."

"I might as well come too," Goliath said.

"Why?" Harmony asked.

Goliath merely shrugged. "I hate being left out."

We made plans to meet later. As much as I wanted Harry to join us, he needed to catch up on his sleep. The theater where Miss Langford was performing happened to be the one where the door to the backstage area opened onto his street. It would be very convenient for him. But I wouldn't disturb him.

I suspected he was going to be annoyed tomorrow when he learned where I'd been and at what time. My uncle's disapproval I could brush off. Harry's bothered me more.

CHAPTER 10

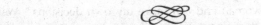

$\mathcal{D}$ressed in my old black woolen cloak, I drew the hood over my head and exited my room. I raced down the stairs, keeping my head bowed, but I met no one on the way. The hotel was almost deserted at this time of the evening. Shows and dinner parties had not yet ended so guests were still out unless they'd gone to bed early. I avoided the foyer altogether and headed into the service area behind the lift. I didn't want to put Philip the night porter in an awkward position by asking him to keep quiet about my leaving.

Harmony met me in the staff parlor then we left the hotel via the service entrance into the lane. Goliath waited for us at the lane's end at the edge of the circle of light cast by a street lamp. We nodded greetings and waited a few minutes until Victor arrived. He'd changed out of his chef's whites and wore day clothes with a long overcoat, the collar flipped up to ward off the chill. His cap perched low over his forehead, almost obscuring his eyes.

Harmony appraised him. "You look like you're going to commit a crime."

He scrutinized her just as thoroughly. "And you look like you're going to break someone's heart. Let's see which of us is right."

He walked off, leaving her staring at his back. I hooked

her arm with mine and dragged her along, trying not to smile too hard lest she scowl at me.

I knew the way, but I let Victor lead. I wouldn't tell the others that Harry lived in the building opposite the theater's back door. I didn't want to endure Harmony's censorial glare. She might not believe me when I denied being inside his flat.

Audience members trickled out of the theater's front door as we passed. The trickle would soon become a torrent. We headed up Harry's street to the back door marked STAFF. Victor asked us to wait while he went inside.

Two women brushed past him as he entered, chatting and giggling. Behind them came some members of the orchestra, carrying instrument cases. They all hurried off, dodging puddles, heads bent into the breeze.

A few minutes later another woman emerged. She crossed the street and unlocked the door to Harry's building. It relocked behind her with a loud click. On the second floor, a light turned off. A few moments later, on the first floor, another turned on. The woman who'd entered the building appeared at the window briefly before closing the curtain.

Victor opened the theater door and signaled for us to follow him. The backstage area of the Regency Theater was laid out in a similar pattern to the Piccadilly Playhouse where I'd been several times while investigating another murder. Small rooms off the narrow corridor were used by the actors, dancers and singers. We caught glimpses of activity as we passed. The lead performers had dressing rooms to themselves, while others shared, jostling for space in front of the mirrors. One of the women dressed only in her underthings began to unlace her corset, not caring that the door stood wide open.

Goliath slowed. Spotting him staring at her in the mirror's reflection, the woman smiled and winked. Harmony grabbed his arm and pulled him along.

Victor stopped at a door where a man stood clutching a clipboard to his chest. A pencil balanced behind his ear, partially covered by wisps of longish brown hair. He looked to be in his early twenties and sported a scar on his cheek. Victor also had a scar, but it was thin and straight. His friend's was circular. He nodded at Victor who nodded back.

"You," he said to Goliath. "Take a bunch of those and give them to Miss Langford." He indicated the flowers on a table outside another door labeled with the name of an actress I recognized.

"Why?" Goliath asked.

Harmony rolled her eyes. "Because Miss Langford likes flowers from big idiots."

Goliath selected a bunch of pink roses. "Aren't these for someone else?"

Victor's friend plucked the card off. "Not anymore."

Goliath straightened his tie. "Do I look presentable?"

"Very handsome," I assured him.

Victor's friend knocked then opened the door. "Visitors for Miss Langford."

The three women seated at the matching dressing tables turned to look at us. Only one was the right age to be Myrtle. The other two were much younger. One hurried out of the room before we even introduced ourselves, blowing kisses to the other two. She disappeared into the corridor but her perfume lingered.

The other young woman beamed at Goliath. "Are those for me?" She took the flowers from him.

"Ummm."

"How lovely." She inspected the bunch, rifling between blooms and leaves. "Where is the card?"

"Ahhh."

Miss Langford smiled sweetly. "Didn't the stage hand say these people were here to see me?"

The younger woman pouted. She passed the flowers over. "Pink isn't my color anyway."

Miss Langford turned to us with a smug smile. If I didn't know she was aged in her fifties, I'd have assumed she was ten years younger. Although she had the lines and sagging jowl of middle age, it was obvious she'd once been a beauty. She needed no makeup to enhance her bright blue eyes and full lips, but she wore it anyway. The effect was a little overwhelming, but it was probably necessary for the stage. I guessed her to be wearing a wig, going by the spare I spotted in the corner of the dressing room. It was identical to the blonde hair on her head in shade and style.

She adjusted the dressing gown over her bosom, revealing more décolletage rather than less, and smiled sweetly. "How lovely to meet you all. Did you enjoy the show? Which song is your favorite?"

"We didn't see the show," I admitted. "I'm a private detective and these are my associates. I need to ask you some questions about Gertrude Lindsey."

Her smile vanished. She tossed the flowers onto the dressing table. "Such a tragedy."

"You're a detective?" the younger woman said. "How curious. That's two in two days."

I blinked at her. "Oh?"

"I met a man who lives across the street who's also a detective." She flapped her hand, but got the direction entirely wrong. She waved it towards the front of the theater, not the back. "Very handsome fellow. Popular with the dancers. With all the girls, really."

"Miss Langford, is there somewhere we can talk alone?" I bit off.

"Here will do." Myrtle made a shooing motion at the younger woman. "Go on, be off with you."

"But I haven't removed all of my makeup yet," the actress whined.

"No one will care."

"But—"

"Go!" Myrtle might no longer be able to command a dressing room all to herself, but she knew how to command authority among the younger cast members. She had once been courted by royalty and cherished by the masses. Her fellow performers might not be old enough to remember that, but they still respected her for it. She must have some interesting stories to tell.

I hoped she had one to tell me.

The other woman took her things and left in a strop. Once the door closed behind her, Myrtle indicated I should speak.

"I noticed your reaction when I mentioned Gertrude Lindsey," I said. "You knew her by that name?"

She opened a drawer and removed a large sapphire and diamond ring. She slipped it onto her finger. "I knew her only as Colette Poitiers. The newspapers reporting her death mentioned her real name was Gertrude Lindsey. I had no idea she wasn't French." She stretched out her arm and admired the ring. "The poor woman. Imagine being strangled to death in your own shop. Shocking."

"Did you know her well?"

"No, not at all. I haven't seen her in years."

"When you wore one of her gowns on stage, it launched her career. She became a highly sought after designer, thanks to you."

She removed a sapphire pendant from the same drawer as the ring. "I'm so pleased I could help her. Such beautiful, elegant clothes."

"More elegant than, say, Worth?"

"Not quite as...exclusive."

"Then why did you agree to wear a Poitiers design?"

She met my gaze in the mirror's reflection. "Because it was lovely."

"But she was an unknown designer and you would have had the likes of Worth courting you to wear their gowns. Why wear Madame Poitiers' dress? What made it—or her—so special?"

She handed the necklace to Goliath. "Put this on me, dear boy."

Goliath bent to the task.

"Did you know her?" I pressed.

Myrtle touched Goliath's hand before he stepped back. "My, aren't you tall. Strong too, I'm sure."

"Did you know her, Miss Langford?"

"No."

I tried not to let my disappointment show. I thanked her for her time and made to leave. Harmony wasn't ready, however.

"You have lovely jewelry," she gushed. I eyed her closely. Harmony never gushed. "I adore sapphires and diamonds." She saw jewels larger than these on the fingers and at the throats of wealthy women every day in the hotel. She'd never shown this much interest in them.

"You should get yourself some." Myrtle touched the sapphire pendant hanging from the gold chain. "They're not very expensive, if you know the right jeweler."

"They're not real?"

"Not anymore. They were once. I had a gentleman caller who gave me jewelry every birthday for almost ten years. We had a falling out and he asked for the jewels back. I refused. He became insistent so I sold them to a jeweler. Mr. Cohen remade the pieces exactly as they were using fake gemstones, and I walked away with a nice sum that has helped support me ever since. You can tell they're not real in the right light, but from a distance, no one notices. I told the gentleman he could have these, but they aren't worth much. He decided not to pursue it." She caressed the sapphire pendant with her thumb. Her smile turned hard. "Every time I put my jewels on, I think of him and how I had the last laugh." She pointed a finger at Harmony and me. "Men are fickle, ladies. Remember that. Be sure to get what you can from them while you're young and pretty."

I'd realized what information Harmony was fishing for, and waited for her to ask the next question.

She didn't disappoint. "If we do find ourselves fortunate enough to be the recipient of lovely jewelry like yours, where should we go to sell them and have good replicas made?"

Myrtle winked at her. "Clever girl. Mr. Cohen's your man. He has a shop in Abchurch Yard. Now, if you have no more questions, it's getting late."

We left the dressing room and the theater, using the back-stage door to exit onto Harry's street.

"What made you think her jewelry was paste?" I asked Harmony as we headed back to the hotel.

"The stones were enormous. If they were real, she would lock them away while she was on stage, but she just left them lying about in a drawer."

"Now we have the name of a jeweler who buys real gems and makes good replicas for the customer to wear instead," I said. "I'll go tomorrow and see if Lady Bunbury was one of his customers. Good work, Harmony."

"Miss Langford was right," Victor said. "You are clever."

Harmony tossed her head. "Merely pragmatic."

The three of them walked me back to the hotel. They all lived in the residence hall not far away, along with many of the other unmarried staff. It made sense for my uncle to pay for their accommodation. It freed up the upper rooms at the hotel where staff used to reside years ago.

"Can I walk you home?" Victor asked Harmony as we drew closer to the Mayfair.

"You're going to anyway. We live in the same building."

He offered her his arm.

She refused it. "You may walk ahead or behind, but not with us."

Victor hunched into his coat as a cold breeze whipped up Piccadilly. "I told you."

"Told me what?"

"That you'd break someone's heart tonight."

He lengthened his strides as Harmony slowed. She stared at his back, looking somewhat dazed. She was always so composed and poised, it was strange to see her unsure what to say or do.

I looped my arm through hers. "He likes you," I whispered.

She made a miffed sound. "He's mad. It's all those cooking fumes he breathes all day."

"Why can't you accept that he likes you?"

"He can't possibly. I've been rude and dismissive. I've discouraged him at every turn."

"Yet he has persisted."

She sighed.

"Why have you discouraged him?" I asked. "Is he that bad?"

"I have my reasons."

"You mean because you're not interested in marriage?" She'd once told me that marriage was simply unpaid drudgery for women. It was impossible to argue with her logic.

We'd reached the lane beside the Mayfair. Harmony extricated her arm from mine and bade me goodnight. The three of them waited for me to enter the hotel through the staff entrance before they departed. I headed up the staircase, my mind on Harmony and the fact she didn't trust me enough to confide in me.

Thanks to my distraction, I forgot to flip my hood up. Floyd and Jonathon recognized me as they descended.

"Cleo?" Floyd raced down the remaining steps to join me. "Have you just come in?"

My mind went blank. Should I be honest or lie?

He knew, however. It was obvious from my clothes that I'd been out. "Where have you been?"

Since I couldn't think of a good lie quickly enough, I decided to keep to the truth. "The Regency, following up a line of inquiry on the Poitiers investigation. I had a chaperone."

He huffed a gruff laugh. "You think that would satisfy my father if he found out?"

"He won't find out, will he?" When he didn't respond, I squared up to him. "Will he, Floyd? If he does, I may have to mention *your* nocturnal activities and how you came home dead drunk the other night after gambling away all your money."

He turned an icy glare onto his friend. "I'm going to kill you for involving my cousin."

Jonathon clapped a hand on Floyd's shoulder. "You'll forgive me one day." He flashed me a grin. "Goodnight, Miss Fox."

"Do try not to lose him again, Jonathon," I said. "I want to get a proper night's sleep."

"You enjoyed the thrill of it. Don't deny it."

"If you think being woken up at an ungodly hour for no good reason thrilled me, then you don't know women as well as you think you do."

He chuckled, apparently unable to determine that I wasn't joking.

I continued up the stairs, this time with my hood up. I heard Floyd growl at Jonathon to get moving. I glanced back down, instantly regretting it. Jonathon saw and winked.

* * *

HARRY REACTED to my report the following morning precisely how I expected him to. The scowl he gave me from the other side of his desk was identical to Floyd's, as was his warning. "If your uncle found out you were investigating late at night—"

"He won't." While I wasn't entirely sure that Floyd wouldn't tell Uncle Ronald, I was positive Harry wouldn't. He knew the consequences; my cousin did not. "If you've finished with your lecture, I'd like to tell you what we learned from Myrtle Langford."

"Why didn't you fetch me? You know I live close by."

"I see you haven't finished." I sighed. This was going to take a little more diplomacy than I expected. "Harry, I didn't fetch you because you needed to rest."

"Let me decide that."

"I know you feel left out, but—"

"It's not that," he snapped.

"Then why does it matter so much to you?"

He leaned back and scrubbed a hand over his jaw. For a moment, I thought he wasn't going to answer and would change the subject, but I wasn't so fortunate. "Your safety is my responsibility. I promised my father I'd take care of you."

"That was in regard to Whitechapel."

"It encompassed everything."

I wasn't quite sure how to react. On the one hand, his concern was touching. He was only acting the way any other gentleman would if he thought himself responsible for me. Floyd had reacted the same. On the other hand, it was unnecessary and even a little demeaning. Did Harry think me so foolish that I'd go to the theater on my own late at night?

"I had Victor and Goliath with me, and Harmony as chaperone. Does that meet with your approval? Or would you like me to call the cavalry next time?"

His jaw hardened. "If there is a next time, I'd like you to fetch me. I'd like it even better if there is no next time."

I stood and snatched up my bag. "I'm going to Abchurch Yard. You can either come with me and find out why, or stay here and brood."

I marched out of the office. He caught up to me at the base of the stairs and pressed a hand to the door to stop me opening it.

He stood very close behind me. I didn't dare turn around or our faces would be mere inches apart. My nerves were stretched enough. "Cleo, this is London. It's a dangerous place at night, even in the theater district and even with escorts. Not only that, whether you like it or not, you're related to the Bainbridges and are a lady of quality because of that connection. It comes with expectations."

I spun around with such ferocity that he stepped back, letting go of the door. "Enough! Enough, Harry! You are not a member of my family so cease with these endless lectures!"

"*You* are the one who insists we are friends. As your friend, I *will* worry about you." His chest heaved with his deep breath, as did mine.

I tried to steady my nerves but they continued to vibrate with my anger. I glared at him, and he glared back. He wasn't backing down. I wasn't used to that.

"I will stop warning you, however," he went on in a calm but steely voice. "I believe I've made my point."

I pulled the door open and strode outside. The air cooled my hot skin but not my temper. It simmered beneath the surface, ready to boil over again at any moment. Harry wisely remained silent.

Until we reached Piccadilly Circus, that is. "Do you know how to get to Abchurch Yard?"

"No."

He kept walking.

"Are you going to tell me?" I asked.

"That depends. Will you start talking to me again?"

"I'll think about it."

He considered this. "That's the best I can hope for. Very well. That omnibus will take us there."

We picked up our pace and climbed aboard the omnibus before it departed. There was only space for one more passenger on the lower deck, so Harry headed up the steps to the upper deck on the roof. Time apart cleared my head. My temper dispersed altogether, but I didn't regret snapping at Harry. If we were to remain friends, he needed to know his lectures weren't welcome. While I appreciated his concern for my safety on one level, it would become cloying and exhausting if he continued to express it. I wasn't a child. I knew the risks, both to my physical safety and my reputation. I'd taken steps to mitigate them.

He had made his point, but I had also made mine. I hoped we could move on from our argument and be friends again.

147

I spotted him through the window as he descended the external stairs and alighted too. He greeted me cheerfully and set off, turning down Abchurch Lane. It led to Abchurch Yard, a small courtyard with a church, cake shop, teashop, photographic studio and accounting office occupying the buildings surrounding it. Cohen and Sons Jewelry was situated between the cake shop and studio. It looked respectable. I'd been expecting a dark shop with iron bars across the windows, tucked out of sight. But this brightly lit shop announced its presence with a bold sign out the front and an unencumbered view through the bay window.

We'd hardly spoken since leaving Harry's office so I told him what Myrtle Langford had revealed about her jewelry and why we'd come here. "I think we should employ honesty when questioning him," I said.

"Lead the way."

I brushed past him and entered the shop. There were no customers. A small bespectacled man looked up from the counter where he'd been examining a clear gem through a loupe. He placed the gem onto a velvet cloth and folded up the cloth.

He smiled. "Good morning, sir, madam. Are you shopping for a wedding ring?"

My face heated. I kept my gaze on the jeweler and didn't look at Harry as he handed over a business card. "We're private detectives consulting for Scotland Yard," I said. "We need to ask you some questions. Are you Mr. Cohen?"

"Y—yes." His face dropped at the mention of the police. "Am I under suspicion for something?" Even though I had spoken, he addressed his question to Harry.

"Not at all," Harry said in the same cheerful tone he'd employed with me outside. "Our questions relate to a customer you may or may not have served. Her name is Lady Bunbury. Has she been here?"

"I'm afraid that's confidential. My customers want absolute privacy."

"Because they don't want anyone to know their jewels are fakes?" I asked.

Mr. Cohen tucked the loupe into his jacket pocket. "I don't sell fake gems."

"No, but you buy real ones and replace them with paste ones that look exactly the same. Unfortunately, the replica Lalique brooch you made for Lady Bunbury wasn't very good."

If Lady Bunbury wasn't his customer, he would have admitted it at that point. He did not. We had the right jeweler. Again, he appealed to Harry. "This is harassment! Sir, make your assistant understand that she can't accuse hardworking businessmen like this. If she insists, I'll have to contact my lawyer."

"She isn't accusing you of anything illegal. We know the customers commission you and all your dealings with them are honest and above board."

Mr. Cohen withdrew a handkerchief and patted his forehead. "I can't help you. As I said, my clients expect absolute confidentiality."

I indicated the black velvet cloth with the uncut stone folded inside. "Is that a fake diamond?" I pointed at the emerald necklace inside a locked glass cabinet. "Is that paste? Is anything in here real? Now that we know you peddle in fakes, Scotland Yard will want to get an expert in here to make sure you're not trying to sell them to unsuspecting customers."

"I'm not!"

"But no one will think that when they see policemen swarming the premises."

Mr. Cohen patted his forehead again. The handkerchief came away damp.

Harry leaned a forearm on the counter, friendly and casual. "Co-operate with us and we'll assume all your transactions are legitimate. No police need to come."

Mr. Cohen pressed the folded handkerchief to his lips. Finally he nodded. "Very well. I do know Lady Bunbury. I've conducted business with the Bunburys a few times in recent years, always buying their real jewels and making identical ones for her. I often use the same setting and replace only the stones. It's less work and the result is almost identical to the original, if one is not an expert and doesn't look too closely. The brooch was different. It wasn't easy to replicate." His defensive tone hinted at his professional pride.

"You did business with both Lord and Lady Bunbury?" I asked.

He nodded. "Sometimes they've come in separately, other times together."

"How many pieces have you reworked for them?

"Dozens. Some large, some small. Some were family heirlooms. They were exquisite pieces. It's a shame they're having difficulty and had to liquidate some assets."

We thanked him for his time. He looked surprised that we had no more questions. Surprised and relieved.

Harry doffed his hat and opened the door for me.

"Are the Bunburys in trouble?" Mr. Cohen called out. "Have they committed a crime?"

"I'm afraid that information is confidential," Harry said with a smirk.

I eyed him as we walked out of the Yard. "You enjoyed saying that, didn't you?"

"More than I probably should. So what do you think?"

"I think Lady Bunbury's visit to Maison de Poitiers before opening was definitely to negotiate a payment plan. I suppose they could have argued about the amount owing and Lady Bunbury strangled Gertrude in anger. But I can't picture it, somehow."

"It does seem a little extreme to kill Gertrude because they disagreed over a payment plan. But what if Gertrude threatened to tell someone about Lady Bunbury's plight? Perhaps she tried to blackmail her, demanding money for her silence."

Blackmail was an excellent motive for murder. But it also didn't quite ring true. "Blackmailing someone in financial difficulty isn't a very wise business decision."

"The Bunburys may be having trouble paying their creditors, but to most people they are still very wealthy. They live in a large townhouse in Mayfair. According to my father, Bunbury owns it. They don't rent."

Then they certainly were wealthy. Yet they didn't have enough ready cash to pay for their lifestyle. They needed to liquidate some assets, as Mr. Cohen put it. Liquidating jewelry was a lot faster, easier and more discreet than selling real estate.

"Who was Gertrude going to tell Lady Bunbury's secret

to?" I asked, not really expecting an answer. "Lord Bunbury knows about the jewelry and is complicit, so it must be someone else."

"Perhaps it was nobody in particular. Perhaps Gertrude told her she would pass along gossip to her other customers unless Lady Bunbury paid her to stay quiet."

"I still don't see her as a murderess, but there is one possibility we haven't considered. That *Lord* Bunbury murdered Gertrude to keep her quiet."

Harry nodded slowly. "We know nothing about him, but it should be easy enough to find out if he left the house with his wife on Friday morning."

I smiled. "We'll question the servants, discreetly of course."

He returned my smile. "Good."

"Why good?"

"I thought I'd irreparably damaged our friendship. I was anticipating begging you to speak to me again. Or, at the very least, buying you lunch."

"I'll never refuse begging or lunch. I'm rather fond of both, as long as I'm the recipient."

He laughed.

"And just so you know," I went on, "you have to try a lot harder to irreparably damage our friendship."

"Good."

This time I didn't have to ask him what he meant.

* * *

HARRY ALREADY KNEW where Lord Bunbury's townhouse was located, thanks to a conversation with his father a few days ago. It was in Upper Brooke Street, not far from the Mayfair Hotel. It was one of the most elegant townhouses I'd seen, and the largest too. Fronted in cream-colored stone with a contrasting fence and balconies in cast iron, it was six levels high with bay windows on three of the levels. Behind one of those windows was the ballroom where their famous ball would be held in a matter of weeks.

The topmost level was narrow, the dormer attic windows small. Servants' bedchambers didn't need to be large. The lowest level was the basement, housing the kitchen and other service rooms. The arched front door was framed by slender Roman columns, adding a classical flavor to the architecture.

We didn't go to the front door, however. We knocked on the basement service door, located down the steep set of stairs. It took some time before a girl of no more than eighteen or nineteen answered. Dressed in a maid's uniform, cap and apron, her cheeks were flushed from hurrying to answer the door.

Harry asked if we could come inside to speak to the lady's maid or valet.

The girl wiped flour-dusted hands on her apron. "The lady's maid isn't here," she said. "But Mr. Holbeck is free." She led the way inside, past storerooms, the larder and kitchen where a cook peered into a pot on the stove. She had no assistants, but going by the flour on the girl's hands, she must help, even though she was dressed in an upstairs maid's uniform, not the clothes of a scullery maid or other staff member who never went above stairs. We continued on to the servants' dining room. A man sat at the table, taking up the hem of a trouser leg.

"Hurry up, Child," the cook called out. "I need you."

The girl bobbed a curtsy then scurried away.

The man introduced himself as Lord Bunbury's valet, Mr. Holbeck. Harry told him we were private detectives but did not elaborate further. Mr. Holbeck regarded us with a frown that deepened the two vertical lines between his brows. Although I guessed him to be about thirty, those lines looked permanent. He must scowl all the time to have put them there.

He took up his mending again. He hadn't offered us a seat. "What do you want?"

"We need to ask some questions about the Bunburys."

"I don't gossip about my betters. I know my place."

"This is important."

He held up the needle and thread. "So is this. I'm busy."

"Is that because you have to work extra?" I asked. "There are few servants here, aren't there? I assume you have to do double duty as a footman when the Bunburys have guests."

He grunted and returned to his sewing.

"Tell us, Mr. Holbeck, was Lord Bunbury home early last Friday morning, or did he leave the house with Lady Bunbury?"

Whatever he'd been expecting us to ask, it wasn't that. "Why do you want to know?"

"Just answer the question," Harry said.

"I told you, I don't gossip. Go away."

Harry placed some money on the table. "The Bunburys are economizing so your wages have probably been cut."

Mr. Holbeck quickly glanced at the door then pocketed the money. "His lordship was at home on Friday morning. Lady Bunbury left on her own. She walked, alone."

"Do you know where she went?" I asked.

Mr. Holbeck shook his head. "You're not the only ones to come here asking questions. A Scotland Yard detective spoke to her. I'm not sure what about. We couldn't hear." It would seem the servants liked to eavesdrop. They also weren't aware of the connection between their mistress and the murder.

This man might be the valet to his lordship, but I suspected he knew quite a bit about her ladyship too. If there were only a few servants, they were probably close and exchanged information about their employers. "Did Lady Bunbury return late on Friday morning?"

"No. She was home by 8:45. It must have been a vigorous walk. Her maid said her ladyship took to her bed when she got back. She was visibly distressed."

"Upset?" Harry asked.

"Angry."

Angry women could kill. "Does she get angry often?" I asked.

Mr. Holbeck stopped sewing and thought about his answer. "She argues regularly with Lord Bunbury, but she rarely shows emotion towards the servants or anyone else. That sort rarely do. In my experience, ladies remain very... contained. Gentlemen will rant and rave at all and sundry, but not ladies, and particularly not Lady Bunbury. Even when she was furious with his lordship, she never raised her voice."

"She wasn't violent towards him?"

He scoffed. "Of course not."

I made to leave, but Harry had another question. "If she doesn't show any signs, how did you know she was angry when she came home on Friday morning?"

"Her maid heard muffled screaming coming from her bedroom. She has seen Lady Bunbury scream into her pillow after a particularly nasty fight with his lordship, so we think she was experiencing similar angry frustration upon her return that day." He'd been sewing the whole time he spoke, but now lowered the garment. "If I return some of your money will you tell me what this is about?"

"No," Harry said.

Mr. Holbeck clicked his tongue and resumed his mending.

I led the way back outside and up the steps. We'd got no more than half way when a carriage rolled to a stop. A stiff-backed butler trotted down the front steps of the house. He hadn't seen us as he rushed past, his focus on the carriage door. He assisted Lady Bunbury down to the pavement and through the front gate.

Perhaps she wouldn't see us, still standing halfway down the steps to the basement. I didn't dare move lest it draw her attention. If she saw me, she'd want to know why I, the niece of Sir Ronald and Lady Bainbridge, was standing on her service stairs with a man.

The butler went ahead to open the front door. Again, he didn't see us. My heart thudded in my chest, and I prayed Lady Bunbury wouldn't look to her left.

But she was sharper than her butler. She saw me before I could turn my face away to hide it. Her gaze held mine for a very long time, unwavering. She was trying to work out why I was there. Her mind would be sifting through the possibilities.

None of those possibilities could possibly align with the innocent, well-bred lady she assumed me to be.

154

CHAPTER 11

*L*ady Bunbury recovered from the shock of our meeting before I did. "Miss Fox? What are you doing here?"

I've come to realize that, when cornered, my mind seizes. I liked to think I was witty and clever, but that wasn't always the case. I couldn't think of a single response that would sound plausible enough to satisfy Lady Bunbury. The seconds ticked by as I grasped for something to say. Anything!

Lady Bunbury's lips pinched tighter the longer I made her wait.

"I...uh..."

"Your button, miss." Harry bent and picked something up from the step below him. He held up a black button between thumb and forefinger, a triumphant look on his face. "I'm glad we finally found it."

I covered one of the buttons on my jacket with one hand and accepted the button with my other. "Thank you, sir. That's very kind of you."

He touched the brim of his hat, smiled amiably, and headed up the steps past me. He tipped his hat to Lady Bunbury too then walked off. She watched him go with a narrowed gaze.

"Is this your home?" I asked her. "It's lovely. I was just walking past when that gentleman noticed my button fall off

155

and roll through your fence and down the steps. If you'll excuse me, I must continue with my errands."

Her gaze fell to where my hand covered one of my jacket buttons at my waist. I wore a double-breasted black and burgundy checked jacket that matched my skirt. It was a simple yet elegant outfit, appropriate for the period of half-mourning I was now in. I hoped she hadn't noticed my jacket possessed all its buttons before I slapped my hand over one.

I headed up the steps, but she moved to block my path. "I'm surprised Lady Bainbridge doesn't insist you take a chaperone on your walks."

"My family agrees that a chaperone is unnecessary at my age." I looked pointedly at the gate.

She looked pointedly at the service entrance at the base of the stairs. She knew I was lying. After questioning the staff, she'd know why I was there. While I doubted Mr. Holbeck would admit he answered our questions, he would have no reason to deny that we tried to gain information from him.

It was only a matter of time before she told my aunt.

She stepped aside and allowed me to pass. "Good day, Miss Fox."

"Good day, Lady Bunbury."

With my heart sinking lower with every step, I hurried along the pavement in the opposite direction to Harry. By the time I reached his Soho office, I'd also reached a conclusion. I had to speak to my aunt before Lady Bunbury did. I must mitigate the damage she could cause and beg Aunt Lilian to keep my investigating activities a secret from my uncle.

Harry sat behind his desk, a steaming cup of tea in front of him. A second cup waited for me. I picked it up gratefully and breathed in the aroma. The familiar scent was a comfort and helped steady my nerves.

The white cups with vertical green and red stripes were a giveaway of the tea's origins. "I thought Luigi only made coffee."

"This is England. He keeps a teapot ready in case someone orders it. He complained the entire time he poured it, saying the puddles in the street had more flavor."

I sipped then set the teacup down as well as the button. I slid it across the desk to Harry. "Thank you for rescuing me."

"Did she saying anything?"

"No, but she suspects something. She'll question the servants." I had not sat and now began pacing the office. "It's only a matter of time before she speaks to my aunt. Or perhaps she'll go directly to my uncle." I clicked my tongue. "I should never have gone to her house. I should have let you speak to the servants alone."

He rounded the desk and stood in front of me, blocking my path. He grasped my elbows and dipped his head to meet my gaze. "It'll be all right, Cleo."

"I appreciate you trying to calm me down. I do. But I think I should go now and speak to my aunt before Lady Bunbury does."

His grip tightened. "Cleo," he said in that stern yet gentle way he had. "It'll be all right. Lady Bunbury won't tell your aunt or uncle."

"I want to believe you."

"Then do." He steered me to the chair then handed me the teacup when I sat. He perched on the edge of the desk beside me. "She won't say anything because if she does, she'll have to admit why we were questioning her staff. The last thing she wants is for people to know she's having financial troubles."

He was right. In my agitation, I'd not thought it through properly. I'd not seen the situation from Lady Bunbury's point of view, only my own. She'd be humiliated if word got out. "Thank you, Harry. It seems I owe you twice over. Once for rescuing me with the button story, and a second time for calming me down."

He smiled. "You don't owe me anything. In fact, I believe *I* still owe *you* lunch."

"I believe it was lunch *and* begging."

"No, it was definitely lunch *or* begging. You can't have both."

"Then I choose lunch, since I expect we'll dine downstairs at Luigi's café, and I know the pasta there is excellent. Certainly more fulfilling than listening to you drone on and on."

"Actually you're missing out. It would have been an eloquent apology, full of wit and big words. You would have learned something and been amused at the same time. It's a shame you won't get to hear it now."

"Is it too late to forgo the lunch and hear the begging?"

"Sadly, yes. You made your decision."

I sighed theatrically as he resumed his seat. We exchanged smiles across the desk.

I felt the heat in my cheeks begin to rise, so in an attempt to hide my blush, I indicated the button. "Where did that come from?"

"My coat." It hung on the stand by the door. "I tore it off when no one was looking."

"She must have noticed you were missing a button that looked exactly like the others on your coat."

"Not necessarily. I distracted her with my charming smile."

I laughed and shook my head. While his charming smile might work on some, Lady Bunbury wasn't that easily distracted. I knew she hadn't fallen for our little charade.

"Do you keep a needle and thread in the office?" I asked. "I'll sew it back on for you. It's the least I can do."

"There's no need. I can sew. My mother taught me."

It was a little early for lunch so we decided to review the case so far. While we couldn't cross Lady Bunbury entirely off our list of suspects, her husband's valet claimed Lord Bunbury hadn't left the house early on Friday morning so he was not a suspect. We both doubted Lady Bunbury was a serious prospect. We didn't strike her off our list altogether, but we placed her at the bottom.

Just like Harmony had done the day before in the staff parlor, I wrote down the known dates of Gertrude's life and pointed out the gaps in our knowledge to Harry. He latched onto something immediately that neither the staff nor I had noticed.

"Everyone says Gertrude returned to England to consult with doctors about her throat disease," he said. "Emmanuel Durant went a step further and claims she had cancer. The only way to treat cancer is to cut it out in a surgical procedure. You saw the body. Did she have a scar on her throat?"

"It was impossible to tell beneath the strangulation marks and the veil without a closer inspection."

"I'll ask my father. The autopsy report should mention it if there is one."

"You think she lied about the disease too?"

"No one has mentioned she spoke differently or that her voice was unusual."

"It wasn't."

"I'm no expert, but I'd expect surgery on the throat to have a lasting effect. We should speak to a specialist. It won't be difficult to find one at a hospital this afternoon."

"There's no need to visit a hospital. There's a delegation of European surgeons staying at the hotel. They represent almost every country from the continent and are here for a series of lectures. The one from Germany specializes in the ear, nose and throat, I believe."

We agreed that I would speak to the surgeon and Harry would call on his father to ask about scars and give an update on our progress. First, we enjoyed a hearty lunch in Café Roma. Despite some silences, which were not at all awkward, we managed to talk about a range of subjects, none of which touched on the murder. Nor did we discuss Harry's biological father or his past. I decided to steer clear of any sensitive topics for now. I still felt raw after our argument over his lecturing and I didn't want to ruin the friendship we'd managed to rebuild.

After lunch, I returned to the hotel. Despite Harry's assurances that Lady Bunbury wouldn't speak to my aunt, I worried nevertheless. Frank greeted me with his usual grumbles but gave no sign that my family were trying to locate me.

"Has Lady Bunbury been here in the last hour or so?" I asked.

He shook his head.

"Have you been off duty in that time?"

"I've been standing here, opening and closing that door for toffs too lazy to do it themselves for the last four hours. I haven't sat down, had a cup of tea, or looked the other way the entire time."

"A simple no would have sufficed. Just think of all the breath you could have saved."

He scowled, not appreciating my teasing.

I opened the door myself, earning another scowl and a

muttered comment that it was his job to open doors and that he would be made redundant if everyone decided to open doors themselves. Frank could find fault with a basketful of kittens.

I greeted Goliath as he wheeled a luggage trolley past me, heading for the service lift in the senior staff corridor. Peter, Mr. Hobart and Uncle Ronald stepped aside to let him pass then all three smiled at me as they joined me in the foyer. They must have been in a meeting together in Mr. Hobart's office.

It was a relief to see my uncle's smile. It meant he was none the wiser about my visit to Lady Bunbury's house. It was still early, however.

"Are you heading out, Cleo?" he asked.

I was dressed in a walking outfit so it was a natural assumption to make. "I've just returned from a walk, as it happens. Is my aunt in her room?"

"I don't know. Excuse me." He strode off to greet a gentleman who'd just emerged from the lift. He was all smiles for the guest and shook his hand heartily.

"Lady Bainbridge hasn't come down today," Mr. Hobart told me.

"Lady Bunbury hasn't called? Or left a message for my aunt?"

"No."

"Why?" Peter asked.

Mr. Hobart frowned at him. "Miss Fox's business is not your business, Peter."

Peter apologized.

"One more question while I have the attention of you both," I said. "I understand there's a German surgeon staying at the hotel. Is he still here?"

"Dr. Gerhardt?" Mr. Hobart said. "He's with us until Thursday." He looked as though he was about to ask me why I wanted to know but swallowed the question before uttering it. He couldn't very well do the thing he'd just scolded Peter for.

"He's out all day giving lectures at Bart's," Peter said.

"St. Bartholomew's Hospital," Mr. Hobart clarified. "If

you require medical assistance, I can provide you with the name of several local specialists."

"It's not for me," I assured him. "I have a general surgery question that may or may not help with the investigation. Can you send word when he returns?"

I went in search of my cousin and found her in her room, reading a magazine. I'd been neglecting her lately so asked if she wanted to spend the afternoon together. Not wanting to miss Dr. Gerhardt's return, I suggested we stay indoors and play cards.

We roped in Miss Hessing, who'd returned to the hotel along with her mother. Mrs. Hessing declined to join us, claiming a headache which had led them to abandon their planned afternoon tour of Hampton Court Palace. We were all rather relieved she wasn't up to playing cards, particularly her daughter. Flossy asked another guest who also happened to be at a loose end to make up a party of four. We spent a very pleasant afternoon in the hotel's private sitting room playing Bridge and nibbling tarts and cakes until we were full.

We were about to disperse for the day when Peter entered. He discreetly signaled for me to join him near the door where he informed me that Dr. Gerhardt had returned and I could catch him in the foyer if I was quick.

I said a hasty good afternoon to my companions and followed him to the foyer. He pointed out Dr. Gerhardt, a tall fellow with a gray beard and mustache ends twirled to points. He was speaking to two other men. Neither Peter nor I wanted to interrupt him.

Mr. Hobart saw me hovering. More self-assured than Peter and me, he approached Dr. Gerhardt and asked if he cared to meet me. Dr. Gerhardt turned away from his companions and greeted me with a polite nod and a click of his heels. Mr. Hobart made the introductions then melted away, taking Peter with him. The manager bent his head to his assistant, perhaps explaining how to subtly break into a conversation without offending anyone.

"I do hope you're enjoying your stay at the Mayfair, Doctor," I began.

"It is very pleasant, thank you. You are Sir Ronald's niece.

Does that mean you live here?" He spoke in the precise, clipped accent of the Germanic people. Having been around many international guests now, I was becoming used to identifying where someone came from by the way they spoke the English language.

"I do. I moved from Cambridge to be with my mother's family in December."

We exchanged pleasantries before I launched into my question. "I have a friend who is worried she may have throat cancer."

"How terrible. But does she not know?"

"She's getting a second opinion tomorrow. The first doctor says she may need surgery to remove it. Is surgery always necessary to remove cancer of the throat?"

"Yes. Tell your friend it is usually successful, if the tumor is not too large. She should not be afraid."

"She is rather frightened, not just of the pain of surgery but also of how it will look afterwards. Will it leave a scar?"

"Unfortunately scarring is inevitable. She can wear a high collar to cover it, however. These are in fashion, I have noticed." He smiled reassuringly.

"And will her voice change?"

"This I cannot say. It will depend on the location of the tumor, its size *et cetera*. Her doctor can advise her. It is possible she may never speak again. I suggest you do not tell your friend this. She must have the surgery to save her life. It is kinder to let her think she will have a complete recovery."

I wasn't so sure. If I was going to have surgery to save my life, I'd still want to know what outcome to expect. "What will happen if she doesn't go through with the surgery?"

"She will die. The tumor will take over her throat, making it difficult to swallow even water. She must have it removed before it is too late."

I thanked him and looked around for Mr. Hobart. I couldn't wait to speak to Harry in the morning and see what his father had to say about scars on Gertrude's throat. Patience was not one of my virtues. Peter said the manager was getting ready to leave for the day and I'd find him in his office. I hurried there before he locked up. Mr. Hobart was putting on his coat.

"May I use your telephone to call your brother at Scotland Yard?" I asked.

"Be my guest." He indicated the telephone. "Lock up when you're finished and give the key to Peter."

I sat in his chair and looked up when he didn't immediately leave.

"Did you spend the day investigating with Harry?" he asked.

"Just until lunch time."

"You two are getting along?"

"Most of the time."

"Good, good." My words seemed to take a moment to register. When they did, he stopped nodding and frowned. "Not all of the time?"

"We both have a stubborn streak and a temper. Also, I am not a conventional female, which tends to be a difficult thing for men to grasp."

"Not all men. And Harry will learn how to bend. He did so here. He managed difficult patrons superbly." He suddenly paled, realizing what he'd implied. "Not that you are difficult! Or require management. Besides, you are hardly unconventional, Miss Fox. Modern in your thinking, yes, but not unusual."

"Thank you, Mr. Hobart. I think." I laughed to show him he hadn't offended me.

"I'd better leave before I put my foot in it any more than I have."

I waited for him to close the door before I plucked the telephone receiver off its hook. The operator put me through to Scotland Yard, but unfortunately Detective Inspector Hobart had gone home for the day. I hung up and stared at the telephone for a few seconds before picking up the receiver again. I asked the operator to put me through to the Hobarts' home.

Very few private homes had telephones in them. They were reserved for the wealthy and places of business, like the Mayfair Hotel. But Harry said his father had one installed last year so he could be summoned at all hours. Crimes often took place at night, and D.I. Hobart wanted to get to a crime scene as quickly as possible. He was dedicated to his work.

Just as I expected, Mrs. Hobart answered. I informed her

163

who it was and asked if her husband was at home as he'd already left the Yard.

"Not yet," she said, her tone crisp despite traveling all that way along a wire. It would seem she still wanted me to know she hadn't forgiven me for getting Harry dismissed from the hotel. "May I take a message?"

"I don't suppose Harry is there?" He often joined his parents for dinner and since he had little to do this afternoon, it wasn't much of a leap to assume he'd visited his mother and stayed for a meal.

"Why?"

"May I speak with him? It's about the case we're sharing."

She paused. "He's setting the table."

I waited. She did not offer to fetch him to the telephone. I heard muffled voices in the background then Harry's voice came on the line.

"Cleo?"

"It's me."

"Sorry about my mother. She..." He expelled a heavy breath, clearly not sure how to explain away his mother's rudeness without admitting the truth.

I decided to make it easy for him. "She hasn't forgiven me. I know. It's all right, Harry. I have a thick skin. I wanted to tell you that I spoke to the surgeon."

"What did he say?"

"That scarring is inevitable, but a change to her voice would depend on where the tumor was located and how big it was. Did you speak to your father earlier?"

"I did. According to the autopsy, there was no scar on her throat."

"So she didn't have surgery," I said. "She lied about that too." I didn't want to mention Gertrude's name in case the operator was listening in to our conversation. News about the investigation into the murder of Madame Poitiers would be fodder for gossip.

"Unless Durant was mistaken and the disease wasn't cancer," Harry went on. "Another disease may not have required surgery."

"True. But let's assume she did lie for a moment. Why?

What purpose did it serve? Why not simply leave the troupe because she wanted to?"

There was a pause on the other end that went on so long I wondered if I'd lost the connection.

"Harry?"

"I'm here. I was thinking about what you said. She must have required a reason because leaving the troupe would have raised eyebrows, and led to questions being asked, perhaps by the troupe members themselves, or family and friends."

"And she didn't want to answer those questions with the truth," I finished. My heart skipped as an answer hit me. "Harry, what's the main reason a woman disappears for a while and lies about it?"

"She's with child," he said without missing a beat. He must have reached the same conclusion at the same time. "If we're right, and she went through with the pregnancy, the child would be about twenty-five now."

"We need to find out if our theory is correct."

"My father will have contacts at the General Register Office. He'll get an answer faster than us. I'll ask him to telephone in the morning." I heard more muffled voices then Harry said, "He just walked in the door. I'll send word to you tomorrow at the hotel when I have news." He hung up before I could ask if he wanted me to call on him at his office instead.

I locked Mr. Hobart's office door and headed up to my room. Harmony suddenly sat up upon my entry and straightened her cap. She'd been napping on the sofa. "Have you been waiting long?" I asked.

"A few minutes. I was just tidying up."

I indicated the book that had fallen onto the floor. "You were reading and fell asleep. You don't have to pretend with me, Harmony. It's your time off. If you want to nap on my sofa, you're very welcome."

"It is quieter than the room I share at the residence hall. My roommate snores. I've heard steam engines that make less noise than her." She picked up the book and placed it on the table near the end of the sofa. "So what have you learned today?"

I told her the jeweler had confirmed that the Bunburys

165

regularly sold their jewels to him and he replaced them with replicas. I went on to mention our visit to the Bunburys' house and my confrontation with Lady Bunbury.

"Harry assures me she won't tell my uncle and aunt that I was there because that will lead to the truth coming out."

"I agree with him. Lady Bunbury's reputation is more important to her than getting you into trouble with your family."

"When you put it that way... Thanks, Harmony. I feel better."

I told her our theory about Gertrude's pregnancy and she agreed it was a strong possibility. After expressing our shared frustration that women often had to bear the responsibility of unexpected pregnancy alone, we sat on the sofa together and read. At eight, we ordered meals through the speaking tube and ate before returning to our books.

I must have fallen asleep because I awoke with a start as Harmony left. It was eleven-thirty, the same time the cooks on the evening shift finished. I smiled to myself. Timing is everything.

* * *

I HAD to wait until late the following morning before Mr. Hobart finally fetched me to tell me his brother had telephoned and left a message for me to call him back. I checked that no one was looking and slipped into Mr. Hobart's office to telephone Scotland Yard. A few minutes later, D.I. Hobart's voice came on the other end.

"Harry is here with me," he said. "I've just received word from my contact at the GRO. You two were right. Gertrude Russell gave birth to a girl in September 1875. She was adopted by a couple from Hedgerley by the name of Newland. They named her Anna."

I gasped. "Gertrude's assistant is her daughter! Do you think Gertrude knew? Perhaps that's why she hired her," I said, answering my own question.

"I don't think so. I interviewed Miss Newland at the boarding house where she lives on Saturday. She resides there because Hedgerley is too far from London to commute every day. I wanted to speak to her away from the shop. I learned nothing, but I managed to talk to one of the other girls and she told me something that only makes sense now, in light of this new information. The witness told me she overheard a heated exchange between Anna and another woman on Thursday evening." That was the night before the murder. "She didn't see the other woman, but I am now convinced it was Gertrude." I heard paper rustling as he flipped through his notebook. "According to the witness, the unseen woman screamed 'How dare you. You are nothing to me.'" His voice was deadpan, devoid of the anger with which those words must have been flung at Anna. "If the visitor to the boarding house was Gertrude, and she is telling the daughter she gave up that she doesn't care for her, then it gives Miss Newland a motive to kill her."

"She must have been terribly upset," I agreed. "Does the record of Anna's birth say who the father is?"

"No."

"Will you go to the shop to speak to Miss Newland now or do you want us to go?"

"Ah. There's a problem," D.I. Hobart said. "Miss Newland left the shop on Monday afternoon at closing and returned to the boarding house. She packed her things and departed without a word to anyone. None of the girls she lives with know why she left, and Mr. Lindsey doesn't either. He only found out yesterday morning when one of the seamstresses came to his flat and told him there was no one attending the shop as Miss Newland hadn't shown up."

"She didn't leave a note on the counter?"

"Nothing. I am about to send a constable to her parents' home in Hedgerley to see if she went there."

"She left on Monday afternoon... Harry and I saw her Monday morning. We spoke to her and the seamstresses. She seemed fine, not in any distress. Nor did she give any sign that she'd just lost her mother."

"Gertrude was not a mother-figure to her."

"Even so, it would be a blow."

Monday... After speaking to Miss Newland and the seamstresses, Harry and I had gone to Mrs. Zieliński's home in

Whitechapel then spoken to Emmanuel Durant. The pieces were beginning to fall into place.

"Miss Fox? Are you still there? You've gone quiet."

"I think I know who the father is and why Miss Newland disappeared."

D.I. Hobart spoke to Harry. There were muffled sounds then Harry came on the line. "Go on, Cleo. We're both listening."

"The witness at the boarding house said she overheard the argument on Thursday evening. Emmanuel Durant told us he met Gertrude after the shop closed on Thursday. So Gertrude spoke to him first then went to speak to Miss Newland."

"Because she learned something from Durant and wanted to confront Miss Newland about it," he finished. "You think he told Gertrude that Anna was their daughter."

"I do, but I don't know how he would know when Gertrude didn't."

"Interesting timing," D.I. Hobart said. His voice sounded a little further away than Harry's, but I could hear him well enough. "This all happened the night before she was found dead."

"Speaking of interesting timing," I went on. "Harry, we spoke to Durant on Monday afternoon at the hotel where he's staying, a few hours after we saw Miss Newland and the seamstresses at the shop. Miss Newland went missing Monday evening. It's possible he told her we were sniffing around and advised her to go into hiding."

"He'd only do that if she was the murderer."

"Or he thinks she is," D.I. Hobart added.

"He's protecting her," I said. "He was protecting her during our interview too. He refused to tell us why he came to London and he never admitted to being Gertrude's lover. He didn't want us connecting Miss Newland to him or to Gertrude in such a personal way."

"A father protecting his child," D.I. Hobart said so quietly I could barely hear him. "It's the most basic human instinct."

"Not for all," I said. "Not for Gertrude. Her rejection of her daughter must have hurt Miss Newland deeply."

"According to her son, Gertrude wasn't very maternal,"

Harry pointed out. "Gerald said she sent him away to school at the first opportunity."

"It's time I paid Mr. Durant a visit," D.I. Hobart said. "I want you two to speak to the husband again. He trusts you, Harry, and won't be surprised that you've continued to dig into Gertrude's past. See if he knew about his wife's daughter. Note his reactions."

"You think he killed Gertrude for keeping it a secret?" I asked.

"It's possible. He claims he left the flat at eight on Friday morning, which would give him time to commit the murder."

Harry and I agreed to meet around the corner from the Lindseys' flat in half an hour. I hung up the receiver and left Mr. Hobart's office with a light step. He emerged from Mrs. Short's office and saw me.

"You look invigorated, Miss Fox," he said. "Was it a productive telephone call?"

"It certainly was. I have to meet Harry. If my family are looking for me this afternoon, tell them I've gone to the museum."

I fetched coat and gloves from my room then left the hotel without any of my family seeing me. I walked to the meeting place and waited for Harry. He arrived at the appointed time a few minutes later and apologized. He smiled at me. I smiled back. We were getting somewhere with the case. Events were moving quickly and the pieces of the puzzle were falling into place.

Although Anna Newland had just become our main suspect, there was always the possibility the murder had been committed by Durant, out of anger that Gertrude had not informed him about their daughter years ago. By that same token, it was possible Mr. Lindsey had become upset at the news too and lashed out.

There was another reason why Mr. Lindsey was now a suspect. Gertrude had been about to make a change to her will that would have cut him out. Could that blow, on top of learning about Gertrude's illegitimate child, have been too much for him?

We were about to find out.

CHAPTER 12

$\mathcal{U}$nfortunately no one was home in the Lindsey household. The only response to our loud knocking came from the neighboring flat. A woman wearing a loose ruby plush tea gown opened the door and glared at us. She couldn't have been more than thirty and was quite beautiful. She looked a little familiar, but I couldn't place her.

"Pipe down out there! Some of us need our rest!" She looked as though she was going to continue with her tirade, but she stopped upon seeing Harry. She put a hand to the doorframe and nibbled on her lower lip. It was a seductive gesture, not a nervous one. Practiced, too.

"We're sorry to disturb you, madam," Harry said.

"It's Miss Adelaide Draythorne." She swept her silky black hair forward over her shoulder. It tumbled down in waves, almost to her waist. "You may have heard of me."

"Indeed, I have. You're a singer, I believe."

I'd heard of her too, and I'd seen her face on some posters in the theater district. I didn't think she was one of the more popular singers, but she must be if she could afford to rent a flat in this building. She hadn't looked at me once, so I stayed back while Harry approached her. I could still make out what she said and see the heated gaze she passed over him. She didn't try to hide it.

"We're private detectives consulting for Scotland Yard," Harry said.

"You're investigating Mrs. Lindsey's murder? Nasty business. Poor woman didn't deserve to die like that, no matter how much everyone disliked her."

"Why was she disliked?"

"She was selfish. She only ever spoke about *her* life. She couldn't even bring herself to ask how my day had been when we passed in the corridor. It was always about *her*, who she knew, who wore her dresses, that sort of thing. I've met more famous people, yet she had no interest in hearing anyone's stories but her own."

"You said everyone disliked her. Are you referring to anyone else in particular?"

"Everyone in the building avoided her. Her and her son." She pulled a face. "Revolting creature, just as selfish as his mother. The husband was all right, though. I don't know how he put up with them."

"Did they argue?" Harry asked.

"The son argued with his mother whenever he visited on holidays, and then when he moved in permanently after he finished school. Honestly, that boy is a turd. The way he looks at me..." She shuddered. "It's unnerving."

"What did he argue about with his mother?"

"It was always about money. He wanted more, and she wouldn't give him any. It's obvious who held the purse strings in that family. The son never asked his father, only his mother. And she always refused, from what I can gather. She told him he had to work for it, like she had done all her life. She called him lazy and pathetic. He called her ridiculous and cruel."

"Did Mr. Lindsey ever argue with his wife?"

"Not that I heard. He was always polite to me and seemed to treat her respectfully. I never even heard him raise his voice to that moronic son. The only time I've heard him speak harshly to anyone was yesterday."

"He argued with Gerald?"

"No. A woman. Tall, dark hair, dressed rather plain. I didn't hear everything, but I got the impression it was related to Maison de Poitiers. She was saying something about Madame promising them, and he kept telling her his wife wouldn't make such a promise and he couldn't do anything without proof. He became quite hot under the collar. When I came out to tell them to be quiet, he apologized and made up an excuse that the woman was from the shop and came to tell him the assistant hadn't shown up. Bald-faced lie, if you ask me."

"Thank you, Miss Draythorne. I appreciate your candor."

She adjusted the tea gown at her shoulder, causing it to slip down a little and reveal bare skin. "Would you like a ticket to my performance tonight? It's sold out but I can get you in."

"Thank you, but I have plans tonight."

Her face tightened. She probably wasn't used to rejection. She watched him walk away then, for the first time, her gaze met mine. I smiled. She wrinkled her nose and disappeared inside, closing the door firmly.

"You must have interesting plans tonight if you turned down free tickets to a sold-out production," I said when Harry rejoined me.

"It was only for one ticket, and I don't enjoy going to the theater on my own. Besides, I didn't think her benefactor would appreciate another man sitting in his seat."

"You shouldn't assume that every singer, dancer or actress becomes a gentleman's mistress, Harry."

"I don't. I used my powers of deduction. The rent here must be high. She can't afford to live in that flat without someone else paying for it. There is also a large portrait hanging on the wall near the door depicting Miss Draythorne leaning against an older man. Before you try to tell me he could be her father, I should point out that her gown in the picture was low-cut and she had a seductive expression that she focused entirely on him."

"I believe you. A portrait like that could only be commissioned by a lover."

We were about to leave the building when Mr. Lindsey and Gerald arrived. The father looked harried. The son bore the same sneering expression as last time.

"We told you that you no longer work for us," he said.

Mr. Lindsey put up his hands, placating. "It's all right, Gerald. Would you like to come in?" He unlocked the door and led us inside to the sitting room. The flat was cool. No one had been there all morning. He invited us to sit. "Gerald, will you make some tea?"

Gerald had just sat on one of the chairs. "You do it. They're here because *you* employed him to spy on Mother."

Mr. Lindsey sighed.

"We don't want tea," I assured him. "We won't be long. We just have a few questions that need clarifying." I paused, letting that sink in. "We heard Miss Newland didn't show up at the shop yesterday."

This produced another sigh from Mr. Lindsey. "I had to go in and serve customers myself, with the aid of one of the seamstresses. I didn't know what I was doing. We've just come from there again today, where the girl seems to be muddling through well enough on her own. We would just have got in the way if we stayed."

"Miss Newland hasn't returned?"

"No."

"Typical," Gerald spat. "You can't trust hirelings."

"She left no word?" I asked. "No indication that she found employment elsewhere?"

"None," Mr. Lindsey said.

"Are you worried about her?"

"Should I be?" Mr. Lindsey's eyes widened. "Is she in danger?"

I quickly assured him that she was not. Going by his deepening frown, I didn't quite convince him.

I glanced at Harry, not sure how to ask my next question delicately. I liked Mr. Lindsey. I felt sorry for him and didn't want to add to his burdens. But it was a question that needed asking.

Fortunately, Harry came to the rescue and took over. "Mr. Lindsey, we've discovered some rather shocking news about your wife's past that we feel you ought to know."

Mr. Lindsey sat forward.

"Your wife had a child before she met you."

Mr. Lindsey's mouth dropped open. He stared at Harry, unblinking.

Even Gerald now took an interest in our conversation. He scoffed. "Don't be absurd. It's a lie, Father. Don't believe them."

Harry ignored him. "She had a daughter who is now twenty-five. It's Miss Newland."

"The assistant?" Gerald blurted out. "Now I know you're lying. Mother is hardly going to hire her own bastard. Tell them, Father."

But Mr. Lindsey just continued to stare at Harry.

"She didn't hire her knowing she was her daughter," Harry went on. "It's more likely Miss Newland applied for the position knowing your wife was her mother. We won't know for certain until we speak to her."

Mr. Lindsey lifted a trembling hand to his mouth. He'd gone pale. "Why didn't she tell me?"

"Perhaps she was ashamed," I said gently. "Or perhaps she knew it would hurt you."

He gave a small nod.

"That's not all," Harry said. "We have reason to believe that your wife was about to change her will but died before she could speak to her lawyer."

This information seemed to intrigue Gerald more than learning he had an older half-sister. "Change it to what?"

"We don't know. All we know is that Mr. Lindsey benefits under the terms of the current will, which has been in place for some time."

Gerald turned to his father. "She must have decided to change it when she learned you were going to divorce her." He wasn't as idiotic as he seemed. "She would have made *me* the beneficiary. There's no one else she would leave it all to."

"Miss Newland?" I offered, just to see what effect it would have.

Both men glanced at me. Mr. Lindsey looked somewhat lost, like a boy in the woods who couldn't find his way out. Gerald, however, looked like a hungry wolf lurking in the shadows.

"Give everything to a girl she gave up and never knew?" Gerald snorted. "Mother wouldn't. She'd have given it to me. That means I can't be a suspect in her murder. I wouldn't kill her *before* she changed her will to benefit me."

It was interesting that he'd concluded that, considering no one had accused him of her murder.

"It doesn't mean that at all," Harry said. "You didn't know

your mother was about to change her will. It's possible you thought the best way to get money was to kill her, let your father inherit, and ask him to increase your allowance. I suspect he would have been easier to get money out of than your mother. We know you argued with her many times about your financial situation."

"Is that what that whore told you?" Gerald jerked his head in the general direction of Miss Draythorne's flat.

"Gerald," his father scolded, without heat. "That's unkind."

Gerald was so absorbed with himself, he didn't realize he'd just implied that his father should be a suspect. By saying that he, Gerald, wasn't a suspect because Gertrude hadn't changed her will before she died, he'd pointed the finger at his father for that very same reason.

But a man about to divorce his wife would know that he wouldn't be her beneficiary for much longer. He would have already come to terms with never inheriting. On the other hand, if Gertrude also told her husband that she was changing her will to favor her illegitimate daughter, the blow could have sent him over the edge.

While I couldn't imagine the mild Mr. Lindsey strangling his wife in anger, Miss Draythorne had told us that he did have a temper. He'd argued with one of the seamstresses yesterday. From the description Miss Draythorne gave, it was Elizabeth Keane.

"It's true that my mother and I rarely saw eye to eye about anything," Gerald muttered. "But I didn't kill her."

"No one is accusing you," Harry said.

Gerald crossed his arms and sank further into the chair. "Good. Anyway, I was asleep when she was murdered."

Indeed he was, according to his father. But parents lied to protect their children. What if Gerald wasn't in bed at eight, when Mr. Lindsey left the flat? What if he rose earlier and went to the shop to kill his mother?

I turned to his father. "You argued with Miss Keane, the seamstress who came to tell you that Miss Newland hadn't shown up at the shop yesterday. What was the argument about?"

Mr. Lindsey didn't look surprised by my question. He

must have suspected it would be asked when he realized we'd spoken to Miss Draythorne. "Miss Keane claimed my wife promised the staff a share in the business. She wanted to know if I'd honor the arrangement. I explained to her that I know nothing of such an arrangement and Gertie's accountant hasn't mentioned anything to me either. Without proof, what can I do?"

"Miss Keane wouldn't accept that?"

"The exchange became heated, as you know. She refused to listen. She became highly agitated, hysterical. I'm a little embarrassed to admit that I raised my voice, but she wouldn't listen otherwise."

Gerald sniffed. "*She* should be a suspect. All of the staff. Greedy, that's what they are. They should be grateful they've got employment at all."

We all ignored him.

"Did she say when this arrangement was due to start?" Harry asked. "Or what it entailed?"

"She just said my wife had promised to set up an arrangement whereby they received a percentage of the profits in addition to their wages. It was an incentive to keep them working for her and working hard. If you ask me, it was an empty promise. Gertie was like that...offering something with one hand and taking it back with the other."

"She liked to use promises to get people to do what she wanted," Gerald muttered. "Especially promises of money."

Father and son exchanged a knowing, almost sympathetic look. "The lack of paperwork about this so-called arrangement is proof that Gertie wasn't going to go through with it," Mr. Lindsey said.

If the staff suspected it was an empty promise too, they would be upset. Perhaps upset enough to kill.

* * *

THE CLOSED SIGN in the window of Maison de Poitiers was upside down. We headed to the lane that led to the workroom and almost bumped into a gentleman emerging from the courtyard behind the shop. He tipped his hat to Harry and me and, with an apologetic smile, stepped aside to allow us past.

We found the seven seamstresses eating sandwiches and chatting quietly. Miss Keane was the only one to stand upon our entry. She wore a simple black dress and had dispensed with the apron. She must be working in the shop.

I asked how she was coping without Miss Newland.

"We're managing," she said. "It hasn't been easy learning where things are, how things are done."

"And the toff accent," one of the other women added with a laugh.

"I'm mostly answering questions about whether orders will be ready on time. How did you know about Miss Newland?"

"We've just come from the Lindseys' flat," Harry said. "Mr. Lindsey told us she didn't show up to work yesterday."

"She didn't even say goodbye."

"It's like she vanished into thin air," the youngest girl said with a little shiver.

The seamstresses exchanged grim glances. All except Miss Keane and Mrs. Zieliński.

"What do you think happened to her?" I asked.

There was a round of shrugs.

"Maybe she decided there was nothing for her here now that Madame is gone," Miss Keane said. "Maybe she got an offer to work somewhere better and took it."

"Does she seem like the sort to leave without as much as a note?"

Again, all except Miss Keane and Mrs. Zieliński exchanged glances.

"When you say there was nothing for her here anymore," I went on, "do you mean because her mother died?"

"Mother?" Mrs. Zieliński echoed.

"Miss Newland was Gertrude Lindsey's daughter, born out of wedlock twenty-five years ago."

The seamstresses gasped. They all looked shocked, even Mrs. Zieliński, the eldest employee who must have known the most about Gertrude's past. I was quite sure she didn't know her illegitimate child had come to work here.

Even so, I needed to confirm. "Did any of you know she had a daughter?"

They all shook their heads.

"Poor girl," Mrs. Zieliński murmured. "To lose her mother like that just as she was getting to know her."

"How do you know they hadn't been in touch for some time?"

"Miss Newland has not worked here long," she said.

"They could have been aware of one another's existence for some time before she came to work in the shop. They could have reconnected years ago."

"That is true, but..." She let the sentence dangle unfinished. Like us, she was sure Gertrude hadn't known Miss Newland was her daughter.

Harry took up the questioning. "You've now all met Mr. Lindsey and his son, Gerald. What do you think of them?"

This time they did not exchange glances. Nor did they meet our gazes. They studied the floor, their feet, their sandwiches...anywhere but us or each other. All except Miss Keane. She didn't hesitate to answer.

"The son is a cabbage-head, fop and a scoundrel. He was rude to us from the moment he walked in. The husband is a weakling. He was too scared of the son to tell him to shut it."

Scared. That was an odd choice of word.

"If you ask me, that boy should have been put over his father's knee and given a good thrashing," one of the other seamstresses said.

Harry leaned a hip against a workbench, his stance casual, unthreatening. His tone turned gossipy. "A witness says Gerald fought with his mother often, usually over money. Apparently she held on tightly to the family's purse strings."

One of the young seamstresses grunted an agreement. The woman beside her nudged her with her elbow. The girl bowed her head and clutched her hands together until the knuckles turned white.

Miss Keane cleared her throat. "Do you have a specific question for us? Because if not, we'd like to continue with our lunch before we have to return to work."

"It's good of Madame Poitiers to allow you time for

lunch," I said, knowing few employers in the clothing business were so accommodating.

Miss Keane's thin smile was as unnerving as it was telling. "She allowed it, but if we took breaks, we didn't get paid for that time. But she's not here, is she? Nor is Miss Newland, Mr. Lindsey or that idiotic son. We are in charge today. We decide how many hours we work now."

It was a sentiment to make an unfair employer quake in his polished shoes. Employees working in trade, particularly women, had few rights. Unless they were fortunate enough to work for an enlightened employer, they were poorly paid and poorly treated. Seamstresses were the lowest of the low.

Since Harry looked as though he wanted to act the friendly one, I took on the role of asking the hard questions. "What is the profit sharing scheme Madame Poitiers promised you?"

Anyone who hadn't been looking at me, suddenly turned sharply in my direction. The young girl bit hard on her lower lip. Mrs. Zieliński looked anxiously at Miss Keane.

And Miss Keane studied me. She was trying to get my measure, perhaps deciding if she should tell the truth or not. After several seconds, she finally answered. "Madame promised each of us shares in the business in return for our loyalty. She said she was reinvesting our share of the shop's profit and when she sold the business, we would get a portion of the sale. The only condition was that we still had to be working here when she sold it."

"That sounds like a good scheme, but it seems to me that it requires a great deal of trust. If she never showed you any paperwork, you had to believe she was being honest with you."

Miss Keane sniffed. "I never believed her. It was too good to be true."

Mrs. Zieliński arched both her brows.

"Yet you were the one who went to Mr. Lindsey and asked him if he would honor his wife's promise," I said. "You argued with him when he refused."

Her jaw firmed.

"Did anyone ask Madame about the scheme when she

179

was alive?" I pressed. "Did anyone ask for paperwork or proof?"

"No," Miss Keane said.

"So you just trusted her."

She merely shrugged.

"You trusted a woman who has a habit of spinning grand tales to impress clients, whom most of you suspected was lying about her nationality and her name? Forgive me, Miss Keane, but I find it hard to believe that no one asked her for an assurance in writing. You strike me as an intelligent, practical woman, and yet you never asked Madame for a contract?"

"I wouldn't be able to understand a contract and I can't afford a lawyer."

"Still—"

"I never confronted her! None of us did."

I let the matter drop. I wouldn't get an answer from her and the other women were once again avoiding my gaze. We might have better luck asking them all individually, but that could wait for a time when they were alone and not under Miss Keane's watchful eye.

Mrs. Zieliński returned her half-eaten sandwich to the basket near her feet. "We should return to work now. There is much to do. Your dresses will not make themselves, Miss Fox." She attempted a smile, but it fell flat.

Miss Keane pushed off and strode for the door leading to the shop. It slammed shut behind her.

I led the way outside, Harry following. Once we were out of earshot, he said, "It seems no one liked Gertrude. Behind her ridiculous façade, she was miserly and mean to her staff, husband and even her own child."

"Is it awful of me to say that I can see why Mr. Lindsey wanted to divorce her?"

"Now that I know him better, and her too, I'm surprised he had the gumption. He's not the bravest of men."

"His patience must have run out," I said. "Perhaps he lied and he *did* find out about Anna Newland. Perhaps *that* encouraged him to divorce his wife."

Harry agreed that it was a possibility. "The staff could have run out of patience too. I can't believe that no one confronted Gertrude about the profit-sharing scheme and demanded proof that she'd set it up."

"The others I can imagine not confronting her, but Miss Keane is no fool. She wouldn't let anyone take advantage of her. She could have stolen Mrs. Zieliński's key, had a copy made then used it to unlock the workshop door on Friday morning before the others arrived, knowing Gertrude had an early appointment with Lady Bunbury."

Harry took up the rest of the story. "When she confronted Gertrude and Gertrude refused to give her any paperwork, Miss Keane became angry. She strangled her with the closest thing at hand."

It was a gruesome summary, and one I could imagine transpiring precisely as he described. Miss Keane was a leader of those women. She would feel responsible for them, perhaps even friendship towards them. Gertrude's betrayal was a betrayal of them all, not just Miss Keane. She would feel it was up to her try to set things right.

"We need to find out where Miss Keane was at the time of the murder," I said.

"My father will have her statement and know where she lives."

We took a hansom to Scotland Yard and found Detective Inspector Hobart in conversation with two sergeants in his office. When he finished, he signaled for us to enter.

"I've just received a report that Mr. Durant checked out of his hotel yesterday," he said. "And Miss Newland did not go back to her parents' house. They're very worried."

We told him about the profit-sharing scheme that Gertrude had promised her staff to ensure their loyalty, and how there was no evidence of it being implemented. "It's possible one of the staff members suspected she was lying, confronted her and killed her," Harry said. "Miss Keane seems to have a leadership role among the seamstresses. They look up to her. Her opinion guides them."

D.I. Hobart nodded slowly. "Money is always the most common motive for murder, in my experience. So you want to know where Miss Keane claims she was early on Friday morning?" He was already reaching for the file before he finished speaking. He flipped through the witness statements until he reached Miss Keane's. He scanned it then set it on the table between us.

Harry and I bent forward to read. According to her statement, Miss Keane had left the boarding house where she lived at seven. She walked to work, arriving at eight.

"That's a slow walk," Harry said, pointing to the home address. "It shouldn't take her more than thirty minutes to get to New Bond Street from Farringdon on foot."

"I asked her about that. She insisted she was merely ambling, enjoying her morning walk." D.I. Hobart took back the file. "I interviewed some of the other girls at the boarding house where she lives and they confirm she left at seven that morning."

"So if we assume the pleasantly slow walk is a lie, where was she for that extra half hour?" I asked. "Did she arrive much earlier, kill Gertrude, leave, then return at eight to make it look like she'd just got there?"

"Did she have a particular friend at the boarding house?" Harry asked. "Anyone she might confide in?"

"The other residents were a little in awe of her, but the landlady seemed to know her best," D.I. Hobart said. "She was wary when I asked about Miss Keane's movements."

"May I speak to her?" I asked. "She might be more forthcoming with another woman."

"Please, be my guest."

"We'll go there now," Harry said, rising.

"Not we," I said. "Just me. I want to play the friendly detective who believes Miss Keane is innocent, if only she can prove it. Woman to woman."

He tapped his finger on the back of the chair. "Very well. I'll wait nearby. Collect me when you leave."

"You don't like missing out, do you?" I asked as we walked along the corridor.

"Not for a moment."

CHAPTER 13

*B*oarding houses provided safe accommodation for young women of good character who worked in respectable employment in the city. Girls needed references and proof they were employed. Strict rules had to be followed, such as curfews and the sort of visitors allowed.

All of the residents were at work but the live-in house-keeper was there. Mrs. Farley couldn't have been more than late thirties or early forties, with only a sprinkle of gray through her hair and few lines on her face. She told me there was no Mr. Farley, but didn't elaborate. He could have died, left her, or never existed in the first place. It wasn't unheard of for women to pretend they were married in order to avoid being labeled a spinster.

Like Miss Keane, Mrs. Farley knew her own mind and was unafraid to speak it. She thought most of the girls who lived under her roof were silly, but she had high praise for Miss Keane.

"She's a hard worker, smart too. If she had half the advantages of some, she'd have made something of herself." By the way she looked at me, I was the "some" she was referring to.

"It's not fair that people like Miss Keane are the first to be suspected of criminal activity by the police," I said in an attempt to befriend her.

She adjusted her shawl to cover the back of her neck. It was cool in the parlor, with no fire in the grate. Delicious scents from the kitchen wafted through the house. It would be some sort of stew for dinner, if my sense of smell was correct. The parlor itself had probably once been quite grand. The large house would have housed a well-to-do family many years ago, but had been divided up. This half was a boarding house, but the other half seemed to be rooms rented out individually. Mrs. Farley was an employee of the landlord, not the owner of the building. She supervised the residents, and she cooked and cleaned for them. She was effectively their mother and housekeeper.

"The police think she killed her employer?" she asked, a hint of alarm in her voice.

"That's the indication I've been given, although as a consultant, I'm not privy to every conversation."

She adjusted her shawl again. "She's not a murderer. She comes across as a hard one, but she's got a good heart. She looks out for the other girls. She advises them and helps if she can, writing letters to parents, potential employers, that sort of thing." She suddenly reached out and grasped my forearm. "You must help her, Miss Fox."

"I will do my very best, but you have to help me help her. According to the detective assigned to the case, Miss Keane claims to have left here at seven, but she didn't arrive at the shop until eight. It's not an hour's walk from here to there, but she claims she went directly to work. If we can't prove she went elsewhere before reaching the shop then..." I let her imagination fill in the rest of the sentence.

Fortunately her imagination pictured precisely what I wanted. After a nibble of her lower lip and a deep breath, she gave in. "I can't let anything bad happen to her. I just can't. The reason she told the police it took her an hour to get to work is because they wouldn't approve. They're men. They think all unwed women should be angels."

"Was Miss Keane with a gentleman?"

"He's not a gentleman, but he's not a bad sort." She adjusted her shawl again. "She regularly meets him here. She pretends to leave for work at seven so the other girls don't know. They all witness her going off. But she comes back and waits for him at the back door. They then go and use the spare room. She has a key."

"Given to her by you."

She nodded. "They're not doing anything wrong! They're in love."

"I agree there's nothing wrong with what they're doing." She seemed to relax a little now that she knew I wasn't judging Miss Keane's behavior. "Did you actually see her double back that morning?"

She chewed her lip again. "No."

"So the last time you saw her was at seven?"

She bristled. "I'm sure she came back here with Paul like she planned. She wouldn't lie to me."

I smiled. "Well, if you're sure then I believe you. You know her best."

Her spine loosened. "That's right. I do."

"What about before seven? Could she have left the house without anyone knowing and returned before seven?"

"No. It's not possible. There are four girls in her room, and a couple are light sleepers. She'd wake them up, for certain."

"Who is the man she was with?"

"His name's Paul Green." She glanced at the wall mounted clock. "He'll be at work now. He's a tunneler for one of the railway companies, working on a new underground line. He's based at the Piccadilly Circus site."

I thanked her and took this information to Harry, waiting around the corner. He tucked the newspaper he'd been reading under his arm and asked me how the interview went.

"We need a cab," I said.

He indicated a hansom waiting up ahead and we hurried towards it. He didn't ask me why we were heading to Piccadilly Circus until after I'd given the driver instructions and we'd set off.

"Miss Keane could have been in the spare room with her lover, Paul Green," I said. "Or she could have left the boarding house at seven. Mrs. Farley insists Miss Keane was with Paul but didn't actually see her after seven."

"And what is Paul Green doing at Piccadilly Circus?"

"He's working as a tunneler for a railway company constructing a new underground line."

"That will be the Baker Street and Waterloo Railway," he said. "Some are calling it the Bakerloo line. There'll be a station at Piccadilly Circus. It's quite an engineering feat. One of the engineers who designed the Forth Bridge is overseeing the project. Brilliant man." He joined his two pointer fingers together, end to end. "There'll be two tunnels, and construction on one began last year." He wiggled one of his fingers. "The other has just begun this month." He wiggled the other. "If Paul Green is based at Piccadilly Circus, that's the one he's working on."

Harry once told me that if he'd received a proper education, he'd liked to have been an engineer. It was a shame that one's situation and birth dictated one's life. It wouldn't have been easy for him to chart a course to university as the son of a teacher and an absent father, but it wasn't unheard of. An excellent pupil can forge the path of his choice these days—as long as he was male and finished his education. But Harry's mother's death had altered the course of his life. It had taken away the opportunity she'd tried to give him.

"Did you know they're tunneling under the Thames for this project?" he asked.

"Considering Waterloo Station is on the other side of the river to Baker Street station, I had guessed."

He lowered his hands to his lap. "I'm boring you."

"Not at all! Do continue. I don't find engineering quite as fascinating as you do, but it is interesting."

By the time we reached Piccadilly Circus, I'd learned all about tunneling shields, compressed air, and cast iron tunnel linings. He continued on, but I tuned out sometime around Bloomsbury.

I knew there were plans to construct a station at Piccadilly Circus to service an underground railway line, but had not thought much about it. With work just beginning on this part of the Bakerloo line, the disruption above ground was minimal and discreet. The station was some time away from being built, however the tunneling had begun.

We were not allowed onto the site so waited for the workers' shift to end. Harry and I did not stand together in case someone from the hotel came by and recognized us. He didn't want my family seeing me with him. The hotel was a short walk away, but I didn't see anyone I knew amongst the throng of pedestrians. The Circus was as busy as always with

pedestrians and vehicles of all types navigating the inter-
section.

I almost bought a mutton pie from a vendor pushing his
cart, but out of the corner of my eye, I caught sight of Harry
shaking his head at me. He nodded at another pie man
further along. Harry had lived and worked in this area for
years. If anyone knew which pie man to avoid and which to
give custom to, it was him. I waited for the good pie man. His
beef pie was excellent.

The afternoon dragged on. Despite the constant stream of
pedestrians and traffic, I grew bored. I wondered why it was
called a circus when it wasn't really circular. I marveled at the
central fountain topped by a winged statue, and I browsed
shop windows. I struck up a conversation with a woman
selling old buttons that she'd probably retrieved from gutters.
I bought several from her. None matched.

Sometimes, I looked around to see what Harry was doing.
He got his shoes shined. He bought a newspaper and a sandwich—not at the same time—and wandered back and forth,
his hands at his back like a policeman on patrol.

Finally the workmen began to emerge from the site. It was
obvious they were tunnelers from the way they blinked in the
light, even though the late afternoon sun was sinking behind
the buildings. They carried drinking canteens and tins with
handles. These men didn't have the luxury of coming up to
the surface to buy pies and sandwiches. They had to remain
underground for the entirety of their shift, dining out on
whatever they'd brought with them.

Harry asked one man after another for Paul Green until
the man himself overheard. He sauntered over, his steps
unhurried. He was a giant, as tall as Harry but thicker with a
square face and brown hair. He was covered in dirt from head
to toe.

He studied Harry with a suspicious narrowing of his gaze
which narrowed further when I joined them. Harry introduced us as private detectives consulting for the police.

Mr. Green did not ask what we wanted. He looked unsur-
prised that he was being questioned. He was expecting it.

"Do you know a woman named Elizabeth Keane?" Harry
asked.

"Aye. She's my girl." Despite being clearly Cockney, I detected a faint foreign twang to his accent.

"Did you see her last Friday morning?"

He folded his arms over his chest and thrust out his jaw. "I don't remember."

Perhaps the boredom of waiting all afternoon got to me, but I was in no mood to be strung along. "Forgive my bluntness, Mr. Green, but we are investigating a murder in which Miss Keane is a suspect. So forget propriety and answer the question. Were you or were you not with Miss Keane on Friday morning?"

He lowered his arms and some of the frostiness left his eyes. "Aye. We met at seven. Mrs. Farley lets us...talk in a spare room. Mornings are the only time we see each other. Most days we both work late." He nodded at the receding backs of his colleagues. "This is a short day for me. There's a problem down below with the machinery. The engineers sent us home early. Bloody useless," he spat.

I wondered why he was so annoyed, but then I realized he wouldn't get paid if he didn't work. Every hour down there meant more money in his pocket.

"Don't tell Betty I told you we were..."

"Talking in the spare room?"

He gave me a sardonic smirk and dipped his head somewhat shyly. "She'd be embarrassed. She's a good girl."

"What time did you leave the boarding house?"

"About seven-thirty or so. We left together and caught a bus. I got off here. She kept going to New Bond Street."

"Thank you for your time, Mr. Green." I stepped aside to let him pass. "If I were you, I wouldn't call Miss Keane a girl to her face."

"Why not?"

Harry huffed a laugh. "When a woman gives you advice about women, just listen and don't question."

Mr. Green tugged on the brim of his cap in farewell and sauntered on his way, his steps once again unhurried.

"What do you think?" Harry asked.

"I think we achieved nothing today," I said on a sigh. "If it wasn't for that excellent beef pie, I would consider the afternoon a complete waste of time."

"Don't ever buy a pie from one of the other sellers around here. Trust me on that. I learned the hard way. So you think Paul Green was telling the truth?"

"I don't know."

We agreed to meet up the following morning. He would apprise his father of the developments, such as they were, which I assumed meant he was dining at his parents' house again.

I returned to the hotel, only to find everyone had been looking for me. Everyone, that is, *except* my uncle. Thank goodness for that.

Apparently Uncle Ronald had been out all day and wasn't yet aware of the crisis that had unfolded inside his own suite on the fourth floor. I knew something was up the moment I saw Frank. He didn't grumble. My apprehension grew worse when Peter, Mr. Hobart and Goliath all swooped on me when I entered the foyer.

"It's Lady Bainbridge and Miss Bainbridge," Mr. Hobart said with an anxious glance at the lift. "They're both in a state."

"Is my aunt unwell?"

He quickly assured me her health was fine. "But she is upset."

"Miss Bainbridge is worse," Goliath said. "I heard her wailing clear through the door. She said her life was over."

Mr. Hobart glared at him. "Thank you, Goliath. Get back to work, please. This doesn't concern you."

"What happened?" I asked, not waiting for Goliath to walk off.

"Invitations for the Bunbury Ball were issued today. All of Lady Bainbridge and Miss Bainbridge's friends have received one. They did not."

My heart sank. I should have expected this. I should have known Lady Bunbury would punish me. Her snub was all my fault.

Feeling somewhat drained after a long and trying day, I took the lift instead of the stairs up to the fourth floor. John the operator seemed to know that I didn't want to talk and remained silent for the journey.

I was about to knock on my aunt's door when Floyd emerged from his own suite further along the corridor.

"Don't, Cleo!" he whispered loudly. "Mother and Flossy are upset about a ball they didn't get invited to. Don't go in if you value your sanity."

"Thank you for the warning, but I'll risk it."

"Suit yourself."

The door to my aunt's suite suddenly opened. Flossy stood there, all red-rimmed eyes and puffy nose. "I thought I heard your voice, Cleo. Oh, it's awful. Just awful. Come inside and sit with us. We could do with the company. You too, Floyd. Mother needs us."

A look of alarm came over him. "I have to go." He hurried off towards the stairs.

I allowed Flossy to drag me inside to the bedroom where Aunt Lilian sat propped up against pillows. The hollows below her eyes were tinged red, but it wasn't a result of crying. She looked fragile in the large bed, and so pale that she was almost luminous. She patted the space beside her, but even that small movement made her wince with pain.

I sat and gently took her bone-thin hand in mine. "Can I get you anything, Aunt?"

She did not look at the table beside her bed where she kept her tonic in a drawer, but we both knew she wanted it. "Thank you, Cleo, but I'm all right. I have my two girls with me."

Flossy sat next to me, making the mattress bounce. Her mother winced again. "Cleo, something terrible has happened. It's a nightmare. A disaster!"

Aunt Lilian sucked in air between her teeth. "Florence, do lower your voice. My head…"

"Sorry," Flossy mumbled.

"I heard that you didn't get invited to the Bunburys' ball," I said. "But perhaps the invitations will come tomorrow. The post may have been delayed."

"They were hand delivered by the Bunburys' servants to everyone currently in London," Flossy said. That was quite a feat considering they had few servants to spare. "Even some of our guests received invitations today. But not us." Her face crumpled but she managed not to burst into tears. "My life is over! I'll never find a husband now."

"I'm so sorry," I said. "This is my fault."

"Nonsense," Aunt Lilian said. "If it's anyone's fault, it's mine. She must have noticed me staring at her brooch during afternoon tea and suspected that I knew it was a fake. I should have hid my curiosity better."

I couldn't let her blame herself. "It's not that. After I spoke to her jeweler I went to her house to speak to the servants. I wanted to know more about Lord Bunbury's movements on the morning of the murder. I'm afraid Lady Bunbury saw me leaving. I am at fault, not you. I'm sorry."

Flossy's face crumpled again and this time tears did flow. She didn't get angry with me. She didn't shout or blame me. I wish she had. I would have felt better being the object of her anger rather than this silent admonishment.

Aunt Lilian patted my hand. "No, Cleo. I won't let you accept all the blame. If Lady Bunbury wishes to be this petty, then so be it. We will manage."

"How?" Flossy exploded. "How will we manage, Mother? The Bunburys' ball is the gateway to the *entire* season. Without an invitation, we won't be invited *anywhere*."

Aunt Lilian closed her eyes. The muscles in her face tightened as she held herself rigid.

"I'll speak to her," I told Flossy. "I'll apologize and beg her to send invitations to you. She should punish me, not you."

Flossy flung her arms around me and sobbed into my shoulder.

Aunt Lilian signaled at me to take my cousin out then pressed her fingers to her temples. She had a splitting headache and Flossy wasn't helping.

I steered Flossy out of her parents' suite and took her to her own, where I spent the remainder of the afternoon and the evening keeping her company. By the time I left and returned to my own room, I wanted to cry myself. Not because I was upset at not being invited but from sheer exhaustion. Flossy was convinced she would die an old spinster because of one snub in one season. Trying to tell her otherwise was an exercise in futility. It was a relief when she finally fell asleep.

* * *

I was about to leave my suite the following morning when a footman delivered an urgent message from Mr. Hobart to meet him in his office. I raced downstairs only to slow when I saw my aunt and uncle in the foyer. They appeared to be having a terse discussion, but were trying not to show it. They did not see me as I slipped past and approached the post desk. I didn't want to go to Mr. Hobart's office in case they saw me.

The lift arrived on the ground floor and the door opened. My uncle and aunt broke apart. Uncle Ronald took the lift while Aunt Lilian crossed the floor to the front door. Her step was determined yet graceful, her manner cheerful as she greeted the staff. She wore a sage green dress trimmed with cream lace and a matching velvet jacket that accentuated her slim waist but padded her form in other areas to disguise her thinness. From this distance, she looked magnificent.

Once she was gone, I made my way to Mr. Hobart's office. He looked up from his paperwork and smiled.

"Ah, there you are. My brother telephoned and asked for you and Harry to meet him at Scotland Yard."

There must have been a development overnight. I thanked him and hurried outside. I would have gone to Harry's office except he was standing on the pavement, waiting for me.

"I hoped you wouldn't be long," he said. "I've been thinking overnight and have a plan for today. We should dig further into Gertrude's past. Have you received any word from the French fashion houses?"

"Not yet." I signaled for him to follow me back to the hotel where it would be easier to catch one of the hansoms that were constantly coming and going. "Your father telephoned. He wants us to meet him."

We met D.I. Hobart in his office a short while later. He looked rather smug as he rose from his chair. "Don't sit down. Follow me."

"Where are we going?" Harry asked.

"The holding cells. Mr. Durant and Miss Newland were caught attempting to leave the country last night. I thought you might like to interview them with me."

This was an unexpected privilege. It was probably highly irregular, but neither Harry nor I questioned D.I. Hobart. His seniority within the police force afforded him the luxury to bend the rules on occasion. Besides, no one particularly cared how answers were gained from suspects. As long as answers were forthcoming, the methods employed to get them were of no consequence to those in charge.

The holding cells were downstairs in the basement. It was chilly, and I was glad I'd worn my coat. We passed door after door until finally stopping at the one that held Mr. Durant. The sergeant on duty unlocked it using one of many keys attached to an iron ring.

The Frenchman sat in the tiny cell on the hard bench that was the only furniture. His head was lowered between his shoulders, and his elbows rested on his knees. His hands clasped loosely in front of him, the fingertips drumming against each other. He only looked up when the inspector greeted him.

"I have nothing to say," he said before we could ask a question. "Go away."

"Were you protecting your daughter?" D.I. Hobart asked.

Mr. Durant's lips thinned. He lowered his head again.

We left. I got the impression the inspector had tried getting answers from him already and had been met with the same response. He'd given up easily. The eager look on his face as the warden opened the next cell door was a clear indication he thought answers would come from Miss Newland, not her father.

She looked terrified. Upon seeing me, she leapt up. "Miss Fox! Please, help—" She cried out and turned her face away as the warden lifted his truncheon.

Harry caught his arm. "There's no need for that."

"Leave us," D.I. Hobart said. The warden left, closing the door behind him.

I put my arm around Miss Newland and steered her to the bench. Her cell was the same as Durant's. Bare, cold and windowless. It was no wonder she trembled. She had a similar hopeless look in her eyes as Flossy had last night. They were red from crying too, and she looked on the verge of tears again.

Harry removed his coat and placed it around her shoulders. He crouched before her. "Miss Newland, are you unwell?"

"No." She clutched the coat tightly at her chest and sat as close to me as our skirts would allow. "Can you tell them to let me out? I've done nothing wrong. I didn't kill her. You have to believe me." Her appeal switched from Harry to me and back again. She didn't once glance at the inspector who'd stayed near the door.

Now I knew why he'd invited us to this interview. Miss Newland was terrified. He hoped the presence of civilians, and a woman at that, might calm her enough to get comprehensive answers from her. A frightened witness might say things that weren't true in an attempt to get early release. The reasoning behind the theory was why torture had been banned as an evidence gathering technique in English law centuries ago.

I took Miss Newland's hand in mine. "We can only help you if you help us," I said. "The only way you can be removed from the suspect list is if you have definitive proof you were elsewhere on Friday morning."

A tear slid down her cheek. "I can't prove anything. No one saw me leave the boarding house that day."

"The only other way we can exonerate you is if we find the real murderer. To do that, we need to know what you know. Any little detail might help."

She blinked damp eyelashes. She seemed so young, like the timid girl I'd met during our fittings. After Gertrude's death, she'd grown more confident in her dealings with us, but there was no sign of that woman now. She looked like she just wanted her mother—the woman who'd raised her and loved her, not the one who'd given birth to her and rejected her as recently as last week.

I put my arm around her. "We know Gertrude Lindsey is your birth mother and Emmanuel Durant your father. We also know Gertrude wasn't aware who you were until Durant told her, and then she confronted you at the boarding house where you live. She told you, in no uncertain terms, that she didn't care about you. That must have been a terrible thing to hear."

Her eyes became huge. "It was, but I didn't kill her!"

I gave her shoulders a light squeeze. "You can see how it looks."

Her gaze flicked to D.I. Hobart, standing passively by the door. She gave a small nod of resignation.

"Tell us how you came to know Gertrude Lindsey was your birth mother," I said.

She drew in a shuddery breath and let it out slowly. "I've suspected for years that I was adopted, but my parents only admitted it a few months ago. I was upset that they'd hidden it from me. I moved out of their house and came to London to find out about my real parents. I went to the General Register Office and saw my birth record. It stated that my mother was Gertrude Russell, but it didn't list my father." We already knew this, but I let her talk uninterrupted. "The GRO staff then cross-referenced my birth record with marriage records and found Gertrude married a man named Lindsey. It listed his place of work. He's a teacher. I didn't expect him to still be working at the same school, but he was. I asked discreet questions and learned which one was Mr. Lindsey then followed him from the school to his home. I watched their building for a while, and then one day I saw him leaving with *her*. I followed her, and that's when I found out she worked at Maison de Poitiers. I didn't know that she *was* Madame Poitiers until I pretended to be a lady's maid collecting a dress. I noticed she seemed very busy and was having trouble reading the order book. We struck up a conversation and she told me her assistant had just left and she'd not yet found a replacement. I said I was available and could start immediately. It seemed like a good way to get to know her. My mother." She said the words slowly, as if trying them out. Then she huffed a bitter, humorless laugh.

"So you worked there for a few months but didn't tell her you were her daughter?"

"It never seemed like the right time."

"How did Emmanuel Durant find out you were his daughter before Gertrude?" I asked.

She gave me a wan smile. "It was Madame Poitiers' own fault, actually. Do you recall the magazine cutout she has framed in the shop, Miss Fox?" I nodded. "She talked endlessly about it. At first she told me what she told the customers, that she was merely fortunate that someone like Myrtle Langford wore one of her designs. But after some gentle probing by me—it really didn't take much—she revealed she and Miss Langford had been close. I knew Miss Langford was performing in a production here in London. So I introduced myself to her one day during rehearsals. She thought I was an avid fan and was more than happy to chat about her past. She and Madame Poitiers both like to talk about themselves, it's a wonder they were ever friends at all."

I resisted the urge to look at Harry. Myrtle had told me she'd simply decided to wear a Poitiers design because she liked it, not because she was friends with the designer. She did not admit they'd been close. "Did they have a falling out?" I asked.

"I don't know."

"Did Myrtle Langford know Gertrude when she became pregnant with you?"

She nodded. "They were in the musical troupe together. She told me Emmanuel was most likely my father as he and Madame—Gertrude—were lovers up until Gertrude left the troupe. She didn't know Gertrude was pregnant. She believed the throat disease story."

"Myrtle helped you get in touch with Durant?"

Miss Newland nodded. "She had an address for him in France. I didn't know if he'd still be there after all these years, but my letter reached him. The next thing I knew, he was in London asking to meet with me. We met at a teahouse." She tried not to smile but it won out in the end. "He's a nice man. Kind. Is he all right, do you know?"

"We've just seen him. He's fine."

Harry spoke for the first time. "He's not saying anything. He thinks he's protecting you."

"But he doesn't need to! I didn't do anything."

I squeezed her shoulders again. "After you met him at the teahouse, Durant went to speak to Gertrude at her flat, but she wasn't home. They spoke later, after she returned from the shop."

She shook her head. "He spoke to her *before* we met. He wanted to ask her before he saw me if what I'd said in my letter was true. She wouldn't confirm or deny it, but he said he came away from that meeting convinced I was right."

"So when did you meet him?"

"Two days later, on Thursday during my lunch break. He confronted Gertrude again at the shop after closing."

"Then she called on you at the boarding house."

She lowered her head and nodded.

I glanced at D.I. Hobart to see if he had any questions.

He stepped forward. "When did you see Durant again after the teahouse meeting?"

She thought for a moment. "Not until Monday. He told me Miss Fox and Mr. Armitage had been to see him and were asking questions. He said the police would think I killed Gertrude once they learned about our argument at the boarding house. He told me to go into hiding and leave the country with him. We'd be safe in France."

D.I. Hobart waited, watching her. She began to fidget under the scrutiny, tugging on her cuffs and touching her face. She was thoroughly agitated by the time he made his point. "You've just found the father you never knew but you don't see him for four days? I would have thought you two had a lot to talk about and would want to spend every possible moment in one another's company."

She splayed her hands across her stomach. "It was Monday, I swear to you! Why don't you believe me?" She started to cry.

Harry produced a handkerchief and handed it to her. "Thank you, Miss Newland. You've been very helpful."

She dabbed at her eyes. "Can I go now?"

"Not yet," D.I. Hobart said. "Kindly return Mr. Armitage's coat. I'll have the duty sergeant provide you with a blanket."

She offered both the coat and handkerchief but Harry told her to keep the latter.

D.I. Hobart knocked on the door and the warden unlocked it. We exited. Before the door closed, I looked back at the small woman crying on the hard bench, Harry's handkerchief clutched to her breast. If she was a murderer, she was a remorseful one.

"Do you want to speak to Durant again, sir?" the warden asked.

D.I. Hobart shook his head.

Once we were out of earshot of the warden, I asked him why.

"He won't say anything," he said.

"Have you considered that Durant may not be protecting his daughter?" Harry asked. "After all, he hardly knows her. Why should he care enough to be imprisoned for her?"

"It's possible he's protecting himself," the inspector said, following Harry's thinking. "Perhaps he visited Gertrude at the shop on the Friday morning, the day after Gertrude confronted Anna at the boarding house. He was angry. Angry that she'd upset their daughter. Angry that Gertrude had not informed him that she'd borne his child. Angry that she'd left him all those years ago. I don't know. There is one thing I do know, however."

"What's that?" I asked.

"We need to employ women in the police force."

"Amen."

"You did well in there, Miss Fox. You too, Harry."

"I was a mere bystander," he said.

"She responded to your kindness. The kindness of both of you."

We made our way to the stairs, each of us lost in our own thoughts. When we reached the corridor on the ground level of the building, Harry paused. "We should visit Myrtle Langford and ask her why she lied to you, Cleo."

I agreed. "I think you were right earlier when you said we need to continue to dig into Gertrude's past. This mystery could be linked to something that happened years ago, and Myrtle Langford might be the key to unlocking it."

CHAPTER 14

*D*etective Inspector Hobart was happy for Harry and me to speak to Myrtle alone since I'd already spoken to her once before. As Harry had pointed out, she'd lied to me about knowing Gertrude before wearing her gown on stage. Why? And what else had she lied about?

It was too early for Myrtle to be at the theater and the manager wouldn't give us her home address. Not until Harry informed him we worked for the police and if he didn't tell us where to find her, he'd be arrested for obstructing the course of justice.

Myrtle Langford lived in an old building in a tiny flat where the walls were covered with posters of her prior performances, as well as framed magazine articles and photographs. She invited us into the parlor with enthusiasm, but I suspected the presence of a handsome man had something to do with that. She couldn't take her eyes off him.

She wore her hair in a simple yet elegant style and without the harsh lights of the dressing room, her beauty shone through. I wouldn't call her ageless, but she had a presence about her that drew attention. Her gown was lovely but the style was at least ten years out of date with its large bustle and the swagged overskirt draped in such a way to reveal the russet colored underskirt. She wore it with a self-assured confidence I could never possess.

Harry took her attention in his stride, but I was still

199

annoyed with her for lying. My tone was curt. "Miss Lang-ford, you owe me an explanation. You knew Gertrude Lindsey well before you wore that gown for her in '83. You knew her when she was Gertrude Russell, singing in the musical troupe. You were in the troupe together, along with Emmanuel Durant."

She touched her chin self-consciously and avoided my gaze. "I see you've spoken to that girl."

"Anna Newland told us how she tracked down her parents and the role you played. But I'm still waiting for you to tell me why you lied to me. What are you hiding?"

"Nothing. Honestly, you're a very suspicious young woman. Mind you stay on her good side, Mr. Armitage, or you'll find yourself on the receiving end of one of her glares." She winked at him. "Pointy." He laughed softly.

I tried to settle my features into what I hoped was a more passive expression.

"Yes, I knew them both," she finally answered. "We performed together in that awful troupe. Honestly, we were quite terrible. Emmanuel and the other musicians had limited skill, at best, and Gertrude was always out of key. The dancers provided the entertainment with our daring outfits." She waggled her eyebrows at Harry.

He blinked back.

"I didn't tell you about it, Miss Fox, because I didn't want to be associated with that troupe. It's an embarrassment. It would ruin my public image if my fans knew. No one here in England knows about it and that's the way I want it to stay. I have a reputation to uphold."

"You say Gertrude wasn't a very good singer," I said. "She claimed otherwise."

"All lies."

"What about the throat disease? You told Miss Newland you believed that story and wasn't aware she left to have a child."

"That's true."

"Did you like Gertrude?"

My question took her by surprise. "I didn't dislike her. We were friends in the troupe together. We drifted apart over time, however."

"So why did you wear her gown in '83? That was a very generous thing to do for a struggling designer. You were at the height of your fame and as you say, you'd drifted apart."

Her hands became busy, smoothing her skirt, picking at a seam, and finally clasping in her lap. The knuckles turned white. "I don't like to say. It brings back difficult memories."

Harry leaned forward. "You can tell us, Miss Langford. Unless it has a direct bearing on the case, we won't tell another soul. You can trust us."

The tension eased from her body. She gave him a small smile and he smiled reassuringly back. She drew in a deep breath. "I felt like I owed Gertrude. She helped me when I needed it most. Wearing the gown was my way of repaying her for the service she rendered me in Poitiers. Yes, I am aware she named herself after the city where I was at my most vulnerable. I have no idea why she chose it."

"What is the service she rendered to you?" I asked.

"My story is not dissimilar to hers, but mine happened first."

I drew in a sharp breath. "You were with child."

Her nod was very slight. "I didn't want to go through with it so she helped me find a...a woman who takes care of such matters." Her fingers twisted together in her lap. "I was ill afterwards. I almost died. Gertrude nursed me back to health on her own and she kept my secret." She blinked back tears. "That was about a year before she left the troupe and returned here. Ever since Miss Newland told me she was Gertrude's daughter, I've wondered if my experience affected Gertrude. Perhaps she went through with her pregnancy because she was too scared to have a procedure and decided on adoption instead."

It seemed likely to me. "You've known Gertrude a long time," I said. "What was she like then? Was she determined? Driven?"

"Oh yes. She wanted to be successful. She wanted money. Not a man's money, but her own. I thought she was mad. I told her women couldn't be successful in their own right."

"You became successful," Harry pointed out.

"Thank you, Mr. Armitage, but take a look around you. There's nothing to show for my success but memories."

"That makes you wealthier than many."

Tears pooled in her eyes again.

I felt teary too. "Could she sew back then?" I asked.

"Yes, but who doesn't sew? We could all put our hand to it, even the men. She wasn't the best seamstress though. She was more of the ideas person when it came to costuming. She had an eye for color and form. She designed all our costumes. Aside from the dancers, I think the audience came to see what we'd wear from one performance to the next. We had very little money to buy fabric, but somehow Gertrude could pull together a marvelous array of outfits from bits and pieces. Despite our different shapes and sizes, she made each piece unique enough to look good on one and all, yet there was uniformity too. I wasn't surprised when I learned she became a designer. I am glad she found her calling. It certainly wasn't singing." She laughed.

The notion that Gertrude hadn't designed her range had niggled at me ever since learning that her eyesight was poor, and no one claimed to have seen her put pencil to sketchbook. But here was proof from someone who knew her that Gertrude had been an excellent designer in her youth. Her eyesight may have failed her lately, and pride had driven her to hide it from others and design only in private, but she'd had a hand in every design right up until the end.

The business wouldn't survive without her.

"She needed good seamstresses to help her shop succeed," Miss Langford went on. "Her skill with the needle was serviceable but not excellent. For such complex designs, she needed the best. She must have found them."

"Indeed," I said. "One of her seamstresses has been with her from the beginning. A Mrs. Zieliński. Do you know her?"

She shook her head. "I never met the back room girls. I was famous by the time I wore Gertrude's gown."

"What about the years before that? You kept in touch for a while after she returned to London, so Miss Newland said."

"Only a little, and only at first. After '83, her career blossomed and mine withered. I don't blame Gertrude for distancing herself from me, but it would have been nice to receive a letter every now and again."

"Did you see Gertrude before she opened the first shop in

Earl's Court?" Harry asked. "Do you know where she worked?"

"In the dressmaking department of Whiteleys department store."

We thanked her and stood to leave.

"Won't you stay for tea?" She directed the invitation to Harry. I might as well not have been in the room.

"We have to work," he said. "Perhaps we can listen to your stories another time."

She put out her hand for him to kiss. "I'd like that."

He took her hand and bowed over it.

Outside, as we went in search of a cab, I said, "She'll hold you to that visit."

"That's why I said *we* would like to listen to her stories, not just me."

We shared a smile. "I've heard of Whiteleys," I said. "But I've never been there. It's like Harrods?"

"Similar. It's in Bayswater. It occupies a row of shops on Westbourne Grove."

We found a hansom and Harry gave the driver instructions then assisted me into the cabin. His hand held mine a few moments longer than necessary before letting go. It took me a few moments more before I could refocus on the case rather than the man sitting next to me.

"What if Gertrude told someone about Myrtle's pregnancy?" I said.

He blinked slowly at me, as if his mind had been elsewhere too. "And Myrtle found out?"

"She would have been deeply upset with Gertrude for betraying her confidence. Perhaps upset enough to kill her."

He tapped a finger against his thigh. "What if Myrtle killed Gertrude to *stop* her revealing the secret?"

I liked his theory better and told him so.

He wasn't convinced, however. "It happened so long ago. Does it matter if the secret is revealed now, after all these years? Myrtle's career has stalled. If the press are interested enough to write about it, would it harm her career further?"

"It might. It would certainly humiliate her. But I do agree there's no reason for Gertrude to reveal Myrtle's secret now, years later."

"At least we have another piece of the Gertrude Lindsey puzzle. Hopefully we'll uncover more at Whiteleys."

"She had a full life," I said. "She didn't need to tell so many stories."

"She made up stories because she couldn't tell anyone the truth. It was either too painful or too scandalous."

I studied his profile as he stared straight ahead, blinking into the icy wind. His own past was painful, but he didn't make up lies to hide behind. He simply avoided talking about it. We all cope in different ways.

I clutched my coat tighter but it did little good. The cold air stung my face. Our cab had no curtain above the half-doors at our legs, and afforded only minimal protection. That's the problem with hansoms on days when winter wasn't ready to release us from its grip and succumb to spring.

Whiteleys department store took up almost the entire length of the street. There was no uniformity to the façade. It was not one building but many and each individual shop had once been independent, only to be eventually overrun by the steady march of Whiteleys. Like most department stores, it had begun life as a drapery. Dressmaking was one of its earliest additions, with that department opening in 1868.

Harry and I learned all of this from the manager of the department, Mrs. Jolly. It was the most inappropriate name for the stiff-backed, pinch-lipped woman who escorted us through the workroom to her adjoining office. The large space hummed with the sound of sewing machines but no chatter. Fifty-odd seamstresses hunched over their work, fingers moving deftly, too busy to even pluck an errant thread off the sleeves of their plain black uniforms. Those who looked up as we passed were snapped at by Mrs. Jolly and ordered to stay back an extra five minutes for every five seconds they weren't concentrating on the task in front of them. I wasn't sure how she'd keep track of it all, but the women seemed to believe she could and obeyed without question.

Mrs. Jolly invited us to sit then took the chair behind the desk for herself. She clasped her hands together firmly on the desktop and regarded us. "What do you want to know?"

It had taken us some time before we'd been given access

to the dressmaking department's workroom. Mrs. Jolly's assistant claimed she was busy, but I got the feeling she didn't believe we worked for the police. It wasn't until Harry instructed her to contact his father at Scotland Yard that she gave in. She fetched Mrs. Jolly who very quickly came to collect us. While we waited, I studied some of the photographs hanging on the walls of the outer office.

"Do you have any records of employees dating from the time Gertrude Lindsey worked here?" Harry asked the manager. "She was Gertrude Russell then."

"No. Unfortunately the fire destroyed them all."

"I remember that fire," Harry said. "The smoke blanketed the city."

"We've had several fires, but the one in '87 was the worst. The store was rebuilt quickly, but we lost all employment records."

"Were any of your current seamstresses working here in the mid to late seventies and might remember her?"

"My girls are all aged under thirty. I find the younger, unmarried ones are best. Once they start a family, they're not as reliable."

From the vacant look on the seamstresses' faces, I suspected they worked hard. Their pay would be meager and the hours long. They couldn't even have a friendly chat with the girl seated next to them or this dragon would bring down her wrath on them. By the time they reached thirty, they were probably worn out.

"I remember Gertrude Russell, however. I was a seamstress too, just like her. There were fewer of us then. The department has grown considerably since I took over management."

"What was she like?" I asked.

She flexed her fingers before re-clasping them. "She was too talkative. She was often getting into trouble for idle chatter. Her work wasn't bad but it was uneven. She was limited with her skill. Her only saving grace was her work ethic. She worked hard, I'll give her that." It was said grudgingly.

"Why did she leave?" Harry asked.

"I don't know. She wasn't forced or anything like that." The lines on her face had settled into a frown as soon as she saw us, but they now deepened. "She left suddenly and without notice. It was around the time of the accident which is why I remember it. The timing seemed too coincidental to me."

"What accident?" both Harry and I asked.

The lines on her face reformed, almost into a smile, but not quite. She was relishing telling us. "The manager of the department fell from one of the windows of the residence hall where the staff live. It's not far from here. We still use it for staff accommodation."

"Fell?" Harry prompted. "Was she pushed? Did she throw herself off?"

"He not she. Mr. Barrymore." She thrust out her chin. "I'm the first female manager of the department. As I said, it was an accident. That was the conclusion the police came to."

"Did you inherit the position after Mr. Barrymore's unfortunate demise?"

"No. There was another before me. And no, he was nowhere near the residence hall at the time. I don't like your insinuation, Mr. Armitage."

"Yet you are insinuating that Gertrude Russell had a hand in Mr. Barrymore's demise. Otherwise, why mention it?"

She unclasped her hands before re-clasping them again. It seemed to be something she did when she was considering her answers. "The general feeling within the company was that he took his own life, but senior management paid the police to conclude it was an accident. It wouldn't look good for the company if one of its department managers killed himself."

"Did you and the other seamstresses think it was suicide?" Harry prompted. "Or did you all believe Gertrude had something to do with it?"

For the first time, she lowered her gaze. "Several of us who'd been here for some time suspected she was responsible. When she suddenly left mere days later, we became even more certain. She was that type of person, you see."

"The murdering type?" I asked, unable to keep the scoff out of my voice.

"The outgoing type. Talkative and forthright. She had

opinions about the working conditions here and wasn't afraid to voice them."

Heaven help the suffrage movement if women with opinions were considered murderesses, and by their own sex too.

"The thing is, long hours are necessary," she went on as if we'd asked. "The company needs to turn a profit or it will not succeed, and then where will we all be? Out of work altogether, that's where. The girls are uneducated. They don't understand the fundamentals of economics. I taught myself, but many lack the skill or the drive to learn." She leveled her gaze with mine, challenging me, daring me to disagree with her. "If the girls don't like it, they may leave. There are others waiting to take their position and are grateful for the work."

"Gertrude must have understood economics," I pointed out. "She started her business from nothing and turned it into a success. Indeed, she's probably the most successful former employee from this department. The company ought to celebrate her achievement and her life. Perhaps you should create some kind of display in the workroom to show the story of Madame Poitiers. It would inspire the girls."

"We don't want to encourage them to look up from their work. Besides, there's no point giving them false hope. They can't all follow in Gertrude's footsteps."

"Nor is it in the company's best interests to inspire the cogs of the empire to change course."

She parted her hands. "I'm glad you understand, Miss Fox. As a woman, I thought you might."

I clenched my teeth to stop my retort. We still needed answers from her.

Fortunately Harry took over the questioning, because I was too livid to keep my tone neutral. "Why do you blame Gertrude for Mr. Barrymore's death?"

"They often clashed. It was obvious to everyone Gertrude never liked him. She said he was mean to the girls, but he was simply doing his job. The manager has targets to meet, you see." She tapped the ledger on the desk. "Time frames and quantities must be met. There is a lot of pressure. I didn't understand this myself in those days, so I admit that we all disliked Mr. Barrymore for his strictness, including me."

"What about inappropriate behavior?" I asked. "Was he too familiar with any of the girls?"

"Certainly not. He was married. He had children."

"Did you raise your concerns about his death with the police or senior management?" Harry asked.

"No. We all kept quiet. They made up their minds early in the investigation that it would be swept under the carpet for the sake of the company. Later, I came to regret my silence, but it was too late to go back. No one wanted to dredge up painful memories for Mr. Barrymore's family. Senior management certainly wouldn't like it. I decided it was best to let sleeping dogs lie. Anyway, it seems as though Gertrude got her just desserts in the end."

Her smugness grated on my nerves. "Do you actually have any evidence of her guilt?" I asked. "Or are you basing your judgement on Gertrude's character and her dislike of Mr. Barrymore?"

"Oh no, there's more. Before the death was ruled an accident, the police questioned all of us. Gertrude had an alibi for the time of death. All the seamstresses did." We waited, but she didn't elaborate. Indeed, she was no longer looking at us again.

"You were each other's alibis," I guessed. "You lied to the police and gave false statements about your whereabouts to vouch for your colleagues."

"Some did, it's true, but not me."

"Gertrude?"

"I know she lied. She says she was working late in here finishing something off with one of the other girls, but I saw her in the residence hall only a few minutes before the accident. She couldn't be in two places at once."

"The other seamstress told the police Gertrude was with her the entire time?"

"Yes."

"Do you remember who the other seamstress was?"

"No."

The door opened and the assistant poked her head through the gap. "There's an issue on the floor that needs your attention, Mrs. Jolly."

"I'll be there right away." Mrs. Jolly stood and indicated we should walk out of the office ahead of her.

We followed the assistant to the outer office, leaving Mrs. Jolly behind to berate one of the girls. The poor thing started to cry, which only earned her a sneering retort from her manager about "useless girls."

I blocked it out and sifted through the information Mrs. Jolly had given us. The more I thought about it, the more I was convinced we now had another motive for Gertrude's murder. Revenge.

I mentioned this to Harry as we stepped foot on the pavement outside Whiteleys. I couldn't hold it in any longer. "What if someone recently learned that Gertrude could be responsible for Mr. Barrymore's death?"

"And what if they confronted her about it on Friday morning?" Clearly he'd come to the same conclusion as me. "Who would care enough about Mr. Barrymore to kill all these years later in retribution? His widow and children, for certain, but perhaps a lover or friend too. We need to find out more about Mr. Barrymore, but his employment records were destroyed in the fire. Scotland Yard should have an old report on the case if it was investigated. We can find out where he lived."

I stopped. "There's something we can do before we leave here that might help. Children sometimes look like their fathers. If we know what Mr. Barrymore looked like, we could determine if any of our suspects resemble him."

"The photographs on the wall in the outer office."

We turned as one and headed back inside, making our way through the shop with its comfortable sofas, gleaming polished counter, and customers flicking through catalogs or having their measurements taken by attentive sales assistants. In the waiting room, Harry asked Mrs. Jolly's assistant if we could look at the photographs on the wall. I didn't wait for assent. I checked their dates, etched into a brass plaque nailed to the wall below each framed image.

The photographs were of the dressmaking staff, taken every year on April first since the department opened. "Why weren't these destroyed in the fire?" I asked.

"They weren't hanging in here then," the assistant said.

"They were kept on display in the residence hall. It was only after the fire destroyed everything that they brought them over. They had to decorate the walls in here with something, I suppose." She looked around and sighed. "These are so drab. I don't know why they didn't put up designs of our best gowns again. They're so much more colorful."

"Here," I said. Harry joined me, standing close behind and peering over the top of my head at the photograph of thirty women in identical black uniforms and three men. The men were seated in the middle front and all the women stood.

"Which one is Mr. Barrymore?" Harry asked.

"Who's Mr. Barrymore?" The assistant approached and squinted through her spectacles at the date plaque. "I didn't work here in '76. If you take it off the wall, the names should be on the back."

Harry took down the picture and turned it over. "Only the men's names are given. The women are simply listed as 'seamstresses.'"

"Typical," I muttered. "Which one is Mr. Barrymore?"

"The left one." He turned it back around.

"He was quite handsome," I said, trying to decide if he resembled any of our suspects.

Harry pointed to one of the women. "This is Gertrude." His finger suddenly moved to point out one of the others. Her face was familiar and didn't come as a surprise.

But I recognized a third person in the photograph, and that one did surprise me.

CHAPTER 15

*N*either Harry nor I mentioned Mrs. Zieliński by
name in the presence of the assistant. There was no
need. We knew it was her in the photograph. She was
younger, but her face had changed little over the years. I
wanted to ask the assistant about the third person, however.
If she couldn't help us, Mrs. Jolly probably could, but I'd
rather deal with the friendlier woman here than the dragon in
there.

I turned the picture over. "Do you know this fellow?" I
indicated the name written in a neat hand on the back. "Mr.
Madden."

"Oh yes, he worked here until six months ago. It was such
a shame when he left. He was an institution. Mr. Madden was
the store manager, Mr. Whiteley's right hand." She pointed
out the man sitting in the middle. "That's Mr. Whiteley
himself."

"Why did Mr. Madden leave?"

"He's going to manage Pritchards, the new department
store opening soon." She sighed. "None of us could believe he
took a position for a rival company. It feels like a betrayal."

Harry returned the photograph to the wall and we
thanked the assistant. Outside, we both agreed we needed to
return to the shop and speak to Mrs. Zieliński. She'd lied to
us about when she first met Gertrude. She hadn't answered

an advertisement. She knew Gertrude *before* Maison de Poitiers opened. They worked together at Whiteleys.

"Gertrude probably approached Mrs. Zieliński while she was still working at Whiteleys and invited her to be her first seamstress," I said.

"As thanks for providing Gertrude with an alibi at the time of Mr. Barrymore's death," Harry finished. "Do you think she killed Gertrude all these years later?"

"If she did, I can't think why."

"Me either," he said, striding towards the line of waiting cabs, "but there must be a reason she didn't tell us they met at Whiteleys."

"We'll ask her. If nothing else, she might be able to tell us more about Gertrude's involvement in Mr. Barrymore's murder. We'll also ask her and the other seamstresses why Mr. Madden called at the workshop."

We'd seen the former store manager of Whiteleys in the lane leaving the workshop a few days ago. It was likely he'd been to see Mrs. Zieliński, his former employee. Was his presence related to Gertrude's murder or was it a coincidence? And did her murder have something to do with Mr. Barrymore's death?

The long-ago events at Whiteleys were yet another piece of the puzzle. But instead of helping me see the bigger picture, I only had more questions and more suspects. There were a lot of puzzle pieces now, and I felt as though I could no longer juggle them all.

The cab deposited us on New Bond Street outside Maison de Poitiers. Miss Keane was on duty, standing behind the counter, studying the order book. She was alone.

She looked up upon our entry and her practiced smile vanished. "Oh. It's you two. Come to harass me again?" she sneered. "Or Paul?"

I dismissed her comments with a flick of my wrist. "We're only trying to get to the bottom of this mystery, Miss Keane. Sometimes awkward questions have to be asked. We're here to speak to Mrs. Zieliński." We headed for the door to the workshop.

"She went out."

Harry opened the door anyway to check. He closed it again and shook his head at me.

I approached the counter. "Perhaps you can answer something for us. Why was Mr. Madden here the other day?"

"Who?"

"The older gentleman leaving the workshop via the lane."

She shrugged. "He was here to see Mrs. Zieliński. I didn't hear their conversation."

"How did they seem? Angry? Worried?"

She shrugged again. "Nothing like that. It seemed like a normal conversation to me. He did most of the talking. She nodded a lot."

"When do you expect her back?" Harry asked.

"In about half an hour."

Harry and I exchanged glances then left the shop. We decided to spend our thirty minutes eating lunch. We headed to Piccadilly Circus to buy something warm and delicious from the pie man.

"I'll never be able to eat a pie from any other pie man now," I said as we walked.

Harry smiled. "You'll never get indigestion after eating them either. At least you can be sure he puts actual mutton in his mutton pies."

"What do the other pie men put in theirs?"

"No one knows, but I've heard people meowing as they pass."

I tried not to think about that.

As Harry purchased our pies, I watched the entry to the construction site for the Bakerloo line. Only two workmen emerged during that time, and both lined up at the cart selling baked potatoes. As the one in front completed his purchase, the second one dusted off his moleskin trousers as if self-conscious of his filthy state among the well-dressed shoppers.

I suddenly straightened, alert.

Harry finished buying the pies. I raced up to him rather than wait for him to join me. "Hungry?" he said, chuckling.

"I've just had a thought."

He gave me his complete attention. "Go on."

"There's a clue we've overlooked. Indeed, I forgot about it altogether until just now."

"Does it involve Mrs. Zieliński?"

"In a way." I bit into the pie and strode towards Piccadilly.

"That's not the most direct way back to the shop."

I waited until I finished my mouthful then said, "I'm not going to the shop. I'm going to the Mayfair Hotel. I want to ask one of the guests something, but I'm afraid he may have already checked out."

"Who? And why do you need to speak to him?"

I told him.

His lips curved into a smile. "Now it begins to make sense."

We finished our pies before we reached the hotel. I strode up to Frank at the door, but Harry hung back. In my enthusiasm, I'd forgotten that he wasn't welcome. Ordinarily, I would encourage him to do as he pleased, but I didn't want to start an argument between him and my uncle. I didn't want any delay. My plan was to speak to one of the doctors and immediately leave again.

I approached Peter as he peeled away from the check-in desk where he'd been speaking to the clerk. "Are any of the European surgeons still here?" I asked. "I believe they were checking out this morning."

"Most have, but some elected to stay on to do some sight-seeing. Do you need to speak to Dr. Gerhardt again?"

"No. Was there a Polish surgeon among them?"

"I believe so." He strode back to the check-in desk and asked to see the reservations book. He flipped back through the pages then turned it around to show me. He indicated one of the names. "The Pole, Dr. Gorecki, checked out this morning, I'm afraid."

I swore under my breath. Both Peter and the check-in clerk raised their brows.

"Why do you need to speak to him?" Peter asked.

"I need someone who speaks Polish to translate for me."

"We have two Polish women on the staff. They're both maids. They should be cleaning rooms at this time. Mrs. Short will know which floor."

I clasped his arms, squeezed and thanked him profusely. Then I went in search of Mrs. Short. I found her in her office.

The housekeeper hadn't been at the hotel very long. I'd taken an instant dislike to her and I was quite sure the feeling was mutual, although she scowled at everyone so perhaps I wasn't so special after all. She narrowed her gaze when I asked where I could find the two Polish maids, but was wise enough not to withhold the information. I suspected my authoritative tone had something to do with it. Sometimes it was useful to be a member of the Bainbridge family.

I hurried to the second floor and looked for housekeeping carts parked outside rooms. I came across Harmony before either of the Polish girls.

"Maria's down there." She pointed along the corridor. "I don't know where Helena is. Why do you need to speak to them?"

"No time to explain," I said as I rushed off.

I found Maria in room two-eighteen. Harmony had followed me, pushing her cart ahead of her to make it look as though she was working if Mrs. Short came past. I introduced myself to Maria, but she seemed to already know who I was.

"I need you to translate something for me," I said.

"Of course, Miss Fox. I would be happy to assist you." There was only a faint hint of an accent in the rolling of the R in "course" and the punchy consonants. She must have been born here or come to England when she was very young.

Just like Mr. Green.

"What is the Polish word for green?" I asked.

"Zielony."

My pulse quickened. "Thank you, Maria."

She returned to her duties while I walked back to the room where Harmony had been working. She pushed her cart alongside me.

"Do you want to tell me what this is about?" she whispered.

"It's about Mrs. Zieliński's son, Paul Green," I whispered back.

"Zieliński...zielony...green. He Anglicized his name to fit in."

"He's also the lover of Miss Keane, one of the other seam-

215

stresses from the shop. Harry and I have just come from Whiteleys where we learned Mrs. Zieliński and Gertrude knew one another."

"What does that have to do with the son?"

"I'm not sure yet. There are still several gaps in my theory, but I now believe Paul Green is involved. It's his clothes, you see. The trousers are moleskin. All navvies wear them. The fabric is coarse, just like the thread I picked up in the shop the day Gertrude was killed."

She gasped. "He was there."

I nodded. "The question is, did he kill her because she lied about the profit-sharing scheme to his mother and lover? Or because he learned something about Gertrude? Perhaps he learned that she killed his father."

She gasped again. "Do go on, Cleo!"

We'd reached the room she was cleaning so I gave her the short version of what we'd learned at Whiteleys about the death of Mr. Barrymore and my suspicion that Mr. Barrymore and Mrs. Zieliński were lovers.

"But why would she give Gertrude an alibi for the time of her lover's murder if she thought her guilty?"

That point troubled me too. "I don't know. As I said, there are still gaps. Harry and I will try to fill them in this afternoon."

She grasped my hand. "Good luck and be careful."

As I headed back outside to meet Harry, all the possibilities swirled together in my head. There were several reasons why Paul Green could have killed Gertrude. He could have been angry that she'd lied about the profit sharing scheme and never meant to go through with it. He could have thought his mother deserved more recognition for her years of service. Or he could be the son of the man Gertrude murdered and sought revenge.

We needed answers. Mrs. Zieliński was still our best chance, but she would also very likely stay silent to protect her son. We had to try, however.

We returned to the shop only to find Mrs. Zieliński had never returned after lunch. Miss Keane seemed a little concerned. The behavior was unusual. Mrs. Zieliński took her responsibilities seriously.

"She's loyal, even though we now know Madame was never going to fulfill her promise." Miss Keane spoke as if she couldn't quite believe it. "Madame never deserved Mrs. Zieliński's loyalty."

"Miss Keane, do you know where she might be?" Harry asked.

She tossed her head. "No. Why should I?"

"She's the mother of your friend, Paul Green."

She drew in a sharp breath. She hadn't expected us to make the connection. "So?"

"So if she didn't come back to work, where would she have gone?"

"Home? Perhaps she felt unwell."

It was the most likely scenario, but there was also another possibility—that she and her son were going to leave the country.

Harry used the telephone in one of the neighboring shops to call his father and tell him our theory. D.I. Hobart agreed to alert the port and railway authorities.

"He's also going to the Piccadilly Circus tunneling site now," he said. "If Paul Green is still at work, he'll take him in for questioning. He also wanted to send men to the Zieliński flat but I asked him to wait. I want to speak to Mrs. Zieliński first using a subtler approach. His men might frighten her."

"That's if she's even there."

We hired another cab and asked the driver to be as quick as he could. Last time, we'd taken a circuitous route to avoid the worst areas of Whitechapel, but this time Harry didn't bother to direct him. We raced through streets where many of the recessed doorways were occupied by drunkards and prostitutes. I was glad to see there were no children here, but there was misery in abundance.

We stopped outside the building that housed the Zieliński flat. We knew which was theirs from our last visit when the shopkeepers had pointed out the window. We didn't wait to speak to the downstairs neighbor but headed directly up to the first floor.

No one answered our knock. I stamped my hands on my hips in frustration.

Harry crouched in front of the door and inserted a set of slender tools into the lock. He was breaking in.

I was about to protest, then decided it was a good idea. It wouldn't meet with the approval of his father, but we could just say the door was open. I kept lookout by the stairwell until I heard the lock click.

The flat was tiny with one bedroom and a small parlor. The parlor was being used as a second bedroom and a work-room for Mrs. Zieliński. Its window overlooked the street. We kept away from it.

"All his things are still in there," Harry said as he emerged from the bedroom. "If he has decided to flee the country, he's prepared to leave everything behind. Including her." He flashed me a creased photograph of Miss Keane.

I felt sorry for her. When this was all over, she would perhaps suffer most from Paul Green's actions. Her and Mrs. Zieliński. I hoped they could find comfort together.

I moved around the parlor, taking in the narrow bed pushed against the wall, the small cupboard and desk. The desk was old and covered with scratches. It looked as though it was only used for sewing. The single drawer contained pieces of fabric and two pairs of scissors. The various tins ranged across the back of the desk contained buttons, beads, needles and other bits and bobs a seamstress needed. A square pincushion had been placed beside spools of thread in various colors and textures, including the coarse one that was an exact match for the thread I'd found on the morning of the murder.

The largest item on the desk was a hand-cranked sewing machine, the sort designed to sit on top of a desk rather than needing a table of its own like a treadle operated machine. It was the most valuable thing in the room. If Mrs. Zieliński left the country with her son, she'd have to leave it behind. Her clothes too. I sat at the desk and watched as Harry looked through the clothes neatly folded and placed on the cupboard shelves.

The door suddenly burst open and the large figure of Paul Green barreled inside, growling like a bear. He rushed at Harry, tackling him. Harry fell back on the bed, taking Paul with him, then they both tumbled to the floor with an almighty thud.

They rolled around, thrashing and grappling, neither able to get in a resounding blow. Paul was the more solid of the two, but Harry held his own, never letting the heavier fellow pin him under his weight. They made an awful lot of noise. Neighbors would soon come to investigate. They might take Paul's side against us. Folk in Whitechapel didn't have much appreciation for law enforcement.

I couldn't allow that.

I grabbed the oil lamp from the corner of the desk and slammed it into the back of Paul's head. He collapsed on top of Harry without a sound.

For a dreadful moment I thought I'd killed him, but when Harry rolled him off, Paul groaned.

"Pass me something to tie his hands together," Harry said.

All I could find was a black ribbon. He eyed it dubiously before tying Paul's hands behind his back. Then he patted his cheek until he regained consciousness.

I closed the door and locked it; then I returned to the desk.

Paul watched me from beneath heavy lids. "What are you doing here?"

Harry stood just out of reach of our captive. "Looking for you."

"Why?"

"Did you kill Gertrude Lindsey?"

"What? No!"

"Did you kill her for your mother's sake?"

"Why would I do that?"

"What about for Miss Keane?"

"Elizabeth?" He shook his head again. "Why would I kill their employer?"

"Because she promised them a share in the shop's profits and then refused to honor it."

"I'm the one who told them she wouldn't follow through with the promise. I warned them not to trust her."

He seemed sincere. I struck that theory off my list. It felt good to narrow them down. "Perhaps you killed her in revenge for murdering your father."

Paul blinked slowly at me, as if his vision was blurred

from the blow. "My father died five years ago of heart failure here in this very flat. No one murdered him."

"I mean your real father. Your mother's lover from her days at Whiteleys. I'm sorry if this comes as news to you, but we believe a man named Mr. Barrymore is your actual father."

He stared at me then he barked a humorless laugh. "You're a fool. Both of you are if you think that. I was born in Poland, not here. I have the birth certificate to prove it. I was two years old when my mother went to work at Whiteleys. I'm twenty-eight, Miss Fox."

"Oh," I murmured. "You look younger."

Harry glanced at me, his brows arched in question.

I simply shrugged. I'd been so sure one of our theories was right.

"We have to take you in for further questioning," Harry said.

Paul spat a few words of Polish at him, but he didn't try to get up off the floor and escape. He knew he couldn't outrun Harry.

"Cleo, ask one of the shopkeepers if they have some rope we can borrow. I'm not relying on this ribbon to hold all the way to Scotland Yard."

I unlocked the door and raced down the stairs and crossed the road to the greengrocer. He was busy with a queue of customers so I headed back outside. On the pavement, I looked up at the window of the building opposite. Harry came into view briefly then moved out of sight. I couldn't see Paul. I couldn't see much from this angle except the ceiling and the top of the cupboard. Anyone standing, like Harry, was visible too, as long as they stood near the window. I'd noticed that on our last visit here, but now I berated myself for not realizing its importance.

If I had, I could have solved this mystery the day we'd first come here.

CHAPTER 16

I bypassed the greengrocer and entered the next shop. The faded sign painted on the window read Rampling's Emporium and it seemed to sell anything a local may require, from second-hand clothes and chipped crockery, to dented pans and wads of dirty wool. The shopkeeper was with a customer so I pretended to admire the red glass beads draped around the neck of the dress form. Last time I'd walked past, a mob cap had sat on the neck stump, but it must have sold as the stump was bare. It looked less lifelike without the cap.

Mrs. Zieliński would have used something like a mob cap to fool the shopkeepers.

The customer left and the shop assistant strode past tables cluttered with odds and ends to me. She moved with purpose and speed, a gap-toothed smile plastered on her face. She could see from my clothes that I was well-heeled and she expected to make a sale.

"How much for this necklace?" I asked, indicating the red beads.

"Ha'penny."

"I'll take it."

Her smile widened. She lifted the necklace off the dress form and held it up to the light to show me how pretty the beads were. "Very nice, this. I've got more out the back if you want to see?"

"I'll just take this one."

She led me to the counter and accepted my money. "I don't have nothing to wrap it in," she said apologetically.

"Never mind. I'd like to wear it anyway." I indicated the dress form. "Where did you get that? It looks like one you see dressmakers use."

"Prob'ly is." She nodded at the door which I assume was her way of pointing out Mrs. Zieliński's flat. "There's a seamstress lives across the way. She was just throwing it away one day. I saw her carrying it out and walking down the street with it. She was struggling. That thing's heavy. I told her I'll take it for display. She gave it to me, for free. I didn't steal it. You can ask her."

I assured her that I believed her. "Are you referring to Mrs. Zieliński? I know her. She used to have the dress form in her room where she did her sewing."

"Aye. You could see it through the window."

"And you could see her through the window when she was using it, couldn't you?"

"Aye."

"But not when she sat at her sewing desk."

She shrugged.

"On Friday morning, did you see her through the window?"

"Friday?" She frowned. "I don't remember. Why?"

I thanked her and accepted my purchase. There was no clasp but the necklace fit over my head. I settled the beads over my bodice, under my coat. They were rather fetching against the black, but were too colorful to be considered suitable for my period of mourning. I'd remove them before leaving Whitechapel.

I was about to leave the shop when I remembered the rope. She sold me a length that should do nicely.

I exited and once again glanced up at the Zielińskis' window. Harry looked out. Seeing me, he moved away from the window again. The dress form would have stood there before Mrs. Zieliński removed it. She must have been worried that we'd see it and realize how she'd tricked the shopkeepers into thinking she was at home on Friday morning when in actuality she was at Maison de Poitiers, confronting and killing Gertrude.

She'd dressed the dress form in her own clothes and added a cap to the neck stump, just as the shopkeeper at the Emporium had done. From the street opposite, the dress form looked like Mrs. Zieliński, head bent over her task as she worked. The shopkeepers saw it when they opened and assumed it was her, but Mrs. Zieliński had already headed off to Maison de Poitiers by then. They'd been too busy throughout the day to look up again, and so didn't realize the dress form had been visible the entire time. Later, after she returned home, Mrs. Zieliński got rid of it as a precaution, in case someone realized she'd used it to create an alibi for herself.

Harry opened the door for me and I handed him the rope. As he tied up Paul, I found the spool of tough thread and cut off a section. I held it up by the end to show them.

"Was your mother mending your moleskin trousers early on Friday morning?" I asked.

Paul Green frowned at me from where he sat on the bed. "Aye. Why?"

Harry looked from the thread to the window to our captive. He expelled a long breath. "You didn't do it," he said flatly.

"I know that!" Paul turned so we could see his tied hands. "Let me go."

Harry took the thread from me and studied it. "My grandmother was a seamstress. She used to have threads stuck to her clothes all the time."

"The seamstresses in the workshop at Whiteleys and Maison de Poitiers do too," I said. "But the threads they used were from fine, delicate fabrics. This thread is used to sew the seams of tough material."

"Like moleskins."

We both looked at Paul. His eyes flared. "What are you saying?"

"I found a thread in Maison de Poitiers on the morning of the murder. It matches this one. It was out of place amongst all the delicate fabrics. I'm not very good with a needle myself, and I haven't sewn anything for months, so I made a mistake with regard to the thread. I assumed it came from your moleskin trousers, but it never made it *onto* the mole-skins. Your mother snipped off the excess thread after finishing her mending. The thread stuck to her clothing all the way to the shop where she used her key to enter the work-room via the back lane. It was before eight o'clock, so the other seamstresses hadn't arrived. Your mother confronted Gertrude in the shop. She was angry. The anger was bubbling away beneath the surface for years, but your mother had finally had enough. She'd been pushed too far. She picked up the closest thing at hand, the veil, and when Gertrude's back was turned, she placed it around her neck and strangled her."

Paul Green rose from the bed. "No! She's not a murderer. She a good woman. She works hard."

"She does. She has worked hard for many, many years in the service of Gertrude Lindsey."

"That's right!" he cried. "She's loyal. So why would she kill her now? What reason could she have to murder the woman who pays her wages?"

The door opened and Mrs. Zieliński entered, only to stop dead when she saw us. The full horror of the situation struck her in that moment. Her face crumpled. But instead of fleeing, she ran into the room. "Let him go!"

I grabbed her arm, but she shoved me away. Harry stepped between us and blocked her. I went to stand in front of the door but I didn't think she would try to escape. She was too intent on her son's predicament.

"It is me!" she shouted. "I killed her. Not him. You must let him go!"

Harry shook his head. "We can't. He must have suspected. He would have wondered why the dress form was missing. That makes him an accessory to murder."

She pushed Harry in the chest with all her might. "No!"

Harry grabbed her and pinned her wrists together. "Cleo, the ribbon."

We'd used all the rope on Paul so the ribbon would have to do for his weaker, smaller mother.

Mrs. Zieliński started crying. "He didn't notice the dress form was gone," she spluttered through her tears. "He didn't!"

"Ma, stop talking," Paul said urgently.

I guided the sobbing Mrs. Zieliński to the bed, keeping her at a distance from her son. "Paul is here in the middle of the day when he should be at work. You were both going to leave the country, weren't you? You went to his work site at lunchtime and spoke to him. You both decided then and there to flee England. You, Paul, came home to pack while your mother made arrangements with her bank or friends."

He shook his head vigorously. "No! She's not guilty." He thrust out his chin. "She was loyal to that woman. Had been for years. Why kill her now?" His eyes gleamed. He was sure he had us stumped. "It's not because of that ridiculous profit-sharing scheme. Ma never believed Madame Poitiers would go through with it."

"You're right," I said. "It has nothing to do with that. Your mother killed Gertrude because she was being blackmailed to stay and work for her."

Paul's mouth pinched. His mother lowered her head. It was the confirmation I needed.

"I see you have the situation well in hand." Detective Inspector Hobart strolled in with four constables behind him. "When I arrived at the construction site and eventually managed to speak to the foreman and learned that Paul Green had left for the day, I hoped to find him here. Is it necessary to restrain the mother too?"

"She's the murderer," Harry told him. "Not her son."

He listened as I told him about the thread and the dress form. "And the motive?" he prompted.

"It all started years ago at Whiteleys department store."

He sat on the chair at the desk, settling in for a lengthy story.

"Mrs. Zieliński and Gertrude Lindsey worked in the dressmaking department as seamstresses. Gertrude was Miss Russell back then. They got along well enough. They may even have been friends. The manager of the department, Mr. Barrymore, worked them hard. He was cruel, at times, making them work long hours. Gertrude clashed with him more than the others. She voiced her dislike of the conditions. When he pushed them to increase their productivity, she pushed back. Their colleagues saw these clashes so when Mr.

Barrymore died under mysterious circumstances, they assumed Gertrude killed him."

"There would have been an investigation," D.I. Hobart said.

"Not a thorough one," Harry told him. "Senior management of Whiteleys thought it was suicide and didn't want any stigma attached to the store."

D.I. Hobart's lips flattened. "Go on."

I resumed. "The police went so far as to gather statements from all the seamstresses. Those that didn't have an alibi for the time of death vouched for one another. Mrs. Zieliński told them Gertrude was with her, working late."

D.I. Hobart grunted. "It's no wonder the investigation never went anywhere. So Gertrude killed Mr. Barrymore…"

"No. Everyone assumed so. But Mrs. Zieliński killed him. And Gertrude knew it."

We all turned to Mrs. Zieliński, sitting mute and calm on the bed. She'd given up. She didn't have any fight left. It had been a long and exhausting road, decades in the making. She'd spent years hiding the truth, lying to everyone and suffering under Gertrude's demands in exchange for her silence.

"Why did you do it?" D.I. Hobart asked.

Mrs. Zieliński remained silent.

"Was it because Barrymore made you work hard?"

Again, nothing.

"Or was it because he tried to…seduce you?" I said.

Her head snapped up. "It was not seduction. It was force. His hands were all over me. So I pushed him away. The window was open. It was a large window. He fell out. It was an accident."

Paul swore silently in English then said something to his mother in Polish. She closed her eyes and shook her head.

"Gertrude saw?" I asked.

Mrs. Zieliński nodded. "She was walking past the door and heard me telling him to get off. She opened the door and saw me push him." She lowered her head again and shook it.

She must know that if she'd waited just a few seconds more, Gertrude could have helped her to escape Barrymore's clutches. Instead, she'd witnessed the entire event and used it to blackmail Mrs. Zieliński. Any remaining sympathy I had for Gertrude vanished.

"Gertrude left Whiteleys days after the incident," I went on. "She must have got work elsewhere. Less than two years later, she met the man she would marry and with his money, opened her first salon. It wasn't a success, probably because, despite wonderful designs, her execution wasn't of the quality her customers expected. So she hired the best seamstress she knew." We all looked to Mrs. Zieliński. "She told you if you didn't work for her, she'd tell the police what really happened to Mr. Barrymore."

"No. She did not blackmail me then. I went to work for her happily. She had been kind to me the day Mr. Barrymore died. She told me what we would do, how she would protect me by lying about where we were. I was too shaken to think properly, but her head was clear. When she came to see me two years later and offered me the position, I took it without hesitation. Mr. Barrymore's replacement was also very strict and cruel. Dressmaking departments in all the big stores worked the girls very hard for little money. Gertrude offered me a better wage and the hours would not be as long. She honored those conditions until the end."

D.I. Hobart looked to me, brows raised in question. He wanted to know where blackmail entered the story.

"Mr. Madden, the man we saw leaving the workshop via the lane," Harry said to Mrs. Zieliński. "He was a senior manager at Whiteleys. He knew your work and remembered you years later when he left Whiteleys to head up Pritchards. They're in the recruitment phase before their grand opening later this year. Because of the Whiteleys connection, he personally sought you out and offered you a job in the dressmaking department at Pritchards. You wanted to take it but Gertrude didn't want to lose you. You're her best seamstress. You work hard and your wages haven't risen much since you started. You were cheap. Newer girls were earning more than you."

"I did not want to ask her for more money. She had been good to me."

"Is that what she said when you approached her about the

job offer?" I asked. "Did you tell her you wanted to take the seamstress position at Pritchards?"

"They didn't want me to be a seamstress. They wanted me to head up the whole department. I was to be manager. It was a good offer."

It was an excellent offer for a woman who'd never risen above seamstress. Mr. Madden must have held her in high regard indeed all those years ago at Whiteleys. He'd probably also kept his ear to the ground in that time. Perhaps he'd heard the rumor that Gertrude didn't design her own gowns but her long-term employee did. Others had made the same mistake, including me.

"Gertrude blackmailed you into turning his offer down," I said. "She told you she'd tell the police you killed Mr. Barrymore if you left. You reluctantly accepted the situation for a short while, but decided to plead with her one more time. You knew she was getting in early on Friday morning to meet with Lady Bunbury, so you entered the salon via the workshop some time before eight."

"You must have gone there expecting to kill her," D.I. Hobart said. "Or why set up the dress form in the window to make it look like you were here?"

"No!" Mrs. Zieliński cried. "I did not plan to kill her. I wanted to frighten her, that's all. The dress form was my insurance, in case she later went to the police. I could say I was here and there are witnesses."

It didn't ring true. I didn't believe she merely wanted to frighten Gertrude.

Harry didn't believe it either. "You lied about the key going missing to throw suspicion onto the other girls. But it didn't go missing, did it? You had it the entire time."

"No!" She would argue in court that she'd not taken a weapon with her, but a good prosecutor would point out that she knew there'd be something lying about that she could use to strangle Gertrude with.

"Mr. Madden approached you again after he heard about her death," Harry went on. "We saw him in the lane as he left. He told you the offer was still open. You discussed terms with him that day and you accepted."

Tears filled her eyes. She closed them but a tear slipped

out. Her son looked just as forlorn and defeated as his mother. "Ma," he murmured.

D.I. Hobart signaled to his men to take them away. I watched mother and son trudge with stooped shoulders from their flat. He'd been loyal to her. He'd been prepared to leave his life behind, including his lover, to flee the country with his mother.

Loyalty made some people do things they might come to regret. Miss Keane had said Mrs. Zieliński was loyal to Gertrude, but she wasn't. Her loyalty was as fake as Lady Bunbury's jewels. Blackmail had been a much stronger incentive to keep her working as a seamstress at Maison de Poitiers.

D.I. Hobart shook my hand and clapped Harry on the shoulder. "Well done. Come down to the Yard tomorrow and I'll see you're both paid your fee."

We followed him out. "Perhaps we can have lunch together to celebrate," I said.

He nodded at the perpetrators being led down the stairs. "I'll be busy, but you two enjoy yourselves."

Harry trotted down the stairs too without as much as a glance in my direction. It would seem I'd be having lunch on my own tomorrow. Now that the investigation was over, he wanted our contact to be over too. He was rather predictable.

"Harry!" D.I. Hobart called after his son. "You seem to be forgetting we're in Whitechapel, Son."

Harry called back without stopping. "I haven't forgotten. I'm going to find a cab to take Cleo back to the hotel."

He did indeed find a hansom but didn't get in himself. He assisted me up to the seat then asked the driver to pull the lever to close the doors. "You're not coming?" I asked. "We can stop at your office on the way."

"I'm not going to the office. I have other things I need to do this afternoon."

"Where? We can divert on the way to the hotel."

He instructed the driver to take me to the Mayfair then raised a hand in a wave to me.

"You promised we'd be friends now," I called out as we drove off.

"No, I promised there'd be no more *lectures*," he called

back. "Not seeing you is the best way to keep that promise." The rat was smiling.

Several curse words seemed appropriate at that point. Indeed, no one would have batted an eyelid if I'd shouted them at the top of my lungs. We were in Whitechapel, after all. But I refrained, stamping down on the urge, and sat back. I would see him again tomorrow at midday. His father had asked us both to his office at the same time.

* * *

WE ATE dinner as a family that night. I was in a good mood, having solved the case. My aunt was in a good mood too, despite clearly battling tiredness and a headache.

My uncle and cousins were less cheerful. Floyd's mind seemed to be elsewhere. He poked his food with his knife and didn't join in with the conversation. His mother had to ask him three times what he'd been up to that day.

"I've been out," he finally said.

"Out where?" she asked.

He glanced at his father, but Uncle Ronald didn't notice. His mind was preoccupied too. "The bank."

She turned to look at Floyd properly. "Why?"

"It's private."

Two guests approached to greet my aunt and uncle, letting Floyd off the hook. When the guests left, Aunt Lilian didn't resume the conversation with Floyd but I could tell she was troubled by his answer and the worried look in his eyes. It troubled me too, knowing that he'd lost an awful lot of money the other night.

Flossy sighed dramatically. When no one paid her any attention, she sighed again.

"Do stop it, Floss," Floyd snapped at her. "We know you're upset about the ball, but do you have to bang on about it? It's done. You're not invited. Time to move on."

Flossy's chin wobbled.

I reached for her hand. "I'm sorry, Flossy."

"It's all right, girls, I've sorted it all out." Aunt Lilian's slender fingers grasped her wineglass. Flossy and I stared at her. "We're invited to the Bunbury Ball after all. All of us are."

Floyd groaned. Flossy sprang up and embraced her mother. "How did you manage it?"

Aunt Lilian's joyful smile turned secretive. "I simply told Lady Bunbury how much I admired her jewelry. Flattery works wonders on some people." Her gaze connected with mine over her daughter's shoulder.

I smiled back. It wasn't flattery that had done the trick, it was blackmail. I suspected my aunt had told Lady Bunbury how much she liked the brooch done in the Lalique style then lamented that our invitations hadn't arrived yet. Not a single threatening word needed to pass my aunt's lips for Lady Bunbury to realize that rumors of her penury would start if we weren't invited.

Flossy resumed her seat with a smile from ear to ear. She tucked into the shrimp croustades with enthusiasm. "This new dish is delicious. Father, you simply must tell Mrs. Poole to keep it on the menu."

"What's the point?" he growled. "She's leaving."

"You will convince her to stay. You're old friends."

"She's given her notice. I have one week to find a new chef."

Flossy deflated a little. "Oh. That is a shame."

Floyd showed some interest in the conversation for the first time. There is nothing like food to get a man's attention. "You have to speak to her again, Father. Tell her how valued she is. Offer her more money."

"I've tried," Uncle Ronald snarled. "I've tried *everything*. She's still leaving." His brusqueness had caused heads to turn in our direction. He smiled and exchanged a few jovial words with our nearest neighbors before turning his attention to his family again. "What have you been doing today, Cleo? I haven't seen you at the hotel much lately."

"I, uh..."

"She was with me," Aunt Lilian said. "She accompanied me when I called on Lady Bunbury. I came home immediately afterwards but Cleo went for a walk. It must have been a good walk, because I noticed she came in with a bounce in her step."

"It was an excellent walk," I said, returning her smile. "It capped off a successful day."

Uncle Ronald accepted our story without question. Floyd narrowed his gaze at me but caught sight of his mother's glare. He cleared his throat and lifted his wineglass in salute. "To successful...walks."

"And to a successful season of husband hunting," Flossy said, raising her glass in my direction.

Floyd smirked at me.

"And wife hunting," his sister added, with a wicked gleam in her eyes.

He swallowed the rest of his wine in a single gulp.

* * *

HARMONY WAS WAITING for me upstairs in my suite when I retired for the night. She flapped a piece of paper at me. "You didn't see this when you came home?"

"No." I accepted the paper from her. It was a telegram. "When did it arrive?"

"This afternoon. Terry gave it to me to pass to you. I placed it on the desk."

"I didn't look at the desk." I hadn't seen Harmony since this morning either. She'd been busy doing the hairstyles for some of our guests before dinner. I'd done my own arrangement this evening.

The telegram was from the French fashion house of Pierre Benoit whom I'd telegraphed on Monday. It confirmed that Gertrude had worked there from late 1876 to Christmas 1877 under one of their senior designers. It filled in the gap between her departure from Whiteleys and meeting the man she would go on to marry. It was one of the few significant events in her life she hadn't lied about.

"Does it help you with the case?" Harmony asked.

"No. But it doesn't matter. We solved it."

Harmony settled in to listen. She asked questions. A lot of questions. They continued while I removed pins and combs from my hair, and while I changed into my night clothes. She didn't finish asking them until eleven-thirty when she promptly decided it was time for her to go.

"Goodnight, Harmony. Enjoy your walk back to the residence hall."

"It'll be cold. I won't enjoy it in the least."

I gave her a somber nod of understanding. "Of course. It'll be awful. Now, do you remember all the details of the case?"

"Yes. Why?"

"I just want to make sure you get them right when you tell Victor on your way home."

She closed the door a little too firmly. I chuckled to myself as I switched off the light.

* * *

I WAS ABOUT to leave the hotel late the following morning when I spotted my aunt coming out of my uncle's office with Mrs. Poole the chef. Both women were smiling. It was pleasing to see.

"Good morning," I said. "You're up early, Aunt. Are you going out?"

"I'm going back to bed. I'm afraid I have a headache. I only got up to speak to Mrs. Poole before she starts in the kitchen."

"Oh?"

"She has agreed to stay on at the hotel as chef de cuisine. Permanently."

I thrust out my hand to the chef. "That's wonderful. I'm so pleased you've agreed to stay."

She shook my hand. "I'm pleased to accept Sir Ronald's offer. It was exactly what I wanted to hear."

"He can be persuasive."

She and my aunt exchanged looks. "Actually, Lady Bainbridge is the persuasive one. But the final offer did come from your uncle, as is right and proper, given he owns the hotel. If you'll excuse me, Lady Bainbridge, Miss Fox, I must get to work."

I watched her go. By the time I turned back to my aunt, she was already opening the door to her suite. "What did you say to convince her?" I asked.

"I offered her what every woman wants and few have. Independence and autonomy. Independence to continue writing for magazines and to run her cookery school, and autonomy to make the decisions she feels are right for her domain here at the hotel. She won't suffer interference from anyone, as long as her work continues at a level your uncle is happy with."

"Those are generous working conditions. He agreed to them?"

"Very readily. He desperately wanted her to stay, he just didn't know how to make it happen."

"He didn't ask her what she wanted?"

"Men like him don't ask, Cleo, particularly when they think that person is beneath them."

"I thought they were friends. I thought he considered her an equal."

She shook her head. "They have known one another for years, but they're not friends. He was only friendly towards her because he thought that would convince her to stay on. He is quite the fool sometimes."

Indeed.

She opened the door to her suite and entered. Before she closed the door, she turned to me. One thin hand rested on the doorframe. It shook, as did her narrow shoulders. She'd been trying to control her trembling in front of Mrs. Poole, but didn't bother with me.

"You should remember that, Cleo. Your uncle tends to do things the way he has always done them. If there's a stalemate in negotiations, you have to make it easy for him. Do the work yourself then present it to him as a done deal that he simply must accept."

"As long as the terms of the deal suit him too?" I finished.

"Precisely." She clasped my hand and squeezed it weakly. "Well done finding Madame Poitiers' killer. You're a clever girl, like your mother, and persistent too."

"I may take after my mother in some ways, but I do wish I had your negotiation skills, Aunt Lilian. You're far subtler than I could ever be."

"Subtlety comes with patience and patience comes with age. You'll be just fine, my dear."

* * *

Maison de Poitiers was open but a policeman stood outside, ordering journalists back from the door to allow customers inside. There were no customers aside from me, however, just Miss Newland and Miss Keane inspecting a white gown together.

They both looked up upon my greeting. "We didn't hear the door over the noise," Miss Newland said. "They've been outside all morning, trying to cajole us into giving them a quote for their articles. Toads. I wish they'd go away."

"Are you all right, Miss Newland?"

She nodded and thanked me. "My ordeal is over, but poor Miss Keane's has just begun."

Miss Keane looked as though she'd been up all night, crying. I imagine the arrest of her beau and his mother had come as an enormous shock. "I haven't been allowed to see him yet," she said. "Perhaps tomorrow."

"The detective in charge is a fair man," I assured her. "Miss Newland, how is Mr. Durant?"

She smiled, hesitantly at first, before it reached her eyes. "He is well. He's an interesting man. He wants me to visit him in France to meet his other children." She grinned. "I have half brothers and sisters younger than me. My parents—the people who adopted me—are eager for me to go, but I want them to come. I need their support, and they need a holiday."

I nodded at the door to the workroom. "How are the other seamstresses?"

"As shocked as we are. They can't believe a murderess worked amongst them and they didn't know."

"I'm going to rejoin them once Miss Newland is back up to speed in here," Miss Keane said. "Mr. Lindsey has agreed to put on two more seamstresses to get on top of the workload. Your dresses will be ready on time, Miss Fox."

"My cousin will be pleased to hear that. Believe me, no one wants to be in her company if she can't wear a new gown to the Bunbury ball."

I left them to their work and walked to Scotland Yard since it was a pleasant day. Spring might still be new, but it was announcing itself today with a cloudless sky and sunshine.

Harry was already waiting with his father in the office. The other detective wasn't there so we had it to ourselves. I accepted the seat Harry offered me.

D.I. Hobart passed a cloth pouch to me and another to Harry. The coins inside jangled. "Mrs. Zieliński has been charged with Gertrude's murder. We're still making inquiries into the Barrymore case."

"And Paul Green?" I asked.

"Charged as an accessory, but he will probably receive a light sentence. He might even get off. His mother is adamant she never told him what she'd done." It wasn't true, but I got the feeling D.I. Hobart wasn't going to fight particularly hard to convict Paul.

He leaned back in his chair and clasped his hands over his belly. He surveyed us each in turn. "So what's next for you two?"

"I'm going to sift through the inquiries that came into my office this week and see if any are worth pursuing," Harry said. "Cleo?"

"I'm going to live a quiet life as the spinster niece of a hotelier. I may take some cookery classes."

Harry snorted. "If only that were true."

"Are you calling into question my ability to learn cookery?"

"No, I'm questioning your ability to live a quiet life."

I refrained from rolling my eyes at him. He was in one of his difficult moods. I stood and thanked D.I. Hobart for trusting me to be a consultant on the case. "Even though you've given no hint of it, I'm sure it wasn't easy to convince your superiors to employ a woman."

His thumbs twiddled and he didn't meet my gaze.

"Inspector? You did tell them I was a woman, didn't you?"

He expelled a breath in resignation. "I have a confession. I told them I was employing Armitage and Associates. They don't know anything about you."

Harry groaned. So he hadn't known either.

"If they do find out, I'll simply tell them you work for Harry. They won't mind that so much, as long as they can't be held responsible if something happened to you."

I began to protest but decided against it. "You could make me a permanent associate," I said to Harry. "We do work better together."

Harry rubbed his forehead. "If I require extra help on a case, I'll ask you."

It was the closest he'd ever come to agreeing to be partners. It was a step in the right direction. Like my aunt, I'd just have to find a way to negotiate my way into working with him. Make it easy for him and present it to him as a done deal, she'd said when referring to my uncle. The advice applied to Harry too. Indeed, to most men of my acquaintance. She'd also said patience came with age. I hoped I didn't reach my dotage before Harry took me on as an associate. Or kissed me.

He walked outside with me then agreed to accompany me as far as the hotel. I wanted to cross through St James's Park, since it was a pleasant day and he made no comment when I took the long way around the lake. His acquiescence gave me a little courage, but I soon doubted my decision and nerves set in. I was mad. Ladies of good breeding should not do what I was about to do, where people could see us, no less.

But do it I did. I caught his hand to make him stop, closed the gap between us before he realized what was happening, and stood on my toes.

I kissed him. It was light and airy, a mere brush really. At first.

Then he placed his hands on my hips and drew me closer. With a soft moan, he deepened the kiss.

The haughty clicking of a matronly tongue had us springing apart. I blushed ferociously, but couldn't stop my smile. Harry cleared his throat and walked off as if nothing had happened. He touched the brim of his hat in greeting to the middle-aged woman who'd interrupted our kiss. She didn't scowl at him. She reserved it for me. No doubt she saw the public display of wantonness as my fault.

Harry didn't talk to me for the rest of the way to the Mayfair. He only spoke when he curtly said goodbye some distance from the hotel. He crossed the road to avoid being seen with me, his back stiff, his focus forward. Next time we spoke, he'd probably be curt with me again. He would pretend the kiss never happened, or that it meant nothing.

But not in private. I suspected—hoped—he would think about it. I knew he'd liked it as much as I did.

Later, when Harmony came to arrange my hair before I went out with my family to dine with their friends, she knew something had happened. With a brush in one hand and a length of my hair in the other, she frowned at my reflection in the dressing table mirror. "What is it?" she asked. "What's going on?"

"The right question is, what have I done?"

"Very well, what have you done that's got you looking like the cat that got the cream and the mouse too?"

"I made it easy for him. Now I just have to wait and see if he accepts it as a done deal or if I misread the situation."

"What are you talking about?"

"The art of negotiating with men."

Look For:
MURDER AT THE DEBUTANTE BALL
The 5th Cleopatra Fox Mystery

A MESSAGE FROM THE AUTHOR

I hope you enjoyed reading MURDER AT THE DRESSMAKER'S SALON as much as I enjoyed writing it. As an independent author, getting the word out about my book is vital to its success, so if you liked this book please consider telling your friends and writing a review at the store where you purchased it. If you would like to be contacted when I release a new book, subscribe to my newsletter at http://cjarcher.com/contact-cj/newsletter/. You will only be contacted when I have a new book out.

ALSO BY C.J. ARCHER

SERIES WITH 2 OR MORE BOOKS

The Glass Library

Cleopatra Fox Mysteries

After The Rift

Glass and Steele

The Ministry of Curiosities Series

The Emily Chambers Spirit Medium Trilogy

The 1st Freak House Trilogy

The 2nd Freak House Trilogy

The 3rd Freak House Trilogy

The Assassins Guild Series

Lord Hawkesbury's Players Series

Witch Born

SINGLE TITLES NOT IN A SERIES

Courting His Countess

Surrender

Redemption

The Mercenary's Price

ABOUT THE AUTHOR

C.J. Archer has loved history and books for as long as she can remember and feels fortunate that she found a way to combine the two. She spent her early childhood in the dramatic beauty of outback Queensland, Australia, but now lives in suburban Melbourne with her husband, two children and a mischievous black & white cat named Coco.

Subscribe to C.J.'s newsletter through her website to be notified when she releases a new book, as well as get access to exclusive content and subscriber-only giveaways. Her website also contains up to date details on all her books: http://cjarcher.com She loves to hear from readers. You can contact her through email cj@cjarcher.com or follow her on social media to get the latest updates on her books:

facebook.com/CJArcherAuthorPage
twitter.com/cj_archer
instagram.com/authorcjarcher